*When Caesar crossed the Rubicon,
the Roman republic died and the age of
the emperors began. We now stand before
a Rubicon of our own. Cross it, and
the American republic will be dead as well.*

RUN

"[A] splendid new political thriller . . . Alexander's gifts are abundant. *Rubicon* provides riveting suspense and action while causing the reader to think about where bloodlust politics, if extrapolated, could take America. . . . Alexander's wordplay is spun gold."

Portland Oregonian

"For those unfamiliar with Roman history, *Rubicon* may seem slightly over the top, but for those of us concerned with the swift drift of the American Republic toward empire post-September 11, the parallels are plausible, prescient, and petrifying. . . . *Rubicon* reminds me of a famous movie line: 'These are dangerous men and they will stop at nothing.' Lawrence Alexander, whoever you are, watch your back."

GARY HART, former U.S. senator from Colorado, author of *The Courage of Our Convictions*

RUBICON

A NOVEL OF SUSPENSE

LAWRENCE ALEXANDER

HARPER

An Imprint of HarperCollinsPublishers

This book was originally published in hardcover May 2008 by William Morrow, an Imprint of HarperCollins Publishers.

HARPER

An Imprint of HarperCollins*Publishers*
10 East 53rd Street
New York, New York 10022-5299

Copyright © 2008 by Lawrence Alexander
ISBN 978-0-06-145641-1

First Harper paperback printing: July 2009
First William Morrow hardcover printing: May 2008

HarperCollins® and Harper® are registered trademarks of Harper-Collins Publishers.

Printed in the United States of America

Visit Harper paperbacks on the World Wide Web at
www.harpercollins.com

10 9 8 7 6 5 4 3 2 1

To J. C.
For everything he taught me

1

B OBBY HART SAT IN HIS OFFICE, REMEMBERING with a kind of rueful nostalgia the cool summer nights at home in Santa Barbara, walking on the beach with a sweater thrown over his shoulders, and the dark, wet sand clinging to his feet. Summer here, in the District, on the other hand, was an endless stay in hell, the heat stifling, breathless, the air heavy and oppressive. It followed you everywhere, the humidity thick and unrelenting, and the nights not much better than the days. It produced a constant, restless irritation, and with it a strange, perpetual suspicion, as if, with weather bad as this, it was hard to believe in anything except the evil side of human nature. He could not wait to get home.

His secretary knocked on the door, the way she did whenever there was something she knew he would want to know.

"Mr. Shoenfeld is on the line, Senator. I thought you might want to take it."

Dieter Shoenfeld was a man of importance, the publisher

of one of Europe's most influential journals, and an old friend. He read everything, could talk about anything, and insisted in all seriousness that he knew nothing.

"I have to see you," said Shoenfeld. "There is something you should know."

Hart glanced out the window at the Washington traffic, barely moving on the street below.

"I've only got two hours before my flight; I don't see how—"

"Cancel it."

It was the strange intensity in Dieter Shoenfeld's voice that told Bobby Hart he was serious.

"Cancel it," repeated Shoenfeld. "Go tomorrow, if you still think you should. This is important, Bobby. I wouldn't ask if I didn't think—"

"Where? When?" asked Hart, reaching for a pen.

An hour later, Hart got out of a cab in Georgetown. He had been on the Senate floor or in committee meetings most of the day. Despite the sweltering heat and humidity he wanted a few minutes outside, where he could breathe, lost in the relative anonymity of a sidewalk crowd. He could not walk down a street in San Francisco or Los Angeles without everyone stopping to stare. Here, the looks were more subtle, more restrained; usually a quick, friendly glance, followed by a brief nod as someone who also worked in Washington passed by.

Two men in their early thirties, the age of ambition, were crossing from the opposite side, moving, even in this debilitating heat, with the brisk efficiency with which they had learned to do everything. With measured smiles, they acknowledged his importance, no doubt wondering, each of them, whether sometime in the future others might look the same way at them.

The restaurant where he was to meet Shoenfeld was crowded, the bar impassable, a sea of hot shining faces, everyone full of news. Shoenfeld stood waiting for him while Hart threaded his way through a maze of tables. He gave him a warm hug as he shook his hand.

"Bobby! It's so good to see you."

Shoenfeld's small eyes were surrounded by drooping lids and large, dark circles. His nose was rather heavy and the nostrils rather wide. His mouth, even when he was sitting still, listening to you speak, was in constant motion, as if he could not help but react with some interest, some enthusiasm, to everything he heard.

"How are you, Dieter?" asked Hart as he sat down at the table. "And how is your lovely wife?" It brought a muted sparkle to Shoenfeld's solemn eyes.

"Very upset, my friend, very upset," he replied, full of soft mischief. His glance became more circumspect, and more serious. "She wanted you to run, you know. She thought you were the only one who could have changed things seriously for the better."

It was the mark of Hart's own unthinking confidence, and perhaps of his own ambition, that the question was, even with Dieter Shoenfeld, one he felt compelled to answer in purely political terms, or rather, not to answer at all, but to deflect with the easy modesty that said one thing and meant another.

"I doubt I could have won."

Shoenfeld studied him more carefully.

"You know what Napoleon told the general who asked how he should take Vienna? 'If you want to take Vienna, take Vienna.'"

Hart laughed and bent toward him.

"Is that what you think Napoleon told himself when he decided to invade Russia? 'If you want to take Moscow, take Moscow.'"

"Think what you could have done in those debates. All those cautious, carefully programmed, slow-thinking . . ."

He shook his head, let the thought finish itself, and then bent forward on his elbows. "You were the one who insisted that the race was wide open, that people were looking for someone new. So why didn't you . . . ?"

For an instant, Hart wondered whether, despite all the difficulties that had stood in the way, he should have done it, taken the chance when the chance was there.

"People were looking for someone new. How long was this supposed to go on? The same two families running the country for nearly thirty years, trading the presidency as if they owned it and could loan it back and forth; the same dull faces, the same dull speeches, the same . . . But I couldn't have done it, even though I voted against the war. Prentice Alworth knew what he was doing. He let everything come to him. He could attack the administration and not have to defend anything he had done."

Forgetting for the moment that he was in Washington and not in some European restaurant, Shoenfeld reached inside his jacket for a pack of cigarettes.

"You don't mind," he remarked as he took one out and lit it. Staring straight ahead he took one drag, and then another. "Do you know where I spent my morning?" he asked, waving his hand to clear away the thin spiral of gray smoke. "With your distinguished secretary of state, along with two of my colleagues from the German press."

"The occasion?"

"She wanted to explain that what happened last week proved that everything the administration has been saying about the threat of terrorism was true, and that she hoped Europe would finally understand that the threat is serious and real," said Shoenfeld. "She remembered that just two months ago, I had told her that the worst thing the United States has done in its history was Abu Ghraib and the other revelations of rendition and torture. I had told her that there was no justification for any of this, and that it had almost destroyed what was left of Europe's faith in America. She reminded me of that and then began to lecture me on having had the presumption to question America's right to defend itself by any means necessary!"

Shoenfeld took another drag on the cigarette. His eyes were immediate, intense.

"It was like listening to an automaton, programmed to repeat certain phrases—sometimes even whole paragraphs—but none of it with any meaning, no connection to the conversation or to the world around her. There is something stunningly superficial about her: all these facts and figures, but no sure grasp of how to put them together, or even what they mean. She is very smart, too smart: she knows so many different things, she makes the mistake of believing that the aim of intelligence is the expansion of knowledge rather than the depth of understanding."

Something occurred to him that he had not thought of before.

"Have you seen her play the piano? Every note correct, exact, but brittle, mechanical, as if she is in a hurry to get to the end, finish it so that she can get to the next busy thing she has to do."

The waiter brought their orders. Hart began to pick at his food, wondering what the real reason was he was there. Shoenfeld lapsed into a thoughtful silence.

"That was the reason, you see," he said suddenly. "What I had said about Abu Ghraib, and the rest of it: torture and anything else they think necessary. There was always this self-righteous assurance that what she and the others in this administration want is a kind of moral imperative and that no one has the right even to question it. That was the reason, you see: when I knew for certain that I could not tell her or anyone else in the government about this threat. I had to tell someone I could trust, someone who might be able to stop it."

"What threat? Stop what?" asked Hart, but Shoenfeld was not finished.

"Do you remember what I told you, just after 9/11? That there were people inside your government arguing that tactical nuclear weapons ought to be used, that both Baghdad and Tehran should be leveled. I don't need to tell you who they were; we both know their names. Or some of them, because I must tell you, Bobby, there are so many secrets inside this government of yours, so many agencies and bureaus that most people do not even know exist, I doubt we'll ever know who was really responsible for half the things that have happened. But never mind that; what I told you then was true, wasn't it? Plans were drawn up to use tactical nuclear weapons in both Iraq and Iran, weren't there?"

Hart pushed his plate aside.

"Yes, you told me; and yes, I checked. Or tried to check, because all I got was the usual runaround. I never got a direct response."

The small faint traces of a smile, a sign of appreciation for a well-told lie, made a brief appearance on Shoenfeld's face.

"You have better sources than almost anyone in Washington."

"I was only a minority member of the Senate Intelligence Committee."

"Your father was CIA."

"My father has been dead for nearly nine years."

"And no one in that business was ever more respected. That was the reason you voted against the war. Some of the people who worked with him told you privately that the intelligence the administration was using was suspect, and that some of it was demonstrably false. And those were the people you talked to when I told you what I had learned, and they told you—"

"But it never happened," Hart reminded him. "Maybe someone thought about it—that's what they do in the Pentagon, come up with plans for every possible contingency."

"Yes, and they get buried in a file. No one takes them seriously. But this was taken seriously, wasn't it: this notion that you could solve the problem of the Middle East by wiping out Baghdad and Tehran at a single stroke?"

"I don't know how seriously. There were discussions; that was all I ever learned."

"Discussions at the highest level," insisted Shoenfeld.

Hart did not disagree. "So I was told."

Staring into the middle distance, Shoenfeld tapped his fingers on the tablecloth.

"I lived in Berlin during most of the Cold War. I was there, a young student, when Kennedy spoke to that crowd that must have been more than a million. Freedom had a meaning then because just the other side of that wall was Soviet oppression. But then the wall came down and the Cold War ended and everybody decided they could go do whatever they wanted. And while everyone went off to live their fortunate private lives, politics and diplomacy were left to amateurs, puffed up with their own importance and no experience of the world. The same thing has happened here."

Shoenfeld reached for the wine bottle and, ignoring Hart's protest, poured them each another glass.

"You have to come to Germany, and you have to do it right away."

Hart started to reply that he could not possibly do any such thing, but then he saw the worried expression on Shoenfeld's face.

"Why? What is it? Why did you remind me of what you told me right after 9/11?"

"To remind you that there are no rules anymore; to remind you that everything is now possible. And to tell you that there is going to be another attack. That's why you have to go to Germany. There is someone there who can tell you, an old friend of your father, who won't talk to anyone but you. I've arranged the meeting."

"You've arranged . . . ?"

Shoenfeld reached inside his jacket and pulled out a plane ticket.

"You're meeting him in Hamburg, tomorrow afternoon."

2

THERE WAS NO ONE THERE TO MEET BOBBY Hart when he landed at Hamburg the next day. Shoenfeld had given him the name of the place he was to go, but not the name of the man he was to meet. No name, no description; nothing, except the vague assurance that someone would be waiting for him at a place called the Cafe Petite at exactly three-thirty in the afternoon.

The cab, a late-model black Mercedes, moved down a wide, leafy avenue, lined with prosperous-looking stone buildings set a discreet distance back from the street. The dockyards, the railway lines, the factories, the entire industrial infrastructure of Hamburg had been destroyed in the war, but the fashionable neighborhoods where the wealthy families lived had been left largely untouched.

"Cafe Petite," announced the driver. He gestured toward a small sidewalk cafe across a narrow side street, just a few yards ahead.

Hart grabbed his overnight bag and got out. It was a quiet, warm afternoon, the kind of day that makes everyone look for an excuse to be out of doors. The sidewalk tables were crowded with smartly dressed women with shopping bags at their feet and gossip on their tongues. Toward the back, under the lengthening shadows of the trees, sat silent young couples lost in each other's eyes.

He moved cautiously across the narrow, shaded street, waiting for someone to catch his eye, to make some sign that he was the one Hart was there to meet. He stepped down two stone steps at the entrance, and went inside. A woman at the cash register asked whether he wanted to be seated in the main part of the restaurant or in the garden in back.

"The garden, if you don't mind," said someone directly behind him.

Hart started to turn around, but the man who had spoken was already moving toward the narrow open doorway that led to the small garden area in back. He was tall, taller than Hart, who was himself nearly six feet, with straight shoulders and long, rather shaggy gray hair. He looked a little like an aging bohemian dressed in an old, but well-tailored suit.

The garden was really a patio, enclosed by a high brick wall. Half a dozen small tables stretched out in a single straight line. The one closest to the door was vacant. As they sat down, the stranger introduced himself.

"My name is Gunther Kramer. I knew your father."

There was nothing particularly unusual about Gunther Kramer's physical features, nothing that would cause someone to take a second look or remark upon them later, nothing that anyone would especially remember. He had a face that could easily blend into the crowd.

"Dieter said you had," replied Hart.

"He was a remarkable man, he—"

"Yes, I appreciate that," said Hart more impatiently than he intended. "But Dieter told me that you had something important to tell me. I've come a long way, Mr. Kramer; and, if you don't mind, whatever it is, I'd like to hear it."

"You have your father's voice, his manner, too—always in a hurry to get straight to the point. And if you made a mistake, if things had not worked out quite the way you had expected, forget about it—that was the phrase he used— forget about it and start thinking about the next thing you were supposed to do. It is the American luxury of always living in the future and never thinking too much about the past. It is probably what got him killed."

"What got him . . . ? My father died of a heart attack, nine years ago next month."

With a look of the utmost seriousness, Kramer leaned forward.

"Your father was killed because of something he knew, something he was not supposed to find out."

"And you know this how?" asked Hart, skeptically.

"There were certain people, a secret group, which had started to assemble their own sources, sources from which they could get the kind of intelligence they wanted."

Kramer had ordered coffee. He sipped on it pensively.

"They say you might one day be president. More important, they say you should. Your father would have been proud of that. Despite what I said a moment ago, he was nothing like the typical American: he was always more interested in what someone was, than in what they did." He paused, smiled, and then, as quickly as that, the smile disappeared. "But they killed him, you can be certain of that. There was no autopsy, was there?"

"No, there wasn't any . . . He told you there was this group that was starting to assemble their own sources? Why did he tell you? Why didn't he tell someone at the agency, someone who might have been able to do something about it?"

"Because he could not yet prove it. That was why he came to me."

"I don't quite understand. I'm assuming you were with German intelligence, so why . . . ?"

Kramer raised his chin, his eyes again distant, remote.

"I was born inside East Germany. When I was old enough to go to university I went to Moscow. I was working for East German intelligence when I first met your father; but I did not meet him in Germany, I met him in Baghdad, in the 1980s. I started working for him a year later, passing on information I gathered about certain governments—governments with which my friends, the Russians, had better relations than the United States."

Kramer seemed to relax a little. A glint of nostalgia entered his eyes.

"We met at various diplomatic gatherings—embassy parties, things like that. I was a cultural attaché—that was the cover we used; everyone knew what it meant. I liked your father; part of it was his name: Maximillian Hart. The moment I heard it, that first time we were introduced, I found myself repeating it out loud. Strange, the things that attract us to people: the name, and the candid look in his eyes. I knew immediately he was someone I could trust."

Kramer stretched his hands, opening and closing them several times. His fingers were long and elegant, with a tremendous reach. Hart stared at him, a look of surprised certainty on his face.

"You're the piano player! My father never talked about what he did, but once, when he was getting ready for a trip, I asked him where he was going. He told me that he had a good friend, a piano player, he was going to see."

"Max always had an eye for the small detail, the thing that distinguishes one person from the next. I might have become a reasonably good concert pianist, but the party thought it had a better use for the skill I had in learning languages. That was something else that drew me to your father: we both spoke Arabic. We could talk together in a crowded room and most of the people there could not understand a thing we said."

Kramer bent forward on his elbows.

"Max discovered that there was this organized effort to develop new lines of contact, new sources of intelligence. Not better sources, not more accurate sources, but sources that would supply intelligence that could be used for their own purposes. People who had been discredited, people notoriously unreliable, people who would invent things to make themselves seem important were suddenly being used again."

He shook his head, gesturing with his hands, trying to get it just right so that Hart would understand.

"If you have one source that says there is no evidence that, say, Syria is trying to develop nuclear weapons, but another source says they are, what is the only reasonable conclusion that you can draw? That Syria may be trying to develop nuclear weapons. You don't have to prove anything, just have sources that will give you what you want, make a threat that does not exist seem as if it might. Because a threat that is possible is real."

"And my father knew this was going on, and that is why you think . . . ?"

"He knew it, but he could not prove that it was anything more than a few overzealous agents using sources that they should have known better than to trust. He could not prove that they were deliberately cultivating sources that would give them whatever they needed to make the case that the only option for the United States was to get rid of certain regimes they did not like. That was why he came to me.

"There was an Iraqi scientist, a brilliant man, Cambridge educated. He knew everything about Saddam's weapons program. He knew that it was all a kind of Potemkin village, a fiction used to prevent other nations, and other groups within Iraq itself, from trying to overthrow Saddam. I knew this man rather well. His wife was German. Max asked me to have him pass on information, a clear statement that the so-called weapons program was all a hoax, to one of the sources, an Iraqi general who had been caught in lies before. That way he could trace who got the information and whether it was accurately reported. That was when your father died; that was when they killed him."

"But you can't be sure of that. You said yourself he did not have any proof. And as for him being murdered . . ."

"You doubt they killed your father? They were going to change the world, bring freedom and democracy to the Middle East! What was one life compared to that? His death was a matter of necessity, the means to an end. One life! How many thousands—hundreds of thousands—have died so that these people could bring about their vision of a world that everywhere looks just like America? Saddam Hussein was a brutal dictator who killed thousands of his own people, but how long do you think he would have stayed in power, how long before he was overthrown, once word got out that all those great, lethal weapons of his did not exist?"

Kramer took a sip of coffee, but it had turned cold. He signaled the waitress for another.

"There are things you would rather not believe," he said with a subtle gaze. "But you know they killed your father, don't you?"

"You're right, I don't want to believe it. But you don't have any doubts at all, do you? Why? What makes you so sure?"

The waitress brought Kramer a second cup. Holding it in both hands, he drank slowly.

"I have seen before what power in the service of a belief makes men do. My father was a decent man before Hitler came to power; but then he became an officer in the SS. Who knows how many men—women and children, too—he may have murdered because he believed in Hitler and the Third Reich. And then the Russians came, and we believed that anything that stood in the way of history—history according to the teachings of Marx and Lenin—deserved to be destroyed. Twenty million kulaks—peasant farmers—were killed in Russia so that progress could be made. And anyone who did not like it, who wanted to leave, who tried to escape East Germany for life in the West, we had to kill them, too. Now it is happening again, all the rules of civilized behavior abandoned, all the forms of decency, because we believe the things we worship—whether it be God or democracy—justifies the use of any means. So, yes, I believe my friend Max was murdered for what he knew. This is the reason I have come to warn you, before things get even worse."

"Warn me of what?"

"That there is going to be another attack, not like before, not like 9/11. It's going to be an assassination, a political assassination."

"Who? Who is going to be assassinated? Who are they? How do they plan to do it?

"My sources in the Middle East, the people I talk to, all heard the rumor of a planned assassination. They didn't know exactly when it was going to happen, only that it would be very soon, sometime before the U.S. election. That was unusual, for things to be that vague. At first I thought that it meant that it was either being done in great secrecy or that it was being done by an organization that none of us had heard of before. Then, just by chance, I found out. I did not believe it at first, I couldn't; but now I know for sure."

Kramer's eyes darted toward the doorway. He was becoming nervous, agitated. He looked at Hart.

"I should go, I've stayed too long as it is."

"You can't go yet. Tell me what you know. You have plenty of time to get back to Berlin."

"I don't live in Berlin, I live in Damascus. It's the only place I'm safe," he explained as his eyes came back around. "I shouldn't have come, but I had to warn you; I owed that much to your father."

Suddenly, Kramer's head jerked forward and twisted to the side. For just an instant, he looked at Hart with a puzzled expression as if he were not quite sure what had just happened. Then there was a blur of shattered glass and broken china and Kramer was falling to the ground. Hart started to reach for him, to do something to help, when he felt a sharp, searing pain in his shoulder. Then he heard it, the sound, the strident, cracking sound of rifle fire and he knew that he had been shot. He saw it now, the blood oozing from the front of Kramer's white shirt as he lay on the ground, staring up at him. Hart stood there, looking around, trying to figure out where the shot had come from, as if, instead of in the middle of a shooting, he were just some distant observer. A bullet whizzed past his ear, another one kicked past his foot; he dove for cover. There was screaming all around him, panic everywhere. Hart turned on his side to see if Kramer was still alive.

"Rubicon," whispered Kramer as Hart bent closer. "The code name is Rubicon. Remember that. It's the key to everything."

"What does it mean?" asked Hart, signaling desperately for someone to get help. "What does Rubicon mean?"

Kramer opened his mouth and tried to answer. Nothing came out, only the slow, gasping sound of his last, dying breath.

3

DIETER SHOENFELD STOOD AT THE RAILING next to the tidal basin. He looked up at the Jefferson Memorial, glistening in the red light of dawn.

"I like to come out here early in the morning just to look at that, the clear upright confidence on the face of Thomas Jefferson. Lincoln saved the Union, but it was the Union that Jefferson made. I wonder if there is a more sublime feeling than the knowledge that you have created something that will be the envy of the world. What a rare thing it is to have great men who aspire to something more than power."

Shoenfeld clasped his hands behind his back and lowered his shoulders. A sad, wistful smile flickered over his mouth. He took Hart by the arm.

"Come, let's walk a little, just around here, close to the memorial. Tell me about Gunther Kramer: everything he said to you before he died. But tell me first that you're okay? The bullet passed through your shoulder? There won't be any permanent damage?"

"I was lucky; another few inches . . . And if I had been sitting on the other side of the table, it would have been me instead of him."

Hart had returned late the night before. He had slept a couple of hours on the plane out of sheer exhaustion; but then, at home, he had not been able to sleep at all. Each time he closed his eyes he saw the face of Gunther Kramer, that strange, puzzled look that seemed to know, and yet knowing, not believe, that in the blink of an eye he was dead. It was as if, in that single instant, the burden of his existence had passed to Hart, and that whatever happened now would in some way be linked to Gunther Kramer's past.

"Who was he working for? I know that he used to be a double agent, that his control in the West was my father, and that he was going to defect. I know that he disappeared and made everyone think he was dead; I know that he had been in the Middle East, living, at least recently, in Damascus. But who was he working for? And if everyone in Germany thought he was dead all these years, how did you know he was still alive?"

Shoenfeld stopped walking. He looked at Hart and nodded slowly as he tried to make up his mind how much he should reveal.

"Gunther Kramer was my brother," he said finally.

"Your brother?"

"Half brother, to be precise. It was the war, or what happened afterward." With his hand on Hart's arm, he began to walk again, but very slowly. "My father, as I think I told you once, was killed at Stalingrad. My mother was trapped in what became the Russian zone. My mother remarried and had a second child."

"Gunther told me that his father had been in the SS. Your mother was a Jew."

"Everyone lied about who they were. All we knew was that, like my father, he had been a soldier in the war. Gunther only found out after his father was dead; we never told my mother. I never suspected anything. He adored my mother, though I think she never really loved him. Things were difficult after the war, and my mother was quite a beautiful woman. She did what she had to do to survive. It is as simple as that. Things that happened in Germany are inexplicable, unless you lived through it."

There was a long silence before Shoenfeld picked up the thread of his narrative.

"I was lucky; I got out and lived most of my life in the West. But Gunther lived his life the way a lot of Germans did, a prisoner of a war that never ended. The war ended in 1945, but if you lived in East Germany all that meant was that instead of living under the Third Reich, you now lived under Soviet Communism.

"I did not have much contact with Gunther until much later, after the wall came down. He wanted me to know that he was alive so that he could arrange to visit our mother. And now he is dead, and there is no one I can tell without giving away the secret that all these years he was living, an exile, in Damascus. You asked who he was working for. I don't know, but he had sources better than any intelligence agency in the West. Gunther could not just speak fluent Arabic and Farsi; he could pass for an Arab when he needed to."

Shoenfeld spun around, a look of urgency in his eyes.

"Now, listen—what I asked you earlier, about what he said to you. When I talked to him the last time, he told me he had discovered something. There was something in his voice. I can't quite describe it; but when he told me that he knew who was behind this, it was as if he still could not quite believe it. He knew he was being followed, that he was under some kind of surveillance. It was the way he cut off the conversation, the way he said he would have to call back later. That's what has me worried."

"Worried?"

"If they were following Gunther, we can't be sure that they have not started following you."

Hart started to object, but Shoenfeld gripped his arm.

"Listen to me—you haven't heard what I said. Gunther is dead. You have to assume that whoever did this knows everything. If they don't know exactly what he told you, they can guess. And remember, they weren't just shooting at Gunther, they shot at you. Now, tell me: what did he tell you?"

"He told me that someone was going to be assassinated and that it was going to happen before the election. He said he didn't know who the target was, but that the code name for this was Rubicon."

"Rubicon—that's what he told you, nothing more?" Shoenfeld nodded quickly and then remarked, "I said that they followed Gunther to Germany, but I wonder if that's possible. I wonder if they didn't follow you."

"Followed me? I don't understand."

"Do you have any idea the skill that was involved—the deception—that allowed Gunther to do what he did all those years? He was a double agent when he worked for your father, and then he disappears, makes everyone believe he's dead. A man like that could sense the danger; he would have known immediately if he was being followed. But you would not know: you're famous; people are always watching you. But that would mean that they weren't there to murder him; they were there to murder you."

"But why? Who would want to murder me? And how could anyone have followed me to Hamburg?"

Shoenfeld glanced back at the statue of Jefferson.

"There are cameras everywhere now; countless images passed through computers that are running all the time, looking for something out of the ordinary: a face that does not belong there, anything that might tell these people in authority something about what might happen next. If there is a group of the sort that Gunther described, people who had your father murdered, do you think it would be difficult for them to keep track of you?"

"You're telling me that I may be being followed all the time?"

"It's possible. It's also possible that you weren't followed to Germany and that what happened to Gunther had nothing to do with you. All we know is that he's dead. Rubicon— that's what he told you? Strange."

"Strange? Why do you say that?"

"Strange that a plot to assassinate someone in the United States, a plot planned in the Middle East, would take a name from Roman history."

"Strange or not, I know some people at Langley. I'll try to find out whether the CIA has come across that name in anything they've intercepted." He paused, thinking over what he had been told. "You say he also knew who was behind it, and that he seemed astonished?"

"Yes, astonished, which itself is astonishing, given all the things Gunther had gone through."

"When are you going back to Berlin, Dieter?"

"I have a flight this afternoon. I have a few other sources in the Middle East—none of them as good as Gunther— but I'll see if they know anything."

Shoenfeld put his hand on Hart's arm.

"It was wise of you not to tell the police Gunther's real name."

"I assumed he must have been using false identification. I told them that I didn't know who he was; that we were just sharing a table."

"The German papers reported it as the murder of a Syrian national traveling on business. We were able to keep your name out of it. It's better this way. There would be too many questions."

Shoenfeld had been right when he said that Hart had grown used to people watching him. But now, as Hart got to his car, he looked first one way, then the other, as he opened the door. Then, as he started the engine, he looked for anything suspicious, anything out of the ordinary, in the rearview mirror. He accused himself of paranoia and the next moment wondered whether, if he had been more careful, Gunther Kramer might still be alive.

He was still thinking about Gunther Kramer and what he had told him when he walked into a meeting of the Senate Intelligence Committee that afternoon.

The meeting had not yet started. Hart's closest friend in the senate, Charles Thomas Ryan, the junior senator from Michigan, pulled him off to the side. Both in their midforties, they were by training and temperament intolerant of liars, pretenders, and fools; which meant that in Washington they had very few allies and, except for each other, no real friends. They did not belong to the same political party, which made it easier to tell the truth about some of the better-known people in the country.

"There's a rumor that Alworth wants you on the ticket, that he's going to ask you to run for vice president." Ryan ran his hand through a thick clump of reddish-brown hair as he tried to suppress a grin. "Some of the people who backed what's his name's wife said you'd be a great candidate, that you could help carry a number of important states, that . . . Well, you know—the usual lies."

Ryan's grin became an impish, eager glow. It had become a kind of game between them, how quickly Ryan could make Hart swear, utter some passing mild obscenity at the latest double-dealing by their fellow politicians. But Hart only laughed.

"They're probably saying that about everyone they know won't be asked. People always feel more indebted to those they think tried to help them when they lost."

"There's more to this rumor than that," insisted Ryan. "Alworth has a short list and your name is on it."

"Whose name isn't?"

Hart had heard that his name was on the short list of candidates; that it was in fact the first name, the one that Prentice Alworth wanted. He was not interested, and he had said so to everyone who had asked, but that had done nothing to stop the speculation.

Ryan checked his watch. "One thing you can always count on about the chairman—he's never on time." He glanced around the committee room. All the other members were there, forced to wait, as usual, for the hearing to start. "You wouldn't take it, would you?" he asked, turning back to Hart. "If Alworth offered it, you'd say no?"

"You know what I think about Alworth. But it's not even a question. If my name is on a list, it's only because they want to keep everyone in suspense. There's no reason to have me on the ticket. He doesn't need me to carry California."

"Clinton didn't pick Gore to help him carry Tennessee. Bush didn't pick Cheney to carry Wyoming. Politics aren't local anymore, they're national. You're the senator who led the fight against private companies making money from the war. You could have had the nomination if you'd wanted it. Alworth was a governor. He doesn't have any experience in foreign policy; he needs someone from the Senate." Ryan searched Hart's eyes. "You know all this. You know he's going to ask you. You're just rehearsing the reasons you're going to give him when you turn him down."

"I couldn't do it even if I wanted to. I'm in the middle of a reelection campaign. I can't just drop that because I decide I want to be vice president instead."

Hart started to turn away, but he remembered something he wanted to tell Ryan, something important he thought he should know.

"Charlie, listen, I heard from someone at the national committee that things in Michigan have tightened up. They tell me that your lead has been cut to a couple of points. Are you in trouble?"

"Not yet, but I could be. Some of my more conservative friends have let me know they aren't particularly happy with some of the things I've done." A wry grin stretched across his mouth, but the look in his eyes was serious. "When I was a kid, tent revivals would come to town. Some wild-eyed preacher with sweat pouring off his face would tell everyone that the Day of Judgment was just around the corner and that they better repent. It was like a sideshow at the carnival, one of those once-a-year diversions that make a few people feel better and leave everyone entertained. No one thought that what was said in one of those summertime meetings—people talking in tongues, people screaming hysterically, full of fear and rapture— was the way you ought to run the country. But now everything seems to be at one extreme or the other. It's what Yeats said: 'The centre cannot hold.'" He looked at Hart, a sheepish grin on his face. "I can't help it. Both my parents were English teachers."

It was also the reason, Hart believed, that whatever the polls might say, Ryan would almost certainly win: the way he always managed to work into a speech or a conversation a serious thought, quoted in the words of another, and with that boyish embarrassment of his make it appear that he was more surprised than anyone by what he had said.

The door at the side opened. Ryan laughed.

"The chairman, and only twenty minutes late! Probably had to explain to members of the press how we won the Second World War. Only man in America who not only remembers the slogan 'Loose lips sink ships,' but every time he repeats it, holds his fingers to his lips to make sure everyone knows what it means."

Sitting at the witness table, directly in front of the committee, Raymond Caulfield, the deputy director of the CIA, listened without expression to an elaborate, and lengthy, introduction by the chairman who, as he liked to point out, had himself "served in some of the nation's wars and knew the vital importance of intelligence."

Hunched over the table, the deputy director tightened his mouth into an expression of puzzled concentration. Caulfield was well into his sixties and looked even older than that. His gray eyes were tired, worn-out with effort, his voice a dim echo of past enthusiasms. Everything about him suggested fatigue.

Caulfield read from a prepared report about the number of particular types of threats that had been uncovered during the preceding three months, the steps that had been taken to combat them, and what, based on the CIA's best estimates, the terrorists were likely to try next. It was all analytical, the world and its dangers reduced to mathematics: X number of electronic transmissions; Y number of telephone calls made from certain places overseas. It was like listening to an insurance agent recite mortality tables to determine how much your insurance would cost, without once mentioning that at some point you were certain to die.

The questioning began in order of rank on the committee and followed the usual, predictable routine. For every question that demanded some thought on the part of the witness, at least a dozen others required nothing more than a cursory nod and a few generalized phrases about the crucial importance of the issue the senator had just raised. There were questions asking for clarification on a particular point, and questions that were not questions at all, but invitations to take credit for the important work that was being done.

"Mr. Hart, do you have any questions for the deputy director?"

Hart sat forward on the edge of his chair.

"All of your testimony here today, and nearly all of your responses to the questions you have been asked, have taken the form of a statistical analysis, an assessment of risk, based on, among other things, the volume of communications traffic. You have not told us anything about a single, definable threat and what might be done about it."

"I was attempting to give the committee an overview of what the electronic surveillance program, authorized by Congress, has allowed us to do."

"Has it allowed you to infiltrate a single terrorist organization?"

"That is not what the program is designed to do; it is designed—"

"To track electronic communications and try to establish a pattern," said Hart. His eyes flashed with impatience. "In other words, the answer is no. It has not helped us get inside a single terrorist organization or network; it has not given us any specific intelligence concerning any specific plan to attack the United States or any of our interests abroad."

Caulfield was courteous and respectful. He had spent too many years testifying before congressional committees to let anything get under his skin.

"No, Senator, but it gives us an important tool by which to determine the size, the scope, and the connecting links of the various cells that make up these networks," he reported methodically. "And with respect to your question about specific threats and what can be done to stop them, we receive information about them every day, dozens, sometimes hundreds of them, from various sources around the world, and we are continuously—"

"How many of these sources are inside Syria or Iran?" asked Hart suddenly and with force. "Let me be even more specific: how many sources do you have inside the intelligence agencies of either country?"

Caulfield moved his eyes in a steady arc from Hart to the chairman.

"I am not at liberty—there is an executive order that specifically prohibits—to disclose operational details of the sort the question asks."

Hart did not give the chairman the chance to agree.

"Let me ask a different question. There is, is there not, a certain established relationship between the Syrian intelligence agency and the CIA?"

"I'm not sure I know what—"

"A number of prisoners—men the United States has held captive at Guantánamo, and other places—have been turned over to the Syrians for further interrogation. *Rendition* is the term usually applied to this arrangement. Presumably, you haven't been doing this only to give the Syrians a chance to refine their own, peculiar methods of extracting information, but to give you intelligence that you did not think you could obtain from your own, more— what shall I say—'civilized' methods."

"What is your question, Senator?" asked the chairman, a polite warning in his voice. Hart ignored him.

"We turn people over to the Syrians for further interrogation. Is this one of the sources—what you learn from Syrian intelligence—of the various specific threats that you were speaking of?"

"Again, Senator, I cannot divulge specific sources of intelligence; I cannot—"

"I'm not asking you to give us their names! I'm asking whether the Syrian intelligence agency—despite all the trouble we have with that government—is cooperating in our effort to discover terrorist threats before they materialize into another attack. Are you going to tell us that you cannot—or will not—answer that, either?"

Caulfield began to repeat the reasons why he could not answer. The chairman cut him off.

"The question seems fair enough. You aren't being asked to name specific individuals. Just tell us what, if any, relationship the CIA has with Syrian intelligence. Anyone who reads the newspapers, Mr. Caulfield, has read the stories about rendition. The question is a logical one to ask. I suggest you answer."

"As I say, Mr. Chairman, I cannot . . ."

The chairman stared hard at him a moment and then, his eyes still fixed on the witness, told his "good friend, Senator Hart," to resume his questioning. "And any question the witness chooses not to answer now, you can ask again when we bring him back under subpoena and put him under oath."

"Mr. Chairman," protested Caulfield, "I'm under an executive order not to discuss certain matters; I don't think that—"

"Senator Hart, if you please."

The other members of the committee turned to see what Hart would ask next. For an instant he hesitated, worried that he might not get it right. The question had to be simple, straightforward, no chance that it might not be understood.

"Mr. Caulfield, what I want to know is this: has anyone in Syrian intelligence provided the agency with any information concerning a plot to kill the president?"

Caulfield sat bolt upright. There was a look of stunned disbelief on his face.

"No," he blurted out before he had time to think about it. "No, we've had no intelligence—from any source— about a thing like that."

"You've had no information, from any source?" asked Hart, pressing hard. "Nothing that would even suggest . . . ?"

Caulfield had recovered from the initial shock. He began to consider the broader implications. He fell back into his favored pattern of ambiguity.

"Senator, there are countless threats made all the time; rumors, most of them, about possible plans to kill Americans, both here and abroad. Obviously, that could conceivably include attacks against our political leaders, including even the president himself."

Hart shook his head in frustration.

"We have a presidential election just a few months away, and the only answer you can give us about the threat we face is a bunch of bureaucratic gibberish that only wastes our time?"

Caulfield started to protest. Hart stopped him in his tracks.

"All of us have heard rumors that something is going on, that someone is planning an assassination before the election. What I want to know—what everyone on this committee wants to know—is what do you know about it and what are you planning to do to prevent it?"

It did not matter that no one had heard this but Hart. Everyone now assumed that everyone else had heard the rumors; no one was about to admit that he was the only one who had not. Everyone leaned forward, eager to hear what Caulfield and the CIA knew, and what they were going to do.

"Mr. Chairman, I believe this is a matter that you should discuss with the director."

Hart jumped on it.

"I'll take that to mean that the agency does have some information. Is it, then, in your estimation, more likely to be an attempt on the life of the president, or on the life of some other political leader?"

"I really could not comment on that. All I can say is that, precisely for the reasons you point out—the near proximity of the election, the importance of protecting the integrity of the democratic process, the knowledge of what terrorist groups have talked about in the past—we're doing all we can to make certain that nothing like this ever happens."

"And I assume that part of your effort to make certain that no one else is assassinated will be to go back to your sources—in places like Syria and other countries in the Middle East—and find out everything they might have heard. I assume, as part of that effort, that you will let those same sources know that if they hold anything back, if they don't tell you everything they know, and something happens, they will be held as much accountable as the terrorists who actually do it?"

Caulfield nodded emphatically and said that of course they would certainly make clear how important this kind of information was.

Hart did not have any more questions. He listened inattentively while a Republican member of the committee told the deputy director something to the effect that "thanks to your efforts there hasn't been another attack since 9/11," and then stopped listening altogether.

When the Intelligence Committee finally adjourned, Hart had to hurry to the Senate chamber for a vote. His administrative assistant, David Allen, walked with him. Short and balding, with small hands and quick-moving eyes, Allen wanted to know how things had gone in committee.

"Not too bad," replied Hart with a weary shrug. "At least everyone now thinks there may be a threat. What do you have for me? I know the bill that's up. I know how I'm going to vote. That isn't why you were waiting."

"It's Alworth. Jenkins called."

"Who's Jenkins?"

"Alworth's campaign manager—the new 'genius' of American politics."

"And what does the genius want?"

"To tell us that Alworth wants to see you."

Hart stopped walking. He glanced around to make sure no one was close enough to hear.

"It's about the vice presidency, isn't it? There isn't any way that—"

"He said Alworth wanted to see you," said Allen in a way that made it sound like the beginning of a joke.

"And?"

"And nothing. That's all he said."

They had worked together so many years they could read whole paragraphs in a single, silent glance.

"And because Alworth is as good as elected president, a word from his man Jenkins and we should all come running." Hart enjoyed it, the thought of it, Allen sitting all cynical and rumpled in his small office, listening in open-mouthed astonishment to the voice at the other end of the line. "How many times did you make him repeat it?"

"Three. Then I asked why." Allen mimicked a hollow, pompous voice. "'The governor would like to discuss several matters of great importance.'"

Hart began to walk briskly toward the door to the Senate chamber, less than a hundred feet away.

"I suppose I have to," he said with an air of resignation. The sergeant at arms opened the door but Hart stopped and looked at Allen with cheerful malice. "Unless you want to call the genius back and tell him I'm just too busy."

The Senate session dragged on for hours. There was no time for dinner. Hart gulped down a sandwich and a cup of coffee back in his office where he was in meetings until half past nine. It was nearly ten-thirty when he finally got home to the house in Georgetown where, in his wife's absence, he lived alone. There was a light on in the kitchen. Someone was waiting for him, and he knew who it was.

"Have you been here long?" he asked as he opened the refrigerator and gathered up two bottles of beer.

"Not long," said Raymond Caulfield; "not long at all." He gratefully accepted the bottle that was handed to him, took a drink and then, with a satisfied look, put it down on the table. "You were a little rough on me today," he said in a quiet, pleasant voice.

4

RAYMOND CAULFIELD GLANCED AROUND THE kitchen with its gleaming appliances and polished tile floor. He liked the air of peaceful domesticity, a place where everything that happened was private. A lifelong bachelor, he often had, when he visited other homes, a sense of what he might have missed. He removed his eyeglasses and rubbed each lens with a handkerchief. Holding the cold bottle of beer, he stared down at the floor.

"You made me look quite the fool, a faceless bureaucrat who won't tell Congress one thing more than he absolutely has to. In short," he continued, raising his eyes, "exactly what I am: a career civil servant about to be pensioned off."

Hart settled into a chair the other side of the ancient wooden table, something his wife had acquired in a small village somewhere in the south of France. It was curious how easily he had slipped into a public attitude of outraged hostility when Caulfield was a witness for the agency. He actually felt enormous respect, and even affection, for him.

"The last thing anyone would ever think to call you is a fool," Hart remarked with a gentle, knowing glance. "As for being a 'faceless bureaucrat,' that is a role you play to protect the anonymity of one of the last great agents the agency has had. And . . . are they really forcing you out? Now, after what's happened?"

"A couple of weeks ago, the director told me that he had just realized—to his great surprise and disappointment, you understand—that I was only half a year from retirement age, and that I was certainly going to be missed. The paperwork has already started."

"But why? Because you know too much? Because they're afraid?"

"Because I know too little. For more than a year now, I have been cut out of things, not invited to the most important meetings." He took a drink. There was a wry look in his aging eyes. "Haven't you noticed how often I'm sent to testify on Capitol Hill?"

He glanced again around the kitchen, taking a kind of comfort in how neat it was, everything in its proper place. It suggested a certain precision, a settled routine, an absence of self-indulgence. It was not the only reason he liked Bobby Hart, but it was one of them.

"They've tried to push me out since the beginning of the war, when I would not give them what they wanted. When the war was going well, that simply meant that I had not understood, that I had not been able to grasp the crucial importance of the intelligence they claimed they had." He paused, concentrating on what he was trying to explain. "Then, when it became obvious to everyone that none of the weapons of mass destruction existed, when it became obvious that the sources on which they had placed such great reliance had either been fools or liars, they wanted to get rid of me even more. They were resentful, and perhaps worried, that I knew what they had done and how badly they had misjudged things."

Caulfield twisted the bottle around, moving it first one way then another, watching that back-and-forth movement as if it were a newfound metaphor for the repeated stupidities of the world.

"I told them at one point—early on, when the vice president and some of his people first started pressing the agency to make the case for war—that Chalabi was an exile, a man who wanted our help to go back to his country, and that everything an exile tells you is always at best an exaggeration."

He shook his head at the irony of what had happened. With a look that was dismissive, unforgiving, and almost cruel, he stared into the middle distance.

"You read these descriptions of the vice president in the public press: the dark view he supposedly has of the world, the belief that it is all a 'Hobbesian' struggle for survival. You read about some of the people who work for him— brilliant, fearless intellectuals; the brave new apostles of an American empire. And yet, once you get to know them, the vice president and his people, you discover that they have not read a thing. Their ignorance is monumental. When I told them that business about not trusting exiles, I added that the thought was scarcely original with me: the principle had been set out as early as Machiavelli. They did not know this, and thought it supremely unimportant. As one of them put it: 'This isn't some graduate seminar.'"

"It is in the Third Book of the *Discourses,* if I remember correctly," said Hart.

"Yes, precisely."

"I should remember; it was just last year you first suggested I read it. But let's get back to the agency for a minute. They can't force you out before you reach retirement age, and that does not happen until after the election. No matter who wins the presidency, the director is going to be replaced. There is even a chance the next president might ask you."

"I've been there too long. They'll want someone new. Besides, I've seen enough; I'm ready to go. What's happened, some of the things we are doing . . . It isn't what I signed up for." Caulfield waved his hand in the air, a signal that he had already said enough. There were other, more important, things they had to talk about.

"What happened?" asked Hart, focused and alert. "After you got back to Langley today, after you testified?"

"I made a full report—a summary—of what was said. I emphasized that there was great concern inside the committee about another attack, a possible assassination."

Caulfield began to run the edge of his thumb around the lip of the dark brown bottle, a thoughtful expression on his mouth. He seemed to sink inside himself, like someone used to being alone, even, and perhaps especially, when he was around other people.

"I said there was a particular concern that we use what sources we had in the Middle East—including especially Syrian intelligence—to find out how real such a threat might be." Caulfield's thumb stopped moving; he looked directly across the table at Hart. "You know something; I knew it right away. What is it—some rumor you've heard, something you picked up from someone you know overseas? You were just in Germany, a sudden trip, and you were only there a couple of days."

"You know about that?" asked Hart. He was a little annoyed, and a little apprehensive. "Am I being watched?"

With a grim laugh, Caulfield threw his eyes toward the ceiling.

"Everybody is being watched, and listened to, and checked on, and kept track of. It's *1984* and *Brave New*

World rolled into one: all the fear and punishment for anyone who gets out of line George Orwell described; all the
mood-altering drugs and soft pornography Aldous Huxley
said would be used to entertain and control the masses.
Were you followed? No, not yet, at least that I know of. But
the moment someone bought that ticket, your name showed
up on someone's computer; and each time you showed
your passport . . ."

"What about you?" asked Hart. "Are you being watched,
and listened to, and checked on, and kept track of?"

"Everything I do; everywhere I go. But I have learned to
take precautions," he remarked with a cryptic glance. He
seemed to be amused by it, the irony that a spy might be
spied upon; amused and at the same time almost embarrassed that things would come to this, watching over your
shoulder for the same people you thought were on your
side. "No one followed me here," he added. "I'm certain of
it. Now, tell me what you know so I can try to help."

"Does the name Gunther Kramer mean anything to
you?"

"I know the name very well. Why? He's been dead for
years."

"He's only been dead for three days. I was with him
when he died. He was murdered."

Caulfield was astonished. He bent forward, his eyes
suddenly eager and intense.

"You're positive it was him? Our information was that
he died in 1989, about the same time the Berlin Wall was
coming down. You're absolutely sure it was Gunther
Kramer?"

"The piano player."

"What?"

"It's what my father called him. It was Gunther Kramer
all right; he understood right away what it meant. And
there is no mistake, given some of the things he said, that

he knew my father—knew him rather well, in fact. He worked for him, became a double agent. He wanted out of the East, and my father was going to help him."

Caulfield nodded in agreement. "We would have, too; but events got ahead of us. No one expected the Soviet Union to collapse. No one had ever imagined that it would happen that quickly, with so little warning. All of a sudden East Germany did not exist. Everyone who had been part of the communist security apparatus changed their names and disappeared, tried to pass for someone else. Kramer must have realized that he could not go back to Germany, that even if he could prove that he had been working for us, he would only be seen as a spy without honor, someone who sold his services to the highest bidder. But he was alive and living in Hamburg all these years?"

"Not in Hamburg; he lived in Damascus."

Caulfield gave a sigh of something more than approval, of appreciation for the talent, the guile, the courage and sheer daring with which Gunther Kramer had pulled it off, managed to make the world believe he was dead, while he lived on, safe in the last place on earth anyone would ever have thought to look for him.

"But you met him in Hamburg. He came there from Damascus to see you?"

"And it cost him his life."

"He could have passed on whatever he had to someone in Damascus, but he chose to tell you. Why? Because of your father, I imagine. He must have thought he could trust you."

"He thought he had to warn me."

"Warn you?"

"He believed that someone was going to be assassinated. I think he thought there was a chance it might be me."

Caulfield pursed his lips, balancing the probabilities, trying to decide whether, from the point of view of what a terrorist might hope to achieve, the murder of a senator made sense.

"If he thought that, he would have been right for two reasons. You're a rising star, someone who might one day be president. If you were to be assassinated it takes away part of the country's future."

"And the other reason?" asked Hart as he got up from the table and put his empty beer bottle in the garbage beneath the sink.

"You don't get Secret Service protection. Killing you is as easy as shooting a stranger on the street."

Hart looked out the window at the moonlit night, wondering at what Caulfield had just said: how easy it would be, if someone wanted to kill him.

"Not in a presidential year," he remarked, surprised at the assurance with which he heard himself say it. He turned around and caught the skepticism in Caulfield's eyes. "If they want to disrupt the election, show the world that democracy isn't safe even in the United States, they'll try to kill the president. Think what would happen: the vice president becomes president, but only for the few months left in the term. The election is thrown into utter chaos, each party blaming the other for what has happened. If we're full of fear and anger now, imagine what that would do!"

"What else did Gunther Kramer tell you? He must have had some basis for what he told you, specific information about a planned assassination."

Hart came back to the table, sat down, and studied his hands.

"It was very strange. He said that everyone he talked to, all his sources, seemed sure that something was going to happen, that something had been set in motion, but no one seemed to know anything about who was involved or where the order was coming from."

Caulfield stroked his chin, a look of grave concern on his face.

"Our worst nightmare: a sleeper cell, waiting to carry out a mission given years in advance. It is the perfect cover: it can't be traced back to anyone. What else did he say?"

"The last thing he told me before he died. The code name for this is Rubicon. Can you find out if anything like that has been picked up in any of the electronic surveillance the agency has been doing? And again, the Syrians—they must know something. If Kramer learned about it, then . . ."

"I'll see what I can find out. I have to be careful; I'm not supposed to be doing much of anything these days except sitting in my office filling out forms."

Hart looked at Raymond Caulfield, nearing the end of his long years of service, ignored and almost forgotten, and wondered whether, had his father lived, the same thing would have happened to him. Theirs was the generation that had fought the great war and then watched, as they grew older, how another generation let others do their fighting for them and forgot how to keep the peace.

"How well did you know Gunther Kramer, back then?"

A wistful look, a remembrance of better times, made a brief, passing appearance in the older man's dark-circled eyes.

"I thought I knew everything about him, though I never actually met him. He was something of a legend, a man of unusual culture and intelligence. That was rare among East German agents. Your father came to admire him, as only your father could."

"I don't quite understand: 'as only my father could.'"

"Max was a very wise, well-educated man. He had read everything on the Russian Revolution; everything of Marx and Engels, and Lenin, too. He studied all the time, and, in addition, had a facility with languages that the rest of us could only envy."

A thin, distant smile, full of the knowledge of the past, slipped almost unnoticed across his lips. He spoke now in a different voice, richer and more secure.

"He understood what it must have been like for someone like Gunther Kramer—brilliant, gifted—to grow up in a regime that brutal and corrupt. Max thought that in an odd way it must have made him even more deeply intelligent than he might otherwise have become—the constant need to watch every word, tailor every action, so that it seemed to be in conformity with what was expected and demanded of a good member of the party. Think of living your life knowing that a single misspoken word could land you in the gulag or in front of a firing squad."

Caulfield rose from the table. He had the slightly distracted air of a man with much on his mind.

"You won't . . . ?" Hart started to ask. Immediately, he shook his head in apology.

"Tell anyone at the agency?" replied Caulfield, not the least bit wounded. "Of course not. There are only four or five people there I still trust; all of them, like me, about to be retired. None of them are in a position to help, and besides, I would not want to put them at risk."

"At risk?"

"The agency frowns on the sort of back-channel communication you and I have had for the last several years. Technically, despite your position on the committee, I could be charged with divulging classified information. The director, and those to whom he reports, only allow themselves to do that. If I were ever caught, the least they would do to me is to take away my pension. It's worth it," he added before Hart could say anything. "There are still some of us left that think the country can be saved from what these people have done to it."

"Kramer told me something else," said Hart as Caulfield got ready to leave.

Caulfield detected the hesitation, the note of caution, in Hart's voice.

"About this assassination plot—or about your father?"

Hart gave him a sharp, searching look.

"Why would you think it was something about . . . ? What is it you know?"

"What did he tell you?" asked Caulfield with a steady, even glance.

Somewhere in the distance a dog barked in the night. Another dog, farther on, answered back.

"That my father was murdered; that he did not die of a heart attack, the way it was reported."

"I never wanted to believe that," said Caulfield after a long, anguished silence. "I never wanted to, and yet, deep down, I suppose I always—"

"Kramer said he was murdered because of something he had learned, something he was on the point of proving. Is that possible? Could that have happened?"

"I don't know that, I don't know what he might have learned."

"Kramer said he found out that there was an organized effort to doctor the intelligence, to establish sources that reported whatever these people wanted to hear. They wanted a way to cast doubt on anything that suggested that there wasn't a threat."

"Max had very good sources—probably the best we had. There were high officials in the Iraqi government who would not talk to anyone else. It must have been frustrating for him," mused Caulfield, "when everything he found out was being discredited by sources he either did not trust or did not know anything about. If he discovered that this was being done on purpose, nothing would have stopped him from getting to the bottom of it."

Hart peered straight into his eyes.

"Kramer said that my father found out that there was a

group that had its own operatives, both here and abroad. Some of them were former agents who had been let go as unreliable or politically motivated. Is that possible? Could there have been—could there still be—an organization like that? Could they have killed my father?"

"The government is full of people who helped privatize a war; who set up phony companies that made fortunes providing private security forces to do things that did not have to be reported. The agency is full of people who believe that nothing is beyond the pale, that any means are permissible if they give you what you think you need. So, is it possible? Yes, without any question. Did it happen? I don't know, but it wouldn't surprise me if it had."

"Setting up different sources, manufacturing intelligence, killing my father when he found out—that isn't something a few disaffected agents could have done. Someone had to be in charge, someone had to be giving direction."

Caulfield gave him a long, searching look. "Someone outside the agency," he said finally, "someone with serious political power, someone who could pull together all the different strings, someone—"

"Someone like the vice president?"

"I told you that he and the people around him hadn't read Machiavelli. That doesn't mean that they weren't fully capable of being Machiavellian. I've seen the way they operate, the threats, the intimidation, the willingness to lie to anyone. There isn't anything they wouldn't do."

"Including murder?"

"If what Gunther Kramer told you is true, your father was a threat to everything they wanted. Would they have murdered him? Without a second thought. But, listen to me, Bobby. Don't try to find out anything; don't ask questions. They're too dangerous; they have people everywhere."

He shook hands and promised to find out what he could.

Hart turned out the kitchen lights, and under cover of darkness Raymond Caulfield disappeared.

It was nearly eleven, eight o'clock on the West Coast. Upstairs in the bedroom he had not shared with her in months, Bobby Hart sat on the edge of the bed and tried to call his wife. The phone rang and rang until, calling anyone else, he would have hung up; but this was Helen, and he let it ring some more, though he knew she would not answer, were he to let it ring all night. He wanted her to know it was he who was calling and that he was there, on the other end of the line, and that he was thinking of nothing else but her. Finally, he hung up and for a long time stared out the window as the trees outside rustled gently, very gently, in the wind.

5

THE HALLWAY OF THE WILLARD HOTEL WAS jammed. People were coming and going, everyone in a hurry, all of them part of a presidential campaign in which changes were still being made. A pair of Secret Service agents stood outside Prentice Alworth's suite. One of them checked Hart's identification while the other spoke into a tiny microphone he wore strapped to his wrist. A few moments later, the door opened and Bobby Hart was invited inside.

"It will be just a few minutes, Senator," said a thin young man in a dark suit. "The governor is just finishing up a call."

Two bookish-looking young men stood together at a window going over what appeared to be the text of a speech. Sitting, or rather slumped in the corner of a sofa, an older man with a shock of unruly gray hair was picking at his teeth while he digested an endless series of polling numbers.

"And to think that all this time I thought you just invented the number you needed."

Startled, Henry Glazer looked up. Embarrassed, he jumped to his feet.

"I'm sorry, Senator, I didn't know you were here. How are you?" he asked as they shook hands. It took only a moment before he caught the mood. "Yeah, well, these numbers—I couldn't make these up." He gave Hart a conspiratorial grin. "You could run a convicted felon and win this one. Doesn't matter who he is, almost doesn't matter what he believes—the only thing that matters is that he isn't a Republican."

Henry Glazer was a pollster always in demand. Inside Washington, he was as famous for his irreverence as for the accuracy of his surveys of public opinion.

"Which means," he continued with a jaded sparkle in his eyes, "that it's the kind of race that only a Democrat could lose." Suddenly, he looked at Hart with a puzzled expression. "They're making you wait? A year ago this guy couldn't get in to see the mayor of Cleveland, and now they're . . . ?" He started to turn toward the door to the private room where Prentice Alworth was huddled with his advisors. Hart stopped him.

"I don't mind waiting. It gives me a chance to talk to someone who knows something. What's the latest on the Senate races?"

"Barring any major new developments, Democrats should pick up four or five. Might even pick up more than that, with a little luck."

"Major new developments," repeated Hart slowly. "What would happen if something major did happen, something serious?"

"You mean . . . ?"

"Another attack. Maybe not like 9/11, but something."

Henry Glazer shuffled his feet and stared down at the

floor. All the irreverence was gone. He had had two friends, two close friends, killed in New York.

"It would depend on exactly what happened next," he said, raising his eyes just far enough to meet Hart's gaze. "And it would depend on the reaction."

"The reaction?"

Henry Glazer squared his shoulders. The off-the-rack suit he wore was a size too large. The coat sagged in the middle and, when he was not smiling, gave him the look of a salesman, tired and depressed by his travels.

"You remember 9/11—the look on the president's face: the deer-in-the-headlights look? Remember Giuliani: the way he took charge? Imagine they were candidates for the same office. It's not too tough to figure out which of them most people would have wanted to vote for. Character counts. The problem is that you can't always know who has it until it's too late."

Glazer had been around Washington long enough to know that politicians seldom asked a question without a reason.

"You're on the Intelligence Committee. Is there something I should know?"

"No," said Hart, shaking his head. "But two years ago there was a lot of talk about how terrorists might try to disrupt the congressional elections. I just wondered what might happen if they really made the attempt."

Hart checked his watch.

"Fifteen minutes," said Glazer, who kept track of both time and numbers in his head.

The door opened and one of the governor's senior assistants greeted Hart with a broad smile and an outstretched hand and took him inside. Prentice Alworth, standing next to a desk, invited Hart to take a chair.

"It's good to see you, Senator," he began with what seemed to Hart a kind of nervous reluctance.

In his early fifties, Alworth was handsome in the rough sort of way that goes with the kind of self-assurance easily mistaken for leadership, but there was something missing in his eyes. Hart had noticed the same thing in other politicians: a dead look, an absence of expression, as if they had been so focused on their own ambition, it was all they could see anymore.

"Let me come right to the point," said Alworth. He flashed a smile that, seen from a distance, would have enveloped you with warmth, but seen close-up, seemed not just artificial but awkward and strangely mistimed. "I would like you to be my running mate. I'd like you to run for vice president. I think we would make an unbeatable ticket."

Hart's mind ran immediately to Henry Glazer and his polling numbers. Was that what Alworth and his people had been discussing while they made him wait outside? Hart sat quietly, waiting, as Alworth pressed his case.

"Look, I know I wasn't your first choice for the nomination. I may not have been anyone's first choice," he added with a shrewd, calculating glance. "And I know there are a great many people, and not just in our own party, who wish you were the nominee. I understand that. I also understand that you're in a reelection campaign in California and—"

"I can't do it, Governor."

Alworth had expected this, or something like it, to be Hart's first response. It was smart, the opening move in a delicate negotiation. He had been told that Hart was always just a little bit ahead of everyone else.

"I don't have to remind you, Senator, that this is an important election, perhaps the most important you or I will ever see," he continued with all the worried sincerity he could muster. "We have to take the country back, save it from what has been happening to it for the last eight years.

We have to win this election, Bobby, we have to. And no one can help do that as much as you can."

Hart stared at Alworth, wondering if the governor ever meant anything he said, whether he ever thought about anything except the effect he wanted to achieve, what he wanted others to believe about what he thought and what he felt.

"You don't need me to carry California, so there really isn't any reason—"

"I need you to carry places like Missouri and Ohio, even some places in the South. There's an enormous respect for you out there in the country. All the polling we've done—"

"If I were on the ticket, you'd have to spend half your time trying to explain away the differences between us. I have six years in the Senate, four more in the House—thousands of votes, not all of which I remember, and not all of which you could support."

Prentice Alworth gave him the look of encouragement with which he had persuaded countless others that they could do anything they dreamed of doing, once he had the power to give them the help they needed.

"We've been through your record. There isn't anything that would cause problems."

"There is some pending legislation that might," said Hart, intrigued by the way Alworth could look right at him as if he were looking at someone filling up an empty space. "One bill in particular."

Alworth gave him a different look, that of growing confidence, the certainty that there were no major difficulties, nothing that could not be handled. It reminded Hart that he was dealing with a man whose mind worked in narrow channels.

"That bill isn't going anywhere, and the session is almost over. It was just a gesture, a symbolic act," said Alworth, starting to talk the way he would when he had to explain it to the press. "A way to show that neither the administration nor the Republicans in Congress were really willing to do everything necessary to win the war."

"I'm afraid it's more than a gesture, Governor. I happen to believe we ought to have the draft." He could not resist using the line with which he had talked to the press about the bill that nearly everyone had opposed. "It's never been clear to me why only the children of the poor should have the chance to serve their country."

Alworth nodded in agreement, the way he always did when he was forced to listen to what someone else had to say.

"It won't be a problem," he insisted. "It's legislation you introduced to make a point, and, the point having been made, you see no reason, at the present time, to continue with it."

"That legislation is a matter of principle with me. I happen to believe in the importance of shared sacrifice."

"We all do, Bobby; but you have to look at the broader perspective. Your principles won't mean anything—and neither will mine—if we don't win this election, if another Republican is allowed to keep control of the executive branch of government. Surely you can see that."

Hart felt like Hamlet, listening to Polonius recite the rules of success followed by fools; a lesson in practical wisdom from a man who could not see anything beyond the end of his nose.

"There are a number of reasons I can't agree to do what you ask. I'm in the middle of a Senate campaign. With so little time left, if the party had to name another candidate it might mean—"

Alworth shrugged aside the objection. "This isn't a year for conservatives, especially in California. Don't worry. A Democrat will hold that seat."

"Yes, and it's going to be me. I appreciate the offer. I'm

quite honored, but I'm not ready to run for national office."

Prentice Alworth lowered his eyes. His manner became stiff, awkward, and hesitant.

"I know about the difficulties you have with your wife. I can certainly understand why you might want to protect her from all the attention that comes with this kind of campaign."

Hart's eyes turned cold and full of warning.

"And what exactly is it that you think you know about my wife?"

"It's none of my business, but it isn't any secret that your wife, Helen, has certain . . . problems, that she—"

"Is mentally ill. Is that what you're trying to say? Why not just say it, then?"

"I didn't mean—I'm not trying to—" Alworth stammered.

Suddenly, Hart felt sorry for him. Alworth was in an impossible situation and it was not his fault. With a slight, sympathetic smile Hart let him know that he did not blame him for anything. And then he lied.

"She sometimes struggles with depression. It's better when she doesn't have to deal with a lot of other people. No one bothers her now, while I'm in the Senate, but what you're asking . . . The press, the media, would never leave her alone."

"Tell everyone what the problem is," Alworth advised. "Explain why she won't be out campaigning. That will be the end of it."

The way he said it, suggesting that this was just another political problem that the governor's people had worked out, that illness and the tragedy of other people's lives were all manageable parts of the process, removed any doubt Hart might still have had about his decision.

"It doesn't matter what some focus group said about

this, I'm not going to do it. I'm not going to run for vice president. I can't."

Prentice Alworth seemed genuinely disappointed. He understood that it was over, that Bobby Hart was not going to change his mind. He shook his hand, told him how much he looked forward to working with him after the election, and then started thinking about who he was going to ask next.

When Hart got back to his Senate office, he told David Allen what had happened. Allen ran his hand over his balding head.

"He obviously isn't afraid to have someone on the ticket that might have a following of his own. That makes him better than I thought."

"Not better, just more ambitious. He'll say anything to get elected. He would have promised me anything, if I'd been willing to run."

"He wasn't willing to support a draft."

"He thinks it would cost him votes, but anything having to do with power, with the authority the vice president would have in his administration . . . Of course, after the election, after I had served my purpose, he'd forget what he's promised me even faster than all the things he promised the voters. But now that I've turned him down, who do you think he'll pick?"

"Someone else from the Senate," said Allen with quiet certainty. "Someone who can bring some knowledge of foreign policy to the ticket. It'll be someone from the Committee on Foreign Relations."

"You're probably right," said Hart with indifference. "I've got a plane to catch and I haven't even packed. Is everything set in California?" he asked as he started to gather up the papers he wanted to take with him.

"Stone will pick you up at the airport," he said, referring to Jeffrey Stone, the campaign manager. "He wants to talk to you before tomorrow's events."

"Tell him I'll meet him for breakfast in the morning. I'm going home. I have to see Helen tonight."

Hart made his way through traffic, angry with himself that he had not thought to pack the night before and bring his bag with him to the office. He could have left from there, gone directly to the airport, instead of going to Georgetown first. Everything was jumbled up, one thing piled on top of the other, no time to think about what he should do next. The word *Rubicon* kept echoing in his head and he still had no idea what it meant. He wanted to tell someone what had happened, how he had been shot and Gunther Kramer had been killed, but unless Raymond Caulfield found something at the CIA, who would believe him?

Charlie Ryan was sitting on the front steps, waiting for him to arrive.

"Shouldn't you be in Michigan, campaigning?" asked Hart as he opened the door.

"Allen told me you were on your way here," Ryan explained as he dusted himself off. "And as for campaigning, I'm not sure it would do any good."

"Sit down," said Hart, glad to see him. "What can I get you?"

Ryan dropped, spread-eagle, into a wing chair, next to the shelves that held the art books Helen had collected.

"Nothing, thanks anyway. I know you have to get to the airport. Go ahead and pack." He opened the louvered shutters just a crack and peered outside. "You ever think you're being followed?"

Hart sat on the edge of the sofa.

"Why? Do you think someone . . . ?"

Ryan frowned, let the shutter snap shut and shook his head.

"It's probably all the things we hear in committee; makes you think half the people you see on the street are about to blow you up. But, still, lately—it's just a feeling . . . That isn't the reason I wanted to catch you before you left. Have you heard anything? I need to know if I'm in trouble. There must be some polling on your side."

Hart knew Ryan too well to believe that he was only worried about the polling results of the other party. Ryan had polls of his own, to say nothing of all the other, public, surveys that were done by the newspapers and the networks.

"So far as I know, no different than what you told me the last time we talked about it. You're running ahead of a popular attorney general who has a fair amount of money, but she's still three points behind and—"

"Which means it's within the margin of error, which means it's competitive," Ryan interjected. He seemed puzzled. "Our polls aren't much different, which means none of it makes sense."

"What doesn't make sense?"

"I thought there was a chance that our polls were just flat-out wrong, that someone else had something showing that I was getting beat and getting beat badly."

"Why would you think that?"

Ryan's eyes were moving everywhere at once, searching for a reason that would explain the inexplicable.

"The money has dried up. I'm in maybe the most competitive race in the country and suddenly the money stops coming."

"That's crazy."

"That's what I told the White House three days ago. I've spent a lot—I've had to—but the national committee always comes through with more. But this time, with everything on the line, with my seat maybe the difference, they tell me that they've already given me what they budgeted, but that maybe, in October . . . So I went to the White House and all they did was say they would see what they could do."

"What makes you think they won't do something?"

Ryan looked right at him, his gaze narrow and intense.

"It was the attitude. It was like they didn't care what happened, that it didn't really matter whether I held the seat or not."

There was an easy explanation, but as Hart understood, Ryan had too much at stake to see it.

"They probably don't care, Charlie. They're on their way out. A few more months and another president will be elected and another administration takes office."

"No, something else is going on," said Ryan, shaking his head emphatically. "Retribution, their chance to get even for all the times I refused to go along, all the trouble I gave them on things they thought important. I started checking, following the money, where it was going and where it was not. The money is there, they're just not giving it to anyone like me."

It did not make any sense. Ryan was reading too much into it.

"Even if the president and his people felt like that, the rest of the party couldn't possibly want to lose a Senate seat to a Democrat."

"Trust me, Bobby—whatever you think you know—the White House still has control. That line about 'you're either with us or against us' did not just apply to people overseas. I was the first Republican member of the Senate to raise serious questions about the war. The vice president hates me for that. He thinks that if I hadn't said anything, everyone else would have stayed in line. He sits in those meetings with all the other principal advisers and never says a word; then he meets privately with the president and decides everything."

"Even if he hates you, it's hard to believe that he would think a Democrat would be an improvement."

Ryan bent forward. His eyes were cold and immediate.

"As long as he holds power, as long as the president is in office, he doesn't care what Congress does. When it comes to the war, no one can stop him."

6

W HEN SHE WAS YOUNGER, WHEN SHE AND
Bobby first started going out, women would stop
her on the street and tell her that she looked just like a
movie star. Bobby used to tease her about it, gently, as a
way of letting her know why it happened, why everyone
thought that she was much too good-looking to be anything but famous. What he had not understood was that
she hated having strangers stare at her, and that the reason
she gripped his hand so hard when they walked into a restaurant or some other public well-lit place was a trembling self-consciousness and a mortal fear that she might
do something wrong. She clung to Bobby, not just because
she had fallen in love with him, but because he made her
feel safe. What she did not understand, what she was then
too young to realize, was that Bobby took his own confidence so much for granted that he assumed that all she
suffered from was a little youthful shyness.

It was strange that she was so quiet and withdrawn
around other people; when it was just the two of them she

was not like that at all. He remembered that now, as he drove up the winding road through Montecito, close to Santa Barbara: the way she used to run to him barefooted when he came home at night; the way her fine, fragile voice, full of bright lights and laughter, made him forget everything that had happened that day. He wanted to hear that voice again; he wanted to see the shining eagerness in her eyes and the easy way she moved; he wanted back again all the things he had loved and in his blissful ignorance thought he could never lose.

He turned in at the gate. The gardener must have come. The long tangled pile of bougainvillea that had worked its way around the hinges, making it difficult to open, had finally been trimmed back. He left the engine running and started fumbling for his key, but the gate had been left unlocked and all he had to do was push it forward. He looked around, remembering how happy and excited they were the day they found it, the house they had dreamed of, with the long view of the Pacific and the lights of Santa Barbara far below, and the rustling brittle leaves of the eucalyptus trees just outside the bedroom windows. It was one of those Spanish haciendas, all white stucco and tile, set far back from the road, surrounded by tall thick hedges and vine-covered fences to keep out the prying eyes of the world.

The house was dark. He started to open the front door, but then he hesitated, wondering if she had heard the car.

"Helen, it's me," he said as he stepped inside.

"Hello, Bobby."

Startled, he looked up to find her standing in the living room just a few feet away. She was holding her cat.

"Look," she said, stroking the cat's shoulder. "Bobby has come to see us." There was a distant, lost look in her large oval eyes that read like an accusation, a silent protest against abandonment and betrayal. "We weren't sure he would, were we?" she whispered to the cat as she knelt down and let it go.

He started toward her.

"Helen, I—"

"Want something to eat? I remember how to cook." She turned away from him and, without another word, walked to the kitchen.

He put down his bag and followed her.

"I could make you eggs; I could . . ." She looked at him with the saddest eyes he had ever seen. "Oh, God, Bobby . . . why?" she cried in a voice from which all the light, and all the laughter, had disappeared. He took her in his arms and told her that things would be all right. She pressed her tearstained face against his chest. "Please don't go; please don't leave."

"I'll never leave you," he promised, the way he always did. "I'll never go."

With a brave smile, she told him that she knew he meant it.

"Not forever, or anything like that, but now, and for a long time, you have."

And it was there again, that haunted, desperate look, that was like a knife through his heart.

"I know I promised that I wouldn't," he began, the words practiced more than once on the long drive from the airport. "I know I promised when I ran the first time, but things have changed, and there are things I need to do, things . . ."

"I know," she said, with a wild, helpless look. She was barefoot, wearing only a white silk nightshirt. Her hair was pulled up in back, the way she often wore it, exposing the long slender neck that was like a white pedestal for her lovely, perfect face. "You said you wouldn't run again, you said that we could come home again. That was the only thing that kept me going, kept me sane—the thought that there would be an end to it, that each day there was one day less to wait until we could be here again."

She took him by the hand and led him to the sitting room behind the kitchen, the room where they used to spend their evenings. She sat in the chair she sat in every night; and he sat next to her, waiting.

"I know you had to," she said after a long silence. She looked at him with a judgment so acute as to seem almost clairvoyant. "I know there are things you have to do. What I'm trying to tell you is that I know that, and that I hope you can forgive me. I must be such a disappointment to you." She stared out the window, thinking about all the problems she thought she had caused him.

"I tried—you know I tried—but I couldn't, I couldn't hide behind a vacant smile, say all the strange, empty things everyone expects you to say." She turned her head and gave him a tender, wistful glance. "Do people really believe it when other people say things like that?"

She looked back, through the glass, out to the vast moonlit ocean, wanting to take back everything that had changed.

"Our life was good, when you just belonged to me, and I did not have to share you with everyone who sees you on television. But I'm okay, Bobby; I'm not unhappy, living here, alone. I know you think of me; I know you call," she said, her voice growing faint as if she had made her peace with loneliness and there was now nothing more to say.

"Come back with me; live in the house in Georgetown when I have to be in Washington; live here—with me— whenever we can get away."

"Every day I tell myself that's what I'll do tomorrow; and then tomorrow comes, and I'm still here." She saw the sadness in his eyes and felt the sadness in her own. "What are you going to do, when are you going to come home? When are you going to remember that I'm the only home you'll ever have? Do you want to save the world, Bobby Hart, or do you want to save me?"

Bobby was not sure he could do either, but he knew he had to try. He had to do whatever he could to help her, whatever the cost might be to his own ambitions.

"Remember Florence—what a good time we had there?" He wrapped both hands around his knee and leaned back, as if they had all the time in the world and he was just reminiscing. "Remember how much you liked it, and how we promised we would go back and see some more of Italy?"

A vague smile floated across her lips as she remembered and, remembering, felt better.

"The hotel with the view across the rooftops to the Duomo, and the drunk laughter in the street that woke us up every night; and the long walks along the Arno and all the old churches we went inside, and all the crooked streets and how often we got lost . . ."

"I thought we could go back—in November, after the election—rent a villa in Fiesole. You liked it there, remember? In the hills outside Florence, with none of the congestion and the noise. No one else but us; no one who even knows my name. You'd like that, wouldn't you—if we went back? We could go other places, too," he went on, warming to the subject. "Rome, or, if you would rather, somewhere in the south of France."

At first she seemed to like it, something to look forward to, something that might finally fill the days and nights with hope; but then, with the strange clarity with which she could sometimes read the future, her smile faded into nothingness and she told him that perhaps they ought to talk about it later.

"Do you have to go so soon?" she asked, as she stood up and took him by the hand. "Or can you stay until morning?" He started to explain, but she looked down at him and put her finger on his lips. "I know you have things you have to do, and I know I should be there with you. I'll try, Bobby; I promise I'll try. But stay tonight, and come back soon, and we'll talk some more and I'll work at being stronger and less afraid. When you're here, I'm not afraid of anything."

He left in the morning, while she was still asleep; but before he did, he wrote a note telling her that he loved her and that he would be back again that night.

JEFFREY STONE was waiting for him at quarter to seven in the back booth of a motel restaurant on the beach in Santa Barbara. He had run Hart's first campaign for the Senate, knew California and its politics as well as anyone else in the business, and had almost never lost a state-wide contest. Hart was not sure he liked him and was not sure he ever would. Stone was too full of calculation, juggling numbers the way a gambler bets on races, always looking for a change in trends, the first signs of slippage or the first evidence of an advance. It was all mathematics, politics devoid of meaning except the statistics it produced. Hart slid into the booth and tried to seem glad to see him.

Stone pushed aside a cheap lined notebook in which he had jotted some notes. He took a taste of the coffee that had gone cold and signaled to the waitress to bring him another cup.

"You said six-thirty."

"I'm late. You going to fire me?"

"If you worked for me I would. I guess I should be grateful. At least this time you made it."

"You mean the one weekend I didn't get out here," replied Hart. He smiled at the waitress while she poured him a cup of coffee. "Something came up. And before you start in about it," he continued, the smile on his mouth now a challenge, "there may be other things that come up as well. Schedule me any way you want, between now and the election, but from now on do it with the idea that it is always subject to change."

Stone studied Hart with clinical indifference.

"Run, don't run; show up, don't show up; win, lose—I don't care. But you might want to make up your mind just what the hell you want to do. I know it's California, I know you have a sixteen-point lead—I also know," he said, bending forward on his elbows, "that leads like that have been lost before."

Stone was ten years older and looked it, in a coat a size too big and a shirt a size too small, a tie that was not tied and socks that even on a good day did not always match. He only ever smiled in anger, and what usually followed—a volcanic torrent of abuse—made the smile seem in retrospect almost pleasant. He had no respect for anyone who did not want to win, and not much more for those who did. He was the most congenitally unhappy person Hart thought he had ever met.

"Why are you in this business, why do you run campaigns? As far as I can tell, you've never liked any candidate, including me, you've ever worked for. What do you care if they win or not—or are you afraid that you'd take all the blame if they didn't?"

Stone lived on confrontation, on verbal combat. His only friends were the enemies he made.

"Why am I in it? To keep the bad guys from winning."

"To keep the bad guys . . . ?"

"From winning. Simple enough. Want me to explain it? There are good guys and bad guys. I help the good guys— even when they don't know they're the good guys."

It was like Alice in Wonderland. Hart started to laugh.

"See, Senator What's Your Name—you're a good guy. It's not your fault," he quickly added, shaking his head as if to absolve him of all responsibility. "It isn't anything you've done; it's what the other side does—the bad guys: Republicans, most of them; conservatives, all of them. I hate them, always have. I was brought up that way. My father fought in the Second World War; my mother was a grade-school teacher. Until I was ten or eleven, swear to God, I thought Franklin Roosevelt was Jesus' brother—their pictures were right next to each other, first thing you saw when you came in the house. I know—you don't have to tell me—lot of Democrats, some of whom I've worked for, aren't any better than the whores on the other side; but the point is that they aren't on the other side. They're on my side, the good side, the side that at least every once in a while tries to do something right. So if I tell you that you would not be the first guy to blow a sixteen-point lead, it isn't because I give a damn whether you win; it's because it would just kill me if that idiot on the other side didn't lose. By the way," added Stone as he pushed across the table the latest figures showing that Hart's lead was holding steady, "maybe you should consider running next time. You probably wouldn't be the worst president we've ever had."

"How could I lose with that kind of enthusiasm," replied Hart, starting to like him despite himself. "Now, tell me, what have I got this morning?"

In a brisk, monotonous voice, Stone reeled off the list of places Hart was supposed to go and the times he was scheduled to arrive at each of them.

"You finish up tonight at a dinner in San Diego. You spend the night there, and then, tomorrow morning—"

"No," said Hart firmly. "I spend the night back here. I spend the night every night I'm in California back here. No exceptions." He waited until he caught the first caustic movement of Jeffrey Stone's embittered lip. "Unless of course you insist I don't; but if it isn't absolutely necessary, then I have reasons why I should."

Rare and almost forgotten, a slender smile made the briefest possible appearance on Stone's crooked, jaded mouth.

"Of course, Senator; there won't be a problem. I'll make sure of it."

They left the restaurant and went to the airport where a plane was waiting for the short flight to L.A. Hart looked out the window as the private jet gained altitude, searching for his house among the shadowed hills. There was a kind of comfort knowing it was there, a place far away from politics and terrorism, a place where he knew Helen was safe.

For the next few hours he seemed to be everywhere at once, giving the same short speech over and over again, pausing at just the right times, saying what needed to be said about the serious threat the country now faced and saying it with a sense of both realism and hope. He seemed to feed on it, becoming stronger, more energetic each time he did it. It was a kind of narcotic: the steady diet of attention and applause, the knowledge that what he said his audience in that moment not only heard but thought; the strange sense that while he did it, stood in front of a crowd, telling them what he thought, what he believed, he could not feel anything he did not want to feel, nothing that could hurt. He had no time to think of Helen and what he might have done to her.

It was past midnight when he got home, but Helen was waiting for him, eager to talk. She was fully dressed, in a simple skirt and blouse. She had even put on makeup and done something with her hair. It was the sign of effort and Bobby Hart felt better than he had all day.

"I saw you on television—when you explained that you did not want to be a candidate for vice president. But you would have run, wouldn't you, if it hadn't been for me? You would have run for president if it hadn't been for me;

if you hadn't had to worry about what would happen, whether I could cope, whether I could . . ."

Hart poured himself a drink, and then sank into the sofa right next to her.

"There isn't anything I wouldn't do for you; but that was not one of them. The truth of it is that I don't like Alworth; I don't trust him. The worst part is that I don't think he really trusts himself. He's like a lot of them are now, the ones who run for president: they're whatever they think everyone wants them to be."

"But you aren't like that; you aren't what everyone wants you to be."

"I told you that if I had run, I wouldn't have had a chance."

She laughed a little and then the laughter died away and she put her head on his shoulder and closed her eyes. He put his arm around her and held her for a long time, staring out into the Santa Barbara night, and the starlight shining silver on the immense solitude of the ocean, sweeping endlessly against the shore.

HE SLEPT LATE, and when he got up, made breakfast for them both. Under the warm morning sun, the blue Pacific was a shimmering sea of bronze. The palm trees just beyond the backyard pool stood motionless in the warm September air.

"I've been thinking about what you said last night. Did it ever occur to you that I might not have wanted to be president?" He held her chair and then sat down on the opposite side of the table. "I didn't think about it when I first ran for Congress. I didn't think about it, six years ago, when I first ran for the Senate. What happens is that other people start talking about it, and then you start wondering if you could, and then you look around and you see the people who have a good chance of getting it and you realize that they're not really better than anyone else you know and you start to think . . ." He pushed his fork through the soft yolk of his eggs. "But, no, I didn't this time, and even if I wanted to, there's no reason to think that things won't be completely different four years from now, or eight years from now." He looked at her in a way that told her he had thought a lot about what he was about to say. "And besides, after what has happened, after what may happen because of it, I may not serve out my term. A year, maybe two— and then I'll quit." He gave her an earnest, almost pleading glance. "Do you think you can get through it, another year, maybe two?"

A sliver of a smile, brave and tentative, came out into the world, ready for whatever judgment was made of it.

"I'll try, Bobby, I promise I'll try."

"Let's get out of here for a while," he suggested quietly. "We'll drive up the coast, out to that beach no one seems to know is there. We won't have to see or talk to anyone."

They spent the day in the simple comfort of being together, safe from all the staring faces, all the familiar strangers who felt the need to introduce themselves and tell the senator what they thought. They packed a lunch, the way they did when they were younger, before he ever ran for Congress, before anyone knew his name. They did not say much to each other—they did not need to. They sat alone on a long stretch of deserted seashore, and when they felt like it, walked barefoot ankle deep in water. They left when twilight came and, after just a few minutes, she fell asleep on his shoulder while he drove the long way home. He carried her inside and, though she woke long enough to smile a protest, put her to bed and sat next to her, waiting until she was sound asleep again.

It had been a long time since he had felt as good as he did that day. He walked around the house, wondering why he had ever thought that he had to be somewhere else, doing other things. He had meant what he told her about quitting after a year or two. After everything that had happened, after everything he had seen, the only ambition he had left was to do what he could to make Helen's life a little better than it had been.

He got a beer from the refrigerator and decided that, for a while, before he crawled into bed next to her, he would see what was on television.

If he had turned it on five minutes later, he would not have heard about it until morning. It was a short, straightforward report, not even the lead item on the local news.

"And in the national news, a tragic accident has claimed the life of the deputy director of the CIA, Raymond Caulfield. Caulfield was apparently on his way home in suburban Maryland when he lost control of his car."

Bobby Hart did not believe it for a minute. Raymond Caulfield had been murdered.

H OW LONG HAD THE DEPUTY DIRECTOR LIVED in the same place?"

Ronald Townsend looked at the senator as if he did not quite understand the question. Hart looked back at him as if he had better be quick with an answer.

"The same place, Director Townsend. You're the director of the CIA. Are you going to sit there, in front of this committee, and tell us that you don't know where the deputy director of your agency lived or how many years he had lived there?"

With small pointed ears and a mouth that seemed to quiver with disapproval, Townsend had the manner of a librarian whose patience was about to give out.

"I will answer—if you will let me. Mr. Caulfield had been with the agency for more than forty years. He would have retired from the agency in approximately four months, if I'm not mistaken. As to the question of where he lived, and how long he might have lived there . . ." He reached back for a file folder an assistant had started to hand him. "I'm sure we have it here somewhere."

"You don't know where he lived? You were never a guest in his home?"

"I'm afraid I never had that pleasure," said the director in a dull monotone. He looked up from the file that now lay open in front of him. "Yes, here it is." He announced the address as a fact of no importance. "As to how long he lived there . . . It appears it is the only address he ever had, I mean since he began at the agency, forty . . . no, forty-two years ago."

"Long enough, I take it," said Hart with an acid look, "that he probably knew the road home. Raymond Caulfield was trained as a field operative, wasn't he? As a matter of fact, he was, for many years, the head of covert operations at the agency."

"Yes, I believe that is correct."

"You 'believe' that is correct, Mr. Townsend? You don't know that to be correct?"

"A figure of speech, Senator. You're right," he said, glancing at the folder in front of him. "He was head of—"

"But you didn't know him then, did you?"

"I became director just eighteen months ago."

"After spending most of your life in the private sector—the defense industry, to be specific."

"That's correct. I was—"

Hart waved it off.

"I'm familiar with your resume—and its limitations. But we're not here to discuss your management of the agency. We're here to find out what you are doing to investigate the death of your own deputy director. My question may strike you as irrelevant, a waste of your time, but does it not seem just a little odd that Raymond Caulfield, who had been driving that same route home for forty years, would suddenly lose control of his car and plunge down a ravine to his death? Doesn't it seem odd that someone that careful—he was deputy director of the CIA, for God's sake—would be that careless?"

"The local police investigated. It was their conclusion that it was an accident, Senator. There is no reason to think that it was not. Unfortunately, things like this happen all the time."

"I sent you a letter asking that you come prepared to answer certain specific questions. I see that you have it with you."

Townsend pulled it from a second folder. He did not bother to look at it.

"Yes, Senator; the answer to all three questions is no."

"If you don't mind, Mr. Townsend, I'll ask them anyway," said Hart with a flash of anger. Then he changed his mind. He tossed the pencil he had been holding between his fingers on the table and sat back. "Your testimony is that the deputy director of the CIA was not working on anything connected with the recent rumors of an attempted political assassination?"

"That's correct. There are certain definite lines of authority inside the agency. Mr. Caulfield had no responsibility for investigating this kind of domestic threat."

"Domestic threat? You mean because it would take place on American soil, though carried out by foreign nationals?"

"Yes, of course that's what I meant."

"But even though it may not have been his responsibility, as deputy director he could have involved himself in the investigation had he wanted to."

It was clear that the senator did not understand the basic rules of organizational efficiency.

"No organization, if it is going to function properly, can

afford to have anyone act outside the established lines of authority. Once that starts to happen, then no one can be sure who is in charge of what."

"He was the deputy director."

"It was not his job. He would not have been allowed—"

Hart shot forward. "Not allowed? By whom? By you? Are you telling me—are you telling this committee—that the director of the CIA expressly prohibited his own deputy director—who had been with the agency for forty-two years—from looking into, or even asking questions about, a plot to disrupt the election?"

"As I've just finished telling you, Senator, there are clear lines of authority and responsibility. I didn't tell Mr. Caulfield that he couldn't do something. I didn't have to. He knew what he was there to do."

"Because that had been made clear to him, when you took over, a year and a half ago . . ." Hart picked up the pencil and tapped it on the table. "And what about you, Director Townsend? Have you been involved in the effort to find whoever might be planning an assassination? Or is that outside your line of authority?"

Townsend bristled at the suggestion.

"I've been directly involved every step of the way."

"You have regular meetings, you're constantly kept up to date—you have a chance to ask questions of everyone involved?" Hart asked this with apparent indifference as he glanced down at a document.

"Yes, of course, Senator; every day."

Hart raised his eyes. A thin smile creased his mouth.

"But Raymond Caulfield wasn't included in those meetings. Was that perhaps because there were things you didn't want him to know?"

"No, that's absurd. Why would I—?"

"The decision to keep the deputy director out of those

meetings, to make sure he didn't know anything about what the agency was doing—"

"I have to object to that characterization, Senator. That was not the intention."

"The decision to keep Raymond Caulfield out of those meetings—was that your decision or did it come from someone at a higher level?"

"I'm in charge of the CIA! Look, Senator, the fact is that Raymond Caulfield was ready to retire. We've gone through a major reorganization; things aren't done the way they used to be. I was brought in to make the kind of changes needed to make the agency better able to respond to the challenges of the world we live in, the world as it is since 9/11. I had great respect for Raymond Caulfield, for everything he had done, his long years of service; but he was not going to be part of the agency's future."

"So you cut him out—or you tried."

"It was not a question of cutting him . . . Tried? I'm not sure I know what you mean."

"In Mr. Caulfield's last appearance before this committee, he was asked to find out what certain intelligence services in the Middle East, particularly the Syrians, might have heard."

Townsend understood at once. There was only an apparent contradiction.

"He wrote a full report of his testimony before the committee. The question about what the Syrians might have learned was passed on to me. Mr. Caulfield was always quite thorough."

"And what did you find out?"

"Nothing more than what we knew already: rumors of an assassination."

"Nothing about the time period within which this is supposed to happen? Nothing beyond the obvious point that if this is an attempt to disrupt the election it would have to take place before the election?"

"No, nothing like that."

Hart leaned back. "I asked you, in that letter I sent, whether the agency had any current information on a former East German agent named Gunther Kramer."

"No, nothing current, but there is no reason we should. He died in 1989. Is there some particular reason why the senator had an interest in someone who has been dead that long?"

"I'm not in the CIA, Mr. Townsend. How would I have known that he was not still alive? The reason I was interested is that I was once told that no one knew more about the Middle East. I thought it might be helpful to find someone who not only knew something, but would actually tell us the truth about it. But you're sure he's dead? There was a rumor that he had not died, that he was living in Damascus, and still had very good contacts on the Arab street."

"We have no knowledge of anything like that. But even if that rumor were true, why would you think a former East German agent would be willing to help us?"

"Because he was also working for the CIA. Gunther Kramer was a double agent, working for the West. That should be somewhere in your files, unless for some reason those files have been destroyed. But let me ask you another question, Mr. Townsend, again about Mr. Caulfield."

Hart chose his words carefully. He did not want to trap Townsend in a lie; he wanted to find out how much he knew.

"As I'm sure he must have mentioned in that report he submitted, the last time he appeared before the committee I told him privately, after the session ended, that in addition to the rumors I had been hearing about an assassination, that this plot had a name."

"A name, Senator? I don't recall that he mentioned—"

"Rubicon."

Townsend's eyes narrowed into a concentrated stare. His mouth twitched at the corners. He nodded twice and then looked straight at Hart.

"Yes, now I remember. He did say something about that; but we haven't found anything to confirm it."

"He reported that to you? It was not something that he tried to check on himself?"

"No, Senator. As I tried to explain earlier, the deputy director was not involved—"

"Thank you, Mr. Chairman, I have no further questions of the witness," announced Hart abruptly.

Caulfield had not known anything about Rubicon until just days before his death. He might have said something to the director, but Hart tended to doubt it. Townsend was just trying to give Hart the answer he thought he was looking for, tell a lie that would keep the senator satisfied.

The chairman was bringing the hearing to a close. "Unless someone else has a question for the director, the committee will—"

"I have a question for the director. Maybe several."

Charlie Ryan bent forward so the chairman, with half a turn, could see him. The chairman, who had other things to do, did not hide his disappointment.

"Yes, all right, Senator, but please keep in mind that this is a short week. With one convention starting this weekend and the other one the week after that, senators of both parties have only a limited amount of time and—"

"I'll be brief. Mr. Townsend, Senator Hart asked you whether the decision to keep the deputy director out of the loop—"

"That's not how I would characterize—"

"Out of the loop, was your decision or whether it came from someone at a higher level. Your answer, to quote you directly, was: 'I'm in charge of the CIA.'" Ryan fixed him with a lethal smile. "Which of course was no answer at all. So I will repeat the question, though, with all due deference to my friend, the distinguished senator from California, in a slightly different way. Was the decision to keep the deputy director out of the meetings when this potential assassination plot was being discussed made in consultation with anyone outside the CIA?"

"Not as the principal subject of discussion."

Charles Thomas Ryan had spent years as a federal prosecutor. In a series of corruption cases, he had taken on the political establishments of both parties. Nothing made him happier than taking apart a witness for the other side. He looked at Townsend and laughed out loud.

"'Not as the principal subject of discussion.' The answer, in other words, is yes."

"Of course I have regular conversations with the head of the Department of Homeland Security, and others in the administration, about the changes being made in the agency, about—"

"'Others in the administration?' You mean the president and the vice president? Neither of whom apparently objected that Raymond Caulfield, who had been with the agency longer than anyone else, who knew more about the way it worked—the way it was supposed to work—than probably anyone alive, be kept away from learning anything about this plot. But I think you have already answered that question. So tell me next, what did you do when you were told about Rubicon? We know you didn't ask Mr. Caulfield to do anything about it. So what did you do? Have a meeting?" Ryan searched Townsend's eyes, almost daring him to lie. "Or did you employ all that advanced technology you've told us would make all the difference and try to find out if that word *Rubicon* came up in all that chatter you can supposedly now intercept and decipher?"

The face of the director grew more rigid the longer he listened.

"I believe I answered the question earlier. We have found nothing to suggest that the name is in usage."

"That was not my question, Mr. Townsend. I asked about your methods. Never mind. There is only one question that matters at this point. Someone out there is planning to kill someone—perhaps the president, perhaps someone else—and we still don't have any idea who it is. Is that a fair statement of the situation, Mr. Townsend?"

"Yes, Senator, I'm afraid it is."

The hearing was over. Cursing under his breath, the director gathered up his neatly filed documents and left. The chairman and the other members of the committee hurried on to the next thing on their schedules. Ryan caught up with Hart in the hallway just outside.

"What's going on, Bobby? You know something the rest of us don't. You didn't tell Caulfield anything in private—you never mentioned Rubicon. You and I left together the day that hearing was over. You never spoke to Caulfield. You know something, Bobby. Tell me what it is."

Hart pulled him off to the side, away from anyone who might overhear.

"Right after the last election, they bring in Townsend and start another reorganization. Why?"

"To cover themselves," replied Ryan without hesitation. "To clean things up, get rid of things that might prove that they knew a lot more than they said they did, that some of the things that happened they knew about from the start. Townsend is someone they can trust. He used to work for the vice president when they were both in the private sector. He was always one of their biggest contributors—must have given millions over the years. He'll make sure there's nothing left, nothing anyone could use to prove that any of it—the torture, the secret prisons—ever existed, and he'll do it with a clear conscience because the president and the vice president were only trying to save the country. Why? Do you think there was another reason?"

"We can't talk here. There isn't time. I've got a Judiciary Committee meeting and a dozen different things I have to do after that, and . . ." He looked at Ryan with a sudden, puzzled expression. "What are you doing here, anyway? Why aren't you home in Michigan, campaigning?"

"I'm here because you called me and told me it was urgent, that I had to be at the committee today, that you knew that Caulfield had been murdered."

"I did, didn't I? He was, too. I'm sure of it."

"I know what you said in there, but . . ."

"Too many coincidences—I know that isn't proof—but Raymond Caulfield was just about the most careful man alive. I'll explain when I see you. Later today—dinner?" he asked as he started down the hall.

"Sure, why not? Why let a little thing like an election stand in the way of trying to unravel a conspiracy that no one but you thinks exists? Maybe you'll loan me a couple points of your lead," he shouted after him. "Where do you want to meet?"

"I'll come by your office," Hart yelled back. "Around six."

The Judiciary Committee meeting was already under way when Hart slipped into his seat in the second row in back. The attorney general had just finished reading his prepared remarks. Alvin Roth of Pennsylvania, the chairman of the committee, now in the middle of his fifth term in the Senate, did not look pleased.

"It's your contention, then, Attorney General Lopez, that for all practical purposes there are no effective limitations on presidential power."

He spoke slowly, with a great sense of each word's importance, listening to the way they echoed back as if, once he had spoken them, they took on a life all their own.

"That isn't what I said, Mr. Chairman. That isn't what I said at all."

Antonio Lopez had a pleasant, almost boyish face, but when challenged on any, even the smallest, point, he looked right through you.

"Well, I could have sworn it was, Mr. Lopez; I could have sworn it was. You said—and I'm quoting now—that 'in a time of war there is no constitutional impediment to whatever the president, acting as commander in chief, decides is necessary to do.' Is this not what you said, Mr. Lopez? I'm not trying to put words in your mouth."

"In a time of war, Senator Roth—that, it seems to me, makes all the difference. Any limitation on the power of the president in a time of war is a limit on the power of the president to win that war."

He said this with utter conviction, as of a thing so obvious as to be self-evident.

"If we follow your logic to its ultimate conclusion, Attorney General Lopez, it would then be your position that should the Congress fail to appropriate moneys the president deemed necessary for the proper conduct of a war, the president could then do—what? Order the Treasury Department to collect what he needed?"

"No, of course not, Senator; but in matters connected with the actual conduct of the war, the executive functions of government, the president remains free to exercise his powers as he sees fit."

"Even if there happens to be a law passed by Congress that says he cannot?"

It is difficult to explain something obvious. Roth was nearly twice his age, but it was Lopez who wore the baffled smile of a frustrated parent.

"Lincoln suspended the law of habeas corpus, because he thought it necessary to save the Union."

"A decision later overturned by the United States Supreme Court," Roth reminded him.

"But only after the Union was saved, Senator."

Roth was not a man to be lectured to, especially on the Constitution or the history of the republic.

"Yes, Lincoln saved the Union; but I don't think that is a claim the current administration is quite ready to make."

"War is war, Senator," replied Lopez, his eyes cold and distant.

"Yes, I know, Mr. Lopez; I was in one or two of them." He started to turn the questioning over to the ranking senator on the other side, but then, suddenly, thought better of it.

"What you are really suggesting, Mr. Lopez, whether you are willing to admit it or not, is that in a time of war the president has nothing short of dictatorial powers. Your position is that the president has all the powers he thinks are necessary in a time of war, and that the war we are now waging—this war against terrorism—may go on for generations. I don't think I need to point out to you that the absence of any and all legal restraints on what the president can do would do nothing less than change our form of government. Don't you think there is more than a little irony, Attorney General Lopez, in the fact that the only way you can think to bring democracy to the world is to end it here at home?"

8

YOU SHOULD HAVE BEEN THERE. YOU SHOULD have seen it."

Charlie Ryan looked into the paper bag Hart had just tossed him across his desk.

"This is dinner? A hamburger and fries." He motioned for Hart to take a seat. He began to unwrap the hamburger. "Where should I have been?" His eyes lit up as he took a bite. "Of course! Judiciary—Alvin Roth had Lopez up today. He hates him. Alvin hates most people, but he has a special hatred for Lopez. Hard to blame him. Lopez is like a lot of the others in this administration who think they're the only ones who understand the threat the nation faces. They were never soldiers and they think they're generals." He put his feet up on the corner of his desk and loosened his tie. "Some guy in a cave somewhere in Pakistan or Afghanistan talks for a few minutes into a video camera saying he's going to blow up America a week from Saturday and they're ready to put the country on full alert. Everything scares them."

Ryan gulped down the rest of the hamburger. He wiped the ketchup off his chin and laughed.

"What are you going to tell me, and why do I think that none of it is going to make me feel better? Start with why you think Caulfield was murdered."

"Because for almost the whole time I've been on the Intelligence Committee, Raymond Caulfield was helping me, giving me information that he could not give to the committee, putting me on to things that no one outside the agency was supposed to know."

Ryan was not entirely surprised.

"You always did seem to be better informed than the rest of us. But why? Why did he do it, and why you? Of course! He knew your father, didn't he? That was how he knew he could trust you. That makes sense. But still, that was quite a chance he was taking, passing classified . . . And you think that's what got him killed?"

"I think he was killed because someone found out he was checking on Rubicon."

"That was the name you brought up in committee, when you were questioning Townsend. The code name—what might be the code name . . . Then Townsend lied. That's why you asked him, to see if he would cover up."

Hart scratched his head. He had not touched his hamburger, which sat, still wrapped, on the front corner of Ryan's desk. He picked it up, started to unwrap it, and then put it down again.

"He probably never heard of Rubicon. He didn't want to admit that Caulfield had held something back from him and was operating outside those sacred lines of authority of his."

"Leave Townsend out of it for a minute, I want to make sure I understand this. You gave the name Rubicon to Caulfield—he didn't give it to you?"

"That's right; I gave it . . ."

"But where did you get it? Who gave you the name?"

Hart unwrapped the hamburger and began to eat. If there was anyone in the Senate he trusted, it was Charlie Ryan, fearless, willing to take on anyone he thought was wrong, no matter how many times that put him on the losing side when the issue came to a vote. Unlike so many of his colleagues, there was not a sanctimonious bone in his body: it was one thing to be gracious in victory, Ryan was gracious in defeat. There was no reason not to tell him, and, after everything that had happened, he knew he needed help.

"Gunther Kramer."

Ryan spilled the coffee he had just begun to drink.

"The East German spy who died in 1989?"

"The double agent who worked for the West; the agent who staged his own death when the wall came down and he knew he couldn't go back to Germany—"

"The rumors you mentioned weren't rumors at all. He's still alive, living in Damascus. He found out about Rubicon and told you. What else did he tell you? What else did he know?"

"That there was going to be an assassination and that the code name is Rubicon." Hart shook his head in frustration. "I was sitting across the table, as close to him as I am to you. A sniper, someone—I don't know who—murdered him right in front of my eyes. Then—Christ, I don't even know how it happened—I was shot . . ."

"You were shot?"

"Yeah, in the shoulder." Hart's hand went to the spot on his left shoulder where he had been hit. "Lucky—went right through me."

"You were shot? And Kramer was killed—like Caulfield? Both of them knew something about Rubicon, and both murdered? When did it happen? Where were you?" he asked with a look of intense interest.

"In Hamburg, where I had gone to meet him."

Ryan pushed the paper coffee cup to the side and leaned across the desk.

"How did you know about him? Why did you go to Hamburg to see him? Did Caulfield put you in touch with him?"

"No, it was Dieter Shoenfeld, the German publisher. He was Kramer's half brother. It's a strange story. Dieter's father was killed in the war; his mother remarried. Dieter wound up in the West; Gunther Kramer stayed in the East. I didn't know any of this until Dieter told me, after Kramer was killed. I talked to him right after I got back, told him what I had learned. He was going to try to find out more, but now he's disappeared. No one has heard from him in over a week. I'm afraid that . . ."

"Shoenfeld is someone you trust, someone you're sure would tell you the truth?"

"Yes, absolutely; no doubt at all."

"All right, let's get this straight: Gunther Kramer finds out about Rubicon and is murdered in Hamburg. Raymond Caulfield learns about Rubicon and, if you're correct, is murdered here, just outside Washington. And now Dieter Shoenfeld has disappeared and you think he may have been murdered as well?"

"I don't know what else to think. I talked to Dieter's secretary in Berlin. She did not know where he had gone, but they were having a board meeting in a few days and she was certain he would be there for that. He didn't make it."

Ryan drew his eyes together into a concentrated gaze. Something was puzzling him.

"Rubicon—strange choice for a code name for something like this."

"That's what . . . Why? What is so strange about it? That it's taken from Roman history?"

"Yes, you would think that . . . but maybe it isn't so strange at all. What does Rubicon stand for, what do we mean when we say that someone has crossed the Rubicon? What did it mean when Caesar did it?"

"That there is no turning back, that it's too late, that once you've taken that first step you can never change your mind. Caulfield said something like that. 'Our worst nightmare,' he called it. A sleeper cell, given a mission, years in advance, and then left alone, with no one to report to, no lines of communication that we might intercept. That would explain it: all the rumors, starting at the same time, about something that is going to happen, and no one with any idea who is really behind it. Though apparently Gunther Kramer found out."

"He knew who was behind this? Why didn't you tell me . . . ? He was killed before he could pass that information on, wasn't he? But he knew—you're certain of that? Do you think Caulfield found out as well?"

"I doubt it. All he was going to do was run the name— Rubicon—through the computers over at Langley to see if it had been picked up in any of their surveillance."

Ryan swung his chair around until he was sitting sideways to his desk. He wrapped both hands around his right knee and tried to think.

"If it is a cell like that, it's even worse than Caulfield imagined. Someone who is a part of it must have infiltrated us." He slapped his hand on the desk and jumped to his feet. "Don't you see? It's the only way to explain what happened, to connect two murders that far apart. Kramer is murdered in Hamburg. There have been a number of terrorist cells found there. Al Qaeda, or some other group, could have done it. But Caulfield is murdered here. And he isn't murdered after making inquiries on the Arab street— what Kramer must have been doing—he's murdered after looking into something at the CIA. That means there is someone inside the agency who doesn't want anything about Rubicon known."

"Or some group within the agency that doesn't."

Ryan did not hear him. He was too worried about something else Hart had said.

"We don't know who is behind this; we don't know for certain what they're going to do, who they are going to try to kill next, and we have . . . ? How long ago did Gunther Kramer tell you this? Two weeks ago! Jesus, Bobby, we have to tell somebody about this, we need to—"

"Who would you suggest? Everyone knows about the rumors; and after today, Townsend and the CIA know about Rubicon. Who else are we going to tell? Besides, the rest of it is just speculation."

"There's got to be something we can do," Ryan mumbled to himself. He paced back and forth. "You're right," he said finally. "All we have is speculation, and it doesn't much matter that it's the only thing that makes sense. But that doesn't mean that all we can do is sit around and wait for someone else to get killed. I know a couple of guys over at Justice, couple of guys I worked with when I was U.S. Attorney—straight shooters, none of these political appointees who do whatever the administration tells them. One of them is a guy I went to college with. Let me talk to him, tell him what I know."

Hart agreed. Never one to waste time, Ryan picked up the telephone and called his old friend from college.

"I'm meeting him for breakfast in the morning," he announced after he hung up. "I'll let you know what happens."

Hart felt relieved, and grateful, that someone else, someone he trusted and respected, was also now involved.

"Thanks, Charlie. I don't know who else I could have told."

He started to get up. Ryan nodded toward the hamburger, now turned cold.

"Don't go. You haven't finished dinner."

The sense of urgency all but vanished from Ryan's clear green eyes. He had taken the first important step to deal with a problem. There was nothing more he could do about it tonight. His mind turned to other things, to politics and what was going to happen at the Republican convention.

"It appears that despite everything this is going to be another typical presidential election: one party nominates a candidate with no principles anyone has been able to discover; the other party nominates a candidate without any principles anyone in their right mind would want to support. You give us Prentice Alworth, we give you Arthur Douglas; they both spend the whole campaign telling the country that the other one does not deserve to hold the office; and the country has to choose between two honest men!"

Ryan shook his head in disgust. "Jesus, Bobby, you should have run—I would have voted for you." A wry expression started onto his mouth and he began to laugh. "Of course, against Douglas, I might even vote for Alworth."

WHILE THE REPUBLICANS held their convention, Hart stayed in Washington, poring over all the intelligence reports he could get his hands on, looking for anything that would tell him who was behind Rubicon and what was going to happen next. He was working in his Senate office with the television set on the last night of the Republican convention, when the face of Charlie Ryan suddenly appeared on the screen. He picked up the telephone and called Santa Barbara.

"Helen, turn on the television. Charlie Ryan is on."

"He's not giving a speech, is he?" she asked. "You told me he said they wouldn't let him."

"No, it's some kind of interview with Charlie and the vice president."

He knew that Helen did not much care for politics and had a particular aversion to most politicians; but she had always liked Charlie Ryan. She liked the way he did not take himself as seriously as the others did; perhaps, she had suggested with what Hart thought shrewd insight, because there was not anything he thought he had to prove. She was excited that he was on television and said she would turn it on right away.

"Call me later, will you? Or I'll call you."

Ryan and the vice president were being interviewed by William Griffin, the editor of a political journal that was must reading among neoconservatives. The first question was for the vice president.

"You've said you're here to support Arthur Douglas, but Douglas has said that he does not agree with the administration's policy on the war; that he thinks mistakes were made, that he thinks—"

"That isn't what he said," said the vice president, who managed to seem irritated, impatient, and bored all at once. "He said that he supported the policy of staying in Iraq until the Iraqis are able to provide adequate security for themselves. That is a sound policy—the only policy, as far as I'm concerned—unless we're prepared to let the terrorists win, which is what the Democrats, and I'm afraid even a few Republicans, seem willing to do."

Eager to stir up a fight, Griffin turned to Ryan.

"I think he means you, Senator."

Ryan did not change expression.

"No, I'm sure he doesn't." He paused just long enough to make Griffin and the audience wonder if that was all he was going to say. "Because if he did, I'm sure he'd say it to my face." He turned to the vice president, who, if he had ever been in a real fight, had not been in one since school. "You don't think that, do you? That I'm in favor of—how did you put it?—'letting the terrorists win.'"

The vice president turned red, and then immediately went back on the attack.

"No, Senator, I'm not suggesting that is what you want. I'm suggesting that the policy you support would almost certainly have that effect."

"What policy is that, Mr. Vice President? Suggesting that we better figure out a way to get out of there before we cause ourselves any more damage? That isn't a policy, Mr. Vice President. You give me too much credit. It's the only remaining alternative we have. And as for letting the terrorists win, every day we stay there we increase their numbers. I may be wrong, but I'm not sure the best way to win a war is to make more soldiers for the enemy you are trying to defeat."

"If Iraq goes, we lose the Middle East," replied the vice president with a look of unyielding belligerence.

"Just when was the Middle East ours to lose? Did you really think that all we had to do was have elections and there would be peace and democracy all through the region?"

"If we don't remake the Middle East," insisted the vice president, "we'll be fighting terrorism for the next hundred years, and it won't be in the Middle East—it will be right here at home. Is that what you want, Senator? Is that what you honestly think we should do?"

"It's the attempt to remake everything, this war you started, is what has led to all the trouble," Ryan fired back.

The vice president lurched forward until his head was down between his shoulders. He glared at Ryan.

"Are you saying that democracy would be a bad thing for the Middle East?"

"No, I'm saying that you can't impose it. We've tried. Look what it brought us."

"What you and people like you don't seem to understand," said the vice president, "is that America has interests and responsibilities all across the globe. We're not some small republic, like we were at the beginning, two hundred years ago. This is a war of civilizations, Senator: radical Islam on one side, America and the West on the other. It's the most important war we'll ever fight, and we have to use every means within our power to win it."

"You're wrong. We're not some empire that imposes its will on others. The only lasting influence we can have is the force of our example. The real question, Mr. Vice President, isn't whether we can remake the Middle East, the real question is whether this country can survive the kind of endless war you describe in which we become no better than the people we're fighting against."

When it was over, Hart walked into David Allen's office next door.

"Did you see that? Every once in a while someone does something and you remember what it is supposed to mean to be a member of the Senate. Charlie Ryan is everything a senator should be. Actually, he's everything a president should be. But I'm afraid that's never going to happen. And now, after he has damn near called the vice president a liar and a fool on national television, he may not even get reelected." Hart exchanged a glance with Allen. "I'm not sure I want to get reelected if I have to listen to Arthur Douglas lecture all of us from the White House about the need to fight with the same unshakable resolve both terrorism and taxes."

9

IT LASTED ONLY TWELVE MINUTES, THE SPEECH that made Bobby Hart even more famous than he had been, the speech that no one who heard it would ever forget, the speech that became the standard by which all of the speeches that followed were measured, and, measured, found to fall short. It was not so much a call to action, the speech a candidate would have given, as a series of stark alternatives, turning on their heads all the false choices and, in the process, making a mockery of the massive and arrogant failures of the last eight years.

"Tax those who can most afford to pay or walk away from the responsibility each generation owes to the next. And who can most afford to pay them—the working poor and the struggling middle class, or the idle and speculative rich?"

The line brought groans to Wall Street, but it brought down the house at the Democratic Convention.

"Decide that you are going to wage war with everything you have—the way we have in every war we have won—or cut and run the way of this administration: too scared to ask for the kind of sacrifice that would include the sons and daughters of every class; too incompetent to know how to stop the bleeding of a war they lied us into!"

There were those who swore that if someone had run to the microphone and said they ought to do it, the convention would have nominated Bobby Hart for president by acclamation.

"I don't think it went too badly," said Hart, his face flushed and full of perspiration. He handed his administrative assistant, David Allen, his copy of the speech. "Put that somewhere. I think I'd like to keep it."

They were just off the stage. The cheering echoed all around them.

"Alworth's people are furious," reported Allen, grinning broadly. "Every speech is supposed to be cleared with them."

Hart gestured toward the arena where the noise, instead of quieting, was getting louder and more insistent by the minute. He did not mind at all if Prentice Alworth did not like what he had done.

"Would they like me to go out there and take it all back?"

Allen pointed to the metal door ahead of them.

"There are about a million reporters out there who are going to ask you everything from the color of your shorts to whether you really think Alworth can win in November."

"As long as they don't ask me if I think he should."

But most of the questions the media started firing at him when he walked through the doorway into the blinding glare of television lights had nothing to do with the Democratic candidate for president; they were all about him.

Did he regret not having been a candidate himself? He flashed the boyish smile that made him seem shy and even self-conscious.

"No, not really," he replied.

Would he consider running four years from now? The smile grew broader and became an irresistible tease.

"Against Prentice Alworth?" he asked back.

Was there any chance that he might reconsider, take the vice-presidential nomination that Governor Alworth had offered him? The smile flickered and died. He was serious now; there was to be no room for misunderstanding.

"I'm a candidate for reelection to the Senate from California. The Senate is where I hope to spend at least the next six years."

They were almost through, only a few more shouted voices trying to be heard. With a friendly wave, Hart turned to go.

"Senator, you're a member of the Senate Intelligence Committee. Is there a plan that you know of to assassinate the president of the United States?"

Hart wheeled around, searching for the face of the reporter. A thin, assertive-looking woman was standing in the middle of the space that had quickly opened at the back of the crowd of cameras and reporters. Hart recognized her at once.

"Norma Roberts," she announced, lifting her chin a defiant half-inch. "Correspondent for the London *Times*. We have been hearing reports, rumors from some of our sources in the Middle East, that something . . ."

Hart nodded as if he were aware of what she was talking about and that there was no reason to be alarmed.

"Just as you say, Ms. Roberts: rumors of various things that might happen, different ways in which some terrorist organization might try to interfere with our elections. But, in answer to your question: no, I have no information about any planned attempt on the life of the president or anyone else." He paused before he added, "That doesn't mean that we don't have to be careful. Just because we don't know about a threat doesn't mean that there aren't people out there who would like to attack us."

Norma Roberts was a highly respected reporter who usually seemed to know just a little bit more than the competition. Hart wondered what else she had heard, and why she seemed to know more than he did.

SECURITY AT THE convention had been tight from the beginning—long lines to get through metal detectors, armed guards both inside and outside the arena—but now, as the convention moved into its final, climactic two days, it became noticeably tighter. The night that Prentice Alworth made his acceptance speech, some of the delegates were forced to wait more than an hour while their credentials were checked.

Hart sat with the members of the California delegation, mixing with the others as if he were simply another anonymous delegate. He rather enjoyed it, the senseless camaraderie of a political convention where the only serious business was to sit around and gossip. The only matter of any suspense was what was going to happen with the vice presidency. There was a rumor that Alworth had decided on Senator Harcourt of Delaware, a respected and knowledgeable member of the Foreign Relations Committee. That rumor was followed by another rumor that while it might be a member of the Foreign Relations Committee, it would not be Harcourt: too liberal, said some; too conservative, said others. Eager for some excitement, a few even claimed that Alworth was going to do what Adlai Stevenson had done in 1956 and throw open the nomination to anyone who wanted to fight for it. Someone asked Hart what he thought Alworth would do.

"He offered it to you, but you turned him down, didn't you?"

With a look that suggested that the whole thing had been exaggerated, Hart replied: "I couldn't run for vice president; I'm a candidate for reelection to the Senate."

It was the reason he had given Alworth, but it was not the only reason he had for not wanting to be on the ticket. Alworth was everything Hart had come to despise about politics and the narrow, single-minded ambitions of politicians.

"So who do you think he's going to pick?"

Hart said that he had no idea what Prentice Alworth was going to do; but then, because the man who had asked was from his own delegation and had a friendly face, he added in a quiet undertone of cheerful malice, "'the greatest statesman of their generation'—in other words, whoever can help him win the election."

Accepting the nomination, Alworth launched into a speech that safely avoided all of the issues that, just days earlier, Hart had said had to be addressed by any candidate who was serious about leading the country. Few noticed. There was so much excitement, so much burning enthusiasm for a candidate who could win back the White House, it did not matter what he said. And besides, Prentice Alworth knew how to give a speech. With smooth, flowing phrases and a sharp pointed wit, he spoke with a beaming smile that, even if nothing he said made sense, seduced you into believing that the bright new future he talked about would still, somehow, manage to come true. He reminded Hart of Bill Clinton.

"Which is probably where he learned it," he remarked to David Allen, sitting next to him. "Watched him on tape, even took over some of the same gestures. Same effect, too. They can't take their eyes off him, and five minutes after he's finished there won't be three people who can quote back to you a single thing he's said."

Alworth was just coming to the end of it. He was about

to announce what they had all been waiting for: his choice for the vice presidency. He looked out at the vast audience, and then looked into the television cameras and the millions watching at home.

"And so I have decided that—"

Suddenly, a shot rang out, a single, sharp report. Alworth, dazed, staggered back. Hart jumped to his feet, searching the upper balcony in back.

"Just a balloon," a distant voice cried out. The convention, stunned into silence, rumbled back to life. Nervous laughter filled the hall.

Alworth was back at the podium, waving to the crowd as if nothing had happened, laughing it off as if they were all a bit too much on edge these days. But Hart had seen it, the instant in which Alworth had shown the fear he might not have known he had.

"And so I have decided," exclaimed Alworth before anyone had time to think back on what had just happened, "that Senator Richard Harcourt will join me on the ticket and after the election become vice president of the United States!"

Some rumors were true after all. More important, Hart explained when the press came to him for his reaction, "Richard Harcourt is the best man for the job: experienced, intelligent, and well informed. No one in the Senate knows more about foreign relations. It is a perfect choice. Governor Alworth deserves a great deal of credit."

Then, as quickly as he could, Bobby Hart left the convention and caught a flight home to California.

The next day David Allen called from Washington.

"The geniuses in the Alworth campaign want to do a day-long whistle-stop train trip out there, starting in San Francisco and ending up in Los Angeles where he'll give a major speech that same night."

"He doesn't need to campaign in California."

"They're doing it because of all the national coverage it will get. They want you on the trip."

"I'll bet they do," laughed Hart.

"You're running for reelection. There are a lot of stories about bad blood over the vice-presidential thing. I don't see how you can do anything but say yes."

"When are they going to do it?"

"Monday, two days from now."

"They have me pretty tightly scheduled. Use that as an excuse. Tell them I can't do it for the whole day. I'll get on at the last stop before Los Angeles. That's where there would be a question if I didn't show up."

Late Monday afternoon, Hart boarded at its next-to-last stop the train that had been temporarily named the Democratic Express and, along with several hundred tired reporters and eager politicians, joined Prentice Alworth for the short trip to Los Angeles.

It was burning hot, the kind of heat that bakes the air and turns the dirt to dust; the kind of day that had always made Bobby Hart feel most alive, the long summer afternoons and the cool California nights, when a T-shirt and a pair of jeans were the only clothes he needed. As the train raced down the tracks under a red, relentless sun, he sat in an air-conditioned car drinking a beer someone had handed him, listening without listening to all the chattered noise around him, wishing he was somewhere out there, in some small California town, with nothing he had to worry about beyond whether he had enough money to take his wife to a movie that night.

He was sitting in the parlor car, with most of the other important dignitaries who had been invited to accompany the Democratic nominee and his running mate. They were there as backdrop, the familiar faces of well-known politicians, the symbolic expression of a united party. There was nothing to do except sit there, part of a select audience in which someone would be noticeable only by their absence.

They were ten minutes from Los Angeles before Prentice Alworth left his private car and made an appearance. Even Hart, who was used to such things, could feel the rush of energy, the burst of excitement that followed a candidate for the presidency like a strong, favoring wind. There was nothing quite like it, the near proximity to the possibility of ultimate power. Prentice Alworth shook hands with Hart with the familiar confidence of a man who no longer needed anything.

"Great speech you gave at the convention, Bobby," he said with the broad smile that was now, at least in public, seldom missing from his ruggedly handsome face. "I don't think we could have asked for anything better."

And then he moved on to someone else, ready with a new set of compliments that would make those to whom they were delivered more certain than ever that Alworth was the candidate they had wanted all along. Hart had seen it all before, this ritual of vanity and ambition, this lesson in how quickly power attracts followers. He watched with a kind of sad amusement the way that people who had once derided not just Alworth's chances, but his qualifications, now told him how eager they were to start campaigning on his behalf. That was the difference, the thing that set him apart, though he could never breathe a word of it to anyone he did not trust: he still did not believe that Prentice Alworth had any business becoming president.

The train rumbled to a stop. The two candidates, Alworth and Harcourt, went out onto the back platform, where, joined by as many of the traveling politicians as could fight their way into the space behind them, they were to make some brief remarks to the huge crowd that had come out to see them.

Hart waited until the others squeezed by, and then,

anxious to get away, walked back through the parlor car and stepped off the train. He walked around to the back of the crowd and, with all the others, watched Prentice Alworth talk about the great things that a new administration was going to do for America. The sun-drenched crowd cheered and cheered again. Alworth fed on it, became a part of it, speaking with their voice, telling them what they wanted to hear. They were cheering louder now, cheering for him, cheering for themselves, cheering for everything he was going to change.

Driven by a politician's need to get close, to make contact with what had become the other part of himself, Alworth told them he wanted to shake as many of their hands as he could before he had to leave. He climbed down onto the tracks and the crowd surged forward, trying to get close to him, pushing hard against the rope line that had been put up to keep a clear perimeter. A dozen Secret Service agents immediately locked hands to hold everyone back.

With Harcourt right behind him, Alworth worked the line, reaching out to touch all the hands that were reaching out to him. Watching from a distance, Hart was struck by the fervor, the excitement on the faces in the crowd, people who, even if they were not close enough to touch the candidate, seemed to be caught up in the strange euphoria of being close to those who could. Everyone was cheering, shouting, laughing at the manic contortions some went through to touch, if just for an instant, the outstretched hand of a man who might be president.

Smiling to himself, Hart turned to go. His campaign manager, Jeffrey Stone, was waiting for him with a car in front of the station and he wanted to beat the crowd. Something drew him back, something that suddenly hit him as odd and distinctly out of place. It was hot, blazing hot, so hot that when you took a breath it seemed to come with a scent of smoke. Most of the crowd had come in shorts and sandals; even older people, senior citizens, were dressed in short-sleeved shirts or summer dresses. But there, near the end of the rope line, waiting without expression, stood a solitary young man in a tan windbreaker zipped all the way up the front. Prentice Alworth, reaching into the crowd, smiling back at all the cheering faces, was less than three short steps away.

The Secret Service agent holding on to the edge of Alworth's sleeve saw the man at just the same moment. Hart watched as the agent dove straight at him. He must have known that it was already too late. The suicide bomber took a step forward. It was the last thing Hart saw before a blinding explosion blocked out everything.

There was an instant in which the world and everything in it seemed to go silent and stop. Hart could not hear anything, and then, suddenly, there was noise, hellish noise, everywhere. People were screaming, some running away in panic, others unable to move because of what they saw. Dozens of people, some of them just children, lay wounded with blood-covered faces and twisted, broken limbs. Hart forced himself to look back to where it had happened. There was nothing left but a pile of burning rubble and a hole several feet deep. Prentice Alworth and at least a dozen others, including the Secret Service agent who had tried to save his life, as well as Richard Harcourt, the vice-presidential candidate and a man Hart had always respected, had all died instantly.

Hart ran into the crowd and tried to do what he could to help. He tore a sleeve off his shirt and used it as a tourniquet to stop the bleeding on a woman with a severed artery in her leg. He left her in the care of her husband and moved on to the next person who needed immediate assistance. When the medics arrived they had to pull him away as he kept trying to revive an eighty-year-old man who had died of a heart attack caused by the horror of the carnage he had seen.

Jeffrey Stone found him sitting on the back of an ambulance, a blanket wrapped around his bare shoulders.

"This is my fault," he said with a bleak, angry stare. "I should have been able to stop it."

10

THE ASSASSINATION OF PRENTICE ALWORTH, Mr. Townsend. Do you want me to repeat it? The presidential and vice-presidential candidates of one of the two major political parties—along with eleven other people—died when a suicide bomber blew himself up, not in Baghdad, Mr. Townsend—in Los Angeles. Assassination, Mr. Townsend! What have you found out about it?"

"Senator Hart, I really don't appreciate that tone. We've been doing—"

"You don't appreciate my tone? You're the director of an agency that has just failed to prevent the most direct attack on the democratic institutions of this country in its history, and you don't appreciate my tone?"

"I'm sorry, Senator; everyone's nerves are a little on edge these days." The director of the CIA opened a black notebook, glanced down the first page, and turned to the second. "We know that the plan was conceived and executed by Al Qaeda. We know that the terrorist who carried it out had been in the United States for almost a year."

Hart looked at him with unconcealed contempt. "We know this because he mailed a videotape to a Los Angeles television station and told everyone what he was going to do, but no one sent anything to Al Jazeera, and no one from Al Qaeda—or any other terrorist organization—has claimed credit for what happened. Don't you find that just a little unusual, Mr. Townsend; just a little strange?"

Townsend's mouth began to twitch nervously. He picked up a pencil and held it tight in both hands, twisting it slowly back and forth.

"I shouldn't think that someone who was about to blow himself up would lie about the reasons he was doing it, Senator—or name the wrong organization."

"I'm sure you're right, Mr. Townsend, but then that doesn't really answer my question, does it?"

When the committee session ended, Charlie Ryan followed Hart to his office. He dropped into a chair the other side of Hart's desk. Hart looked past him, to the far end of the room and the windows streaked with rain from a passing storm.

"We could not stop it," said Hart, his gaze still on the window. "The FBI, the CIA; we did not even know where to start. If anyone had said anything about an assassination attempt we would have assumed that the president would be the target. We should have known better. What better way to show that democracy is not safe anywhere than to murder one of the two candidates for the most important office in the country?"

Slowly, and with an effort, Ryan pulled himself up. The world since Los Angeles had become harsh and oppressive. Everything now seemed a burden. There were no good times anymore.

"People are scared to death. No one knows what to do. It's a little hard to tell everyone that they ought to go about the normal business of their lives when one presidential candidate is dead and the other one has canceled all public appearances."

Hart looked straight at him.

"And everyone is looking for someone to blame. You heard it in the committee. People want to go after someone and they don't much care who it is. You heard what the president said the other night, that the only way to stop something like this from happening again is to stay with the fight, go after the terrorists wherever they are and for as long as it takes. Remember what he said: 'If we don't change the world, the world will change us.' We both know what is going to happen next. They'll want even fewer restrictions on what they can do, and given the mood of the country, Congress will give them anything they ask for."

"There might be one or two members who object," said Ryan as they exchanged a glance.

Hart's gaze drifted off, his mind on other things. Dull thunder echoed softly in the distance. A fragile shaft of sunlight broke the gray darkness and painted everything in shades of yellow.

"It's been difficult, hasn't it?" asked Ryan. He tried not to sound too sympathetic. He did not want Hart to think that he had any doubts about his ability to deal with what had happened.

Hart looked back at him, started to apologize, and then, because they were friends, gestured helplessly with his hands.

"Every night I have the same nightmare. It's always in slow motion: that kid in the tan windbreaker, the terrorist who did not look like a terrorist at all, standing there as calm as anything. Then the Secret Service agent—Albert Humphreys, as brave a man as I ever saw—diving for him. He seems to float in the air, just hang there, his arms stretched out. And then, a split second later . . ."

Hart closed his hand into a fist and beat it gently against

his chin. He shuddered at what he knew he would never for the rest of his life forget. He shook his head as if to say he was all right; then shook it again because he was not really sure.

"There is a story in the *Times* this morning," he remarked after a short pause. "There is some suggestion that the election should be delayed. The Democratic National Committee meets this weekend to pick another candidate, but with barely two months left there isn't much time for someone to mount a serious campaign."

"I read the article. There is a group over at Justice looking at how it could be done."

Hart was surprised, though when he thought about it, he realized that it was bound to happen.

"There were those who wanted to postpone the city elections in New York after 9/11. And after Katrina, there were those who wanted to postpone the election for mayor of New Orleans. But they didn't do it then and we shouldn't do it now. We've never postponed a presidential election. That would be like surrender, don't you think, if we did that?"

"You're right, we can't," agreed Ryan. "Or at least we shouldn't. But what's going to happen this weekend? The Douglas campaign is worried. No one wants to talk about any of this in public, but they think there could be a terrific wave of sympathy, the kind of situation where people believe the only way to show the terrorists that they can't decide the election is to vote for whoever takes Alworth's place." Ryan gave Hart a searching glance. "The one they're really worried about is you. After that speech you made at the convention, after what you did in Los Angeles after the attack, the nomination is yours for the asking."

"I didn't run before, when I had the chance; and now . . . No, not after what I saw. It would seem like taking something from the dead, something that had never belonged to me. It should be someone who ran in the primaries."

"That isn't a good reason, Bobby," insisted Ryan. "Everyone who ran in the primaries against Alworth lost. You could pull the country together. Douglas is a fool. He'll be worse than what we have now, if that's possible."

"I can't. I couldn't before because of Helen, and now, after what's happened . . ."

It was what Ryan had long suspected: Hart had given up his chance at the presidency because of his wife. He admired him for that.

"How is she, anyway? Better?"

Hart looked away.

"Better? Yes, I suppose."

Ryan got up to leave.

"Don't worry," he said with a grim smile. "The country will get through this. We've been through worse."

"Yes, we have, haven't we?"

Hart remembered the panic he had seen all around him that awful day in Los Angeles, but he also remembered countless acts of heroism. People, some of them with severe wounds of their own, rushed to the assistance of others. And if there had been some congressmen and senators who could think of nothing better to say than shouted outrage and mindless cries for revenge, there had been those like Charlie Ryan who had counseled patience and fortitude and a decent respect for the opinions of others. The country had done about as well as could have been expected, and a good deal better than almost any other country would have done.

Hart stayed in Washington the rest of the week. Both the House and the Senate had been called back into session within days of the assassination. Political campaigning had been brought to a halt while the country buried its dead and tried to come to terms with what had happened. American forces had been put on alert throughout the world and the National Guard had been called out to help protect against another attack at home. Everyone was waiting to see what would happen next.

On Friday afternoon, David Allen had the news everyone, or at least everyone in Washington, had been waiting for.

"It's going to be Jeremy Taylor. That's what I'm told by sources inside the national committee."

Taylor, the senior senator from Illinois and a ranking member of the Senate Foreign Relations Committee, had run for the nomination but had not been able to generate wide popular support. He had been one of the first candidates to drop out.

"Solid, respectable—but he didn't win a single primary."

"No one cares about that," replied Allen. "He's what you just said he is—solid and respectable, someone people trust. He has the kind of stability the country needs. And he knows more about defense policy and the armed forces than almost anyone around. He'll run rings around Douglas in the debates."

"What about the other question? What's the national committee going to do about delaying the election?"

"No one wants to do it now. Taylor will bring over some of his own people, but the organization put together for Alworth will stay in place. They think they can win, and I'm not sure I don't agree with them."

Hart glanced at his watch. "It's after nine. Why don't you get out of here?"

Allen threw a quick glance at the pile of work on his desk. That was not the reason he was still here, and Hart knew it. There were always stacks of paper on Allen's desk.

"You wouldn't be here if I wasn't still here. You don't have to guard me. Nothing is going to happen here."

Allen started to deny it, but Hart stopped him with a look.

"I'm leaving in a few minutes anyway. It's been a long day. I'll see you tomorrow."

Still protesting that he had work to do, Allen grabbed his coat from the rack and headed out the door. Hart went back to his office, jotted down a few notes about what he wanted to do the next day, and then gathered up his things. With his briefcase tucked under his arm, he closed the door to his private office and left the building.

The moon had passed behind the clouds and a heavy mist hung over the tree-lined street. A dark wind sighed through the thick autumn leaves. Hart thought he heard something. He stopped and looked behind him, but there was nothing there. He taunted himself for how easily since Los Angeles he let his imagination play havoc with his senses. Between that and watching Gunther Kramer die, he wondered if his nerves were shot, whether he was having the kind of delayed reaction he had often read about. He was always telling people not to let their fears run away with them, and yet fear, not of what might happen to him, but just fear of what might happen, seemed to follow him everywhere he went.

He reached the car and started to open the door. He thought he heard it again, a footstep right behind his own.

"Fool!" he cried out loud, ashamed of his own weakness, but then a hand suddenly came out of nowhere and grabbed him by the arm. Spinning around, he found himself face-to-face with a ghost.

"It can't be!"

Dieter Shoenfeld assured him that it was. And then, before Hart could say another word, Shoenfeld hurried around to the other side of the car.

"Get in!" he cried. "We have to get out of here. We can't afford to be seen."

11

DIETER SHOENFELD HAD CHANGED. HIS FACE had become gaunt and the circles around his eyes deeper, and darker, than before. He was a man on the verge of exhaustion.

"Why didn't you call me?" asked Hart. "Why didn't you let me know you were here? When I didn't hear from you I thought—"

"That I was dead." He looked across at Hart, who had begun to drive. "There have been times the last few days when I thought I was, or was about to be. It's a miracle I'm still alive. It's a miracle you're still alive."

There were a dozen questions Hart wanted to ask. He did not think in terms of destinations, places they could go; he drove at random, staying close to the Capitol. He turned his head just long enough to catch Shoenfeld's eye.

"A miracle I'm still alive? Tell me what's going on. Why this sudden need for secrecy?"

"After what I have to tell you, that won't be a question

you will need to ask." He looked ahead. "Where are we going?"

"Where are you staying? We can talk there."

Shoenfeld sat in the darkness, staring out at the Capitol all lit up at night. He did not say anything, he just kept looking out the window, a strange expression on his face.

"Rome," he said finally, and to no apparent purpose. "Years ago, the first time I came here, that was the immediate, almost overpowering impression I had. Rome, what it must have been like, two thousand years ago, a city at the center of the world, every building, every street, the outward expression of its greatness. Washington was built to be a city just like that, with long broad avenues and the Capitol, the center of government, up on a hill, dominating everything else."

"Dieter, I don't think I quite understand what all this has to do with—"

"Rome," repeated Shoenfeld. "I forgot what Rome became."

There was something tired and frantic in the way Shoenfeld was talking. Nothing he said made sense.

"When is the last time you had any sleep?" asked Hart, certain that must be the cause of it. "Tell me where you're staying. I'll drive you there. You can take a shower, change clothes, and then we'll get something to eat and you can tell me everything that has happened the last couple of weeks."

Shoenfeld reached across and put his hand on Hart's shoulder.

"I know you think I'm rambling, and perhaps I am a little, but there is something I am trying to say."

"Tell me after dinner. Now, where am I taking you?"

"I'm not staying anywhere. I didn't check into a hotel; I came right from the train station—"

"The train station? You didn't fly into Washington?"

"New York, I took the train down. I couldn't take the chance."

"What chance? I don't understand."

Shoenfeld shook his head. He would explain later.

"I have something you need to see. Can we go to your place, your house in Georgetown? It should be safe there. I don't think anyone followed me. I think I lost them in New York."

"Lost them in . . . Yes, of course we can go to my place. You can stay there, too. There is plenty of room. But why are you afraid someone might be following you?"

"Because I found out what Rubicon means. It isn't over, Bobby. Gunther was right: Rubicon has just begun."

Shoenfeld was nervous, cautious, and so high-strung he could barely sit still. He kept looking around to see if anyone was following them. Each time they passed through an intersection, his eyes darted from one side of the street to the other as he sank lower in his seat. He held a black briefcase in his arms, the only luggage he had.

"I had a letter from an attorney in Damascus, a man of shall I say doubtful character, but someone Gunther had apparently known for years, someone with whom, at least on occasion, he had done some business. He wrote to tell me that Gunther had left a package with him that was to be delivered to me should anything ever happen to him. Because Gunther was now 'unfortunately dead'—that was the phrase he used—he wished to turn it over. He went on to detail certain expenses—rather exorbitant expenses, as it seemed to me—which he had incurred in keeping this package in his custody. He said that because Gunther had been a friend of his, he was willing to bear something of a loss, and would accept no more than the equivalent of ten thousand dollars for his trouble. There was of course the further difficulty that for obvious reasons he could only accept cash. He suggested I come to Damascus where we could make the exchange in person."

"And so you went to Damascus . . ."

Shoenfeld glanced over his shoulder, out the back window.

"The same car has been following us for blocks . . . No, he turned. It's all right. What? Yes, I went to Damascus. I was going there anyway. I had to find out what happened to Gunther and what he had learned about Rubicon. I thought there might be something in his apartment—a scrap of paper, perhaps even a journal—something he had written down that might give me a start."

"And was there?" asked Hart, eager to know what Shoenfeld had found.

But Shoenfeld had too much to tell and he did not want to leave anything out. He blinked his eyes in quick succession, waving his hand to ward off interruption.

"I got to Damascus two weeks ago. It seems like two years. The lawyer was waiting for me in his office, a dark, fly-infested hole of a place in a walk-up third-floor landing. There was only one window, but a cheap curtain kept out the light. I thought at first that it was because the heat in Damascus was almost unbearable, but then, as my eyes adjusted to the darkness, I decided that the curtain probably always covered the window, at least when the lawyer was not alone. He had the most singularly repulsive face I have ever seen: fat, with thick, blubbery lips and tiny, evil eyes. That would have been enough to make him ugly, but something had been done to him, something that . . . You could not tell at first. He had a habit of keeping his head turned at an angle, so that what you saw was mainly the left side of his face, but even with that, he could not keep it hidden, not all of what had been done to him. The right side of his face, starting with his eye and going down to the corner of his lip, was a cruel, gruesome disfigurement, what was left after the flesh had been eaten away with acid. He told me that it had been done by the secret police when he was a young law student and had made the mistake of circulating a petition calling for free and fair elections.

"'I had not realized,' he told me with a truly ghastly grin, 'that we already had free and fair elections and that President Assad always won them with more than ninety-nine percent of the vote.'"

Shoenfeld held the briefcase tighter to his chest. For a moment, remembering what he had seen, he stared straight ahead. A look of grim resolve came into his eyes.

"He managed somehow to finish up his studies; but there was never a chance, after what was done to him, that he would have much of a career. He lived on the fringe, a kind of outcast, and took what work he could get. He became a part of the Syrian underground, to the degree to which there is one. That was how he met Gunther; or rather, how Gunther met him. He doesn't know how Gunther found out about him. All he would tell me was that Gunther seemed to know everyone."

Shoenfeld paused, looked across at Hart, and nodded in agreement with what the Syrian had said.

"That was a talent Gunther always had. He knew everyone, and not just his friends, his enemies, which makes what happened . . ."

Hart drove across the bridge into Georgetown. The long main street, normally crowded even on a weekday evening, was almost deserted. Since the attack in Los Angeles, no one was going out much, and they tended, when they did, not to stay late. Hart made a right turn and then, two blocks later, made another right. The street he lived on was darker than it used to be. The street lamps were still on, but most of the narrow brick houses were barely lit up, only an

occasional lamp from a second- or third-story window behind shutters that were now, almost all of them, closed.

"We're almost there," said Hart, trying to put him at
ease. "Just at the corner, then down the alley in back."

Shoenfeld looked behind him; then, just to be sure, he
looked again.

Hart pulled into the garage off the alleyway in back.
He started to turn on the backyard light to see his way to
the kitchen door. Shoenfeld put his hand on his arm and
suggested he leave it off. Stumbling on the first step of the
porch, Hart cursed under his breath. With some difficulty,
he managed to get the door unlocked, and then, with Shoenfeld finally safe inside, he remembered to lock it again.
He did not turn on a light until he had led him from the
kitchen, through the dining room, to the living room in
front.

Shoenfeld sat down in the middle of the sofa, still
clutching the black briefcase in his arms. He gazed at the
bookshelves with the practiced eye of a well-read man. He
seemed to relax, to take some comfort in the close presence of familiar things, hundreds of books in a well-
furnished room. Setting the briefcase off to the side, he
began, almost unconsciously, to examine the titles. Hart
made him a drink.

"You were telling me in the car about Damascus—the
Syrian lawyer who was holding something from your
brother."

Shoenfeld casually rattled the ice in his glass and then,
slowly, took a drink.

"Thank you for this," he said, nodding toward the drink
as he set it down on the coffee table in front of him. "And
for everything."

He moved to the end of the sofa and leaned back. Hart
was sitting in the easy chair on the opposite side of the
coffee table.

"Yes, the Syrian lawyer. I felt sorry for him. It was impossible not to feel sorry for him after what they had done to him. But that did not change the fact that he was a thief, and I told him so.

"'You tell me what a good friend Gunther was to you, how much he tried to help you, and yet you insist that I give you ten thousand dollars before you'll give me what he asked you to?'

"He was not offended by the question, you understand. He simply spread open his hands—soiled, dirty hands—and explained that, as Gunther quite well understood, he was a poor man who had to earn money any way he could."

"And so you paid him?"

"Of course I paid him. I was always going to pay him. I had to know what Gunther wanted me to have. I gave him the money, all of it in cash, the way he had asked. Then he reached into a drawer and pulled out a large, bulky envelope, which, as was obvious immediately, had already been opened. There was nothing in it.

"It was the Syrian's idea of a joke. A man like that . . . well, I imagine he did not have many occasions to laugh at anything. He thought it was funny, the look I had on my face. Before I could say anything, tell him what I thought of him and his little tricks, he reached inside the same drawer and pulled out a small package. It had been inside the envelope, but it had not been opened. He seemed—the Syrian—to take a certain pleasure in that, as if, having found what was inside the envelope, what Gunther had meant for me, he had done the honorable thing by not looking any further. It's hard to explain to someone not familiar with the Syrian mentality, but it was a little like a man who breaks into a bank but would not think of touching the money. It's not something I could ever understand."

"The package—what was in it?"

"I'm getting to that." He reached for his glass, took a

drink, savored it for a moment, and then turned sharply to Hart. "A key—and a letter, a letter which I did not read—not there, in that office—but only later, when I got back to my hotel.

"At first I thought the key was to a safe-deposit box somewhere—Switzerland, perhaps—where he might have kept whatever money he might have made from . . . well, from whatever he was doing all the years after he left Germany for good. But it was not that at all. It was a key to a box he kept hidden in his apartment. The letter gave a list, a kind of inventory of what the box contained. I went to the apartment. I bribed the landlord to let me in. There was nothing in it, the place had been stripped bare. The landlord said that someone had broken in. I asked if I could be alone a few minutes. In the bathroom, under a loosened tile behind the toilet, exactly where Gunther had said it was, I found the metal box."

Hart was growing more curious, and more impatient, by the minute.

"The letter—was there anything about Rubicon? Was there anything inside the box that would . . . ?"

Shoenfeld shook his head. His eyes were luminous, intense, seeing everything all over again that he had seen in Damascus.

"The letter. Yes, the letter. It contained that list, that inventory, I spoke of, but there was another list besides that one, a list of seven names, each with an address somewhere in the Middle East, three in Cairo, two in Damascus, one in Baghdad, and one in Tel Aviv. He said that if I was reading this letter it would mean that he was dead, and that these seven were people I could trust: people who would be willing to help, if I needed help, finding out what had happened."

"But nothing about Rubicon?"

"Yes, but only later."

"Something he left in the metal box that you found?"

"Yes, but only indirectly. There were several passports, all with slightly altered photographs, all with different names. There were bundles of cash, currencies from several countries. And there was a book."

"A book? What kind of book?"

"An old book, a very old book, a famous book, written in Greek. I have it with me." He gestured toward the black briefcase that lay next to him on the sofa. "That, and a few other things that helped me learn what Gunther was on to when he was killed."

Dieter Shoenfeld was one of the most urbane and worldly-wise men Hart had ever known. Nothing had ever seemed able to disturb his equanimity. Hart thought that nothing ever could. And yet here he was, just a few feet away, with a look as close to complete astonishment as any Hart had seen.

"There are passages that have been underlined, notes in Gunther's hand written in the margins, but nothing that would tell you much beyond the bare fact that for some reason he had begun a serious study of Roman history. The first passage he marked is the description of Caesar and his army when he crossed the Rubicon."

"But what would that . . . other than the name—?"

Shoenfeld's eyes were shining with the knowledge of something that still seemed almost too impossible to believe.

"And then I found it, wedged between the last page and the back cover: a single thin piece of paper, folded into quarters. Gunther had traced out a diagram, certain historical parallels. At the bottom of the page—here, let me show you!"

He opened the black briefcase and carefully removed a single thick volume. The leather cover was scratched and torn at the corners, proof of age and usage. The onionskin paper had been left where he had first found it. He handed the book to Hart, who unfolded the paper on which an elaborate diagram had been sketched. Hart looked at it, and then gave it back.

"It appears to be in German, and . . ."

"Yes, forgive me. I should have remembered. Well, but see there, the name Rubicon scribbled at the top of the first of the two columns, the list of historical parallels. The first column is a kind of outline of Roman history. But now—the second column—see the name again. But this time it isn't at the top, it's at the bottom. Gunther had worked it all out. Rubicon was the start of something in Rome, but it was meant to be the end of something in America. Rubicon means more than what happened in Los Angeles. That was only the beginning."

"But how do you know this—from a few marked-up passages in an old book and a strange diagram written on a piece of paper?"

"There's more, a lot more. Those seven names Gunther gave me. I found six of them. I learned that Gunther was not killed by a terrorist organization; Gunther was—"

"You said you found six of them," said Hart, wondering if he had missed something. "Didn't you say there were seven?"

"Mohammed al Farabi. He was supposed to be in Cairo, but he isn't there anymore. From what I could learn, he moves constantly. I'm supposed to meet him next week. He may have the final piece of the puzzle, the—"

The telephone upstairs began to ring. Helen was the only one who used that number.

"I have to take this. I won't be long," said Hart as he left Shoenfeld in the living room and hurried to the bedroom upstairs.

It was Helen, and she sounded better than she had in a long time.

"I just wanted to hear your voice," she said. She laughed a little and started to tease him about what he was missing. "I'm sitting here, watching the sun go down on maybe the most perfect day I've ever seen. The sky is painted all orange and red and purple and the ocean has that glimmer like liquid gold. You'd like it here this evening, Bobby Hart, you would. Why don't you come home and stay with me?"

"I have a morning flight. They have me doing a few things in the afternoon, but, I promise, I'll be there for dinner."

She laughed again, that same teasing sparkle in her voice.

"I think I've forgotten how to cook. Why don't we go out somewhere, just the two of us?"

He could see her face across the candlelight, a smile like forever dancing gently on her lips. He could hear the thrilling way she laughed, the way she used to, before things had started to go bad.

"We have a date. I'll see you around—"

Suddenly, there was a tremendous, violent noise, followed by the sound of shattered glass.

"What is it, Bobby?"

He heard heavy footsteps running on the floor below, and then a shout, Dieter's voice, and a burst of gunfire. The house went silent.

12

I'M ALL RIGHT," HE WHISPERED INTO THE RE-
ceiver and then hung up.

He moved across to the open bedroom door and tried to
see downstairs. He caught a glimpse of two armed men
searching through the house. He pressed back against the
wall and held his breath.

"Where's the other one?" said one of them in a hushed,
hurried voice. "There were supposed to be two of them!
He's not down here—try upstairs!"

Hart looked behind him, across the bedroom to the
windows at the front. His only chance was to jump.

"Never mind," said the other one, "there isn't time. The
cops will be here any minute. Grab the briefcase and let's
get out of here."

Lights were coming on all over the neighborhood. The
sound of sirens could be heard in the distance, coming
closer. Hart went downstairs and found Dieter Shoenfeld
slumped back on the sofa, his eyes wide open, the front
of his shirt soaked in blood. The black briefcase had been

taken, but the book, that ancient book of Roman history with the all-important single folded piece of paper inside it, was still sitting there in plain sight on the coffee table.

The sirens were getting louder. He put the book high up on a shelf, well out of view, and then, as quickly as he could, went through Dieter's pockets, looking for anything that might tell him something about what Shoenfeld had learned about Rubicon. He found a small notebook, slipped it into his own pocket, and then ran to the front door, waving frantically for the police.

A police car screeched to a halt and two uniformed officers, weapons drawn, moved quickly toward the house. "Are you all right?" asked one of them, peering down the empty hallway. "What happened?"

"They came in through the back. I was upstairs, but Dieter . . ." Hart gestured toward the living room. "In there . . ."

More police cars pulled up, and, within minutes, a crowd had started to form in the street outside. The police cordoned off the front of the house and began a slow, methodical search of the grounds in the back.

"This wasn't some burglary gone bad," said one of the officers to his partner. "Not the way these assholes came through the back door. Broke it right off the goddamn hinges—kicked the sucker in, and took all the glass with it. This wasn't some robbery, this was a fucking execution."

Twenty minutes after the uniformed officers arrived, a plainclothes detective found Hart alone in his study next to the bedroom on the second floor.

"Lieutenant Coleman, Senator—Leonard Coleman. Sorry about all this."

Leonard Coleman was nearly sixty, a black detective who spoke in a quiet, understated voice.

"What can you tell me about what happened? I know that someone—two men, I gather—broke in through the back door and shot to death your friend, Mr. Shoenfeld. It's clear that they came here intending to kill someone, so the obvious question, Senator, is whether it was you."

"How long have you been a detective, Lieutenant?"

"Nearly twenty years."

"Most murders are what they call crimes of passion, aren't they?"

"Most—yes, sir, but not this one. But you know that, so, if you don't mind, why do you ask?"

"I'm not sure; maybe I'm just trying to put things in the right categories. I was in Los Angeles, and . . ."

"I know, sir; I know where you were—and what you saw."

"And then again tonight, though I didn't actually see it happen, I know what happened tonight. What happened in Los Angeles—that was not a crime of passion, either. He stood there, waiting, as calm as anyone you've ever seen: no fear, no anger, no hatred in his eyes. He was a believer—a zealot if you want—but someone who did not think for a moment that what he was about to do was wrong. But now, tonight, two men—" He gave the lieutenant a quick, clear-eyed glance. "White men in their late thirties, early forties. One of them had a mustache, and one of them—I couldn't tell you which—had an accent: New York, maybe New Jersey—I'm not sure. They weren't terrorists, and they sure as hell weren't from the Middle East. Almost forgot—one of them was at least six foot; the other was shorter, and broader at the shoulders—"

"That's very good, Senator. That will help."

"I doubt it."

"You . . . ?"

"They didn't come here to settle a grudge. It wasn't anything personal. They were hired professionals. And in answer to your question, they came here to kill both of us. I was here, upstairs, just down the hall in the bedroom. My wife had called—from California. I left Dieter in the living room. They broke down the door, murdered Dieter, and then came looking for me. Or started to. The only reason I'm still alive is that they realized that with all the noise they were almost out of time."

"And you know for sure that they meant to kill you, too?"

"That's the interesting thing. They didn't know who they were after, who they had been sent to kill. One of them said to the other, right after they murdered Dieter, 'There were supposed to be two of them.'"

"What else, Senator? There's something else, isn't there?"

"I'm not sure. At first I thought that . . . Dieter thought that he might have been followed and . . ."

"Why would he think that, Senator? Why would Mr. Shoenfeld—I gather from the identification in his wallet that he was a German citizen—why would he think he was being followed?"

"There are certain things I can't tell you. He had been working on something, trying to find something out."

Coleman made an educated guess.

"Given what happened in Los Angeles, Senator, I would assume it must have had something to do with that."

Hart looked at him with added respect, but still did not answer directly.

"I didn't know he was coming. He showed up outside my office and we drove around a little and eventually came here. Whoever was following him must have followed us here. But now that I think about it, part of it doesn't make sense. We had only been here fifteen or twenty minutes, so how could they have contacted two hired killers, unless . . ."

"Unless the hit had already been arranged. Which means, Senator, that they were coming for you; that someone was watching the house so they could let them know when you were here."

Coleman took a long, slow look around the study, at the walls lined with books and photographs, pictures of statesmen and politicians, all of them smiling as if none of them had a care in the world. His eyes came back to the only photograph on the senator's desk.

"Your wife?" He bent a little forward to get a better view. "Very beautiful," he remarked, nodding his head in approval. "She's in California, you say?"

"Yes, our place in Santa Barbara."

Coleman listened for a moment to the commotion downstairs.

"That might be a good place for you, as well. I'm not sure why anyone wanted to have you murdered, but if they went to all this trouble there isn't much reason to think that they'll stop after tonight."

Coleman took a notebook out of his pocket and flipped it open. In a small, crabbed hand, he jotted down a short summary of what he had learned. Then he asked Hart to come outside and walk him through everything that had happened from the moment he and Shoenfeld had first arrived.

"We came down the alley," explained Hart. He pointed from the back of the garage where they were standing to the street at the end. "The same way I do every night."

Coleman bent down. Carefully, with his handkerchief, he picked up the crushed remains of a cigarette.

"Do you smoke, Senator, or did Mr. Shoenfeld?"

"Dieter did, but not tonight."

Coleman put the cigarette in a small plastic bag. He pointed back to the street where Hart had pointed before.

"They were probably parked out on the street somewhere, waiting. It's dark out there. No one would have noticed. They walked up the alley—a car would have made too much noise. One of them smoked a cigarette—out of habit, maybe to calm his nerves. Probably stood here a moment, looked around, made certain no one was coming, then went for the door. We'll put this through forensics," he added as he put the bagged cigarette inside his pocket, "and see what we get."

They stood a while longer next to the garage.

"You get out of the car—you and Mr. Shoenfeld—and you go directly to the house. Did you turn on the lights, the way they are now?"

"No, I started to, but Dieter asked me not to. He was so afraid that someone might have followed him that . . ."

"Yes, but that confirms what you said earlier about what you heard. One of them said that there were 'supposed to be two of them.' That means they hadn't seen you both. They couldn't have been following you. Yes, okay—go on. You walked across the yard, all the lights were out. You went inside the kitchen. What happened next?"

Hart led Coleman back into the kitchen, and then, just as he had Shoenfeld, led him through the dining room into the living room in front. A police photographer was taking the last pictures of the body. Hart could not watch. He walked away. Coleman said something to the photographer who quickly finished.

"You said Mr. Shoenfeld was going to stay here tonight, but he doesn't seem to have brought any luggage."

"All he had was his briefcase," replied Hart. He was standing next to the bookshelf near the front windows, staring down at the floor. He forced himself to raise his eyes and point to the bloodstained sofa. "He had it there, next to him."

"It's not there now."

"No, one of them—I remember now—told the other one to grab it just before they left."

Coleman looked at Hart, and then at Shoenfeld's body as it was being placed inside a black bag and lifted onto a gurney. There was a worried look in his eyes.

"But this wasn't a robbery. They didn't come here to steal. So why would they bother to take his briefcase unless they had some idea—unless whoever sent them had some idea—what was in it?"

Hart understood the implications, or thought he did.

"Which would mean that Dieter was right. He was being followed, because otherwise how would anyone have known he was here. But that means . . ."

"That the people who were having him followed are the same people who want you murdered." Coleman gave Hart a searching glance. "What happened in Los Angeles—both of you were looking into that. I read the papers, Senator. Everyone knows the kind of questions you've been raising. That was the reason Mr. Shoenfeld came here tonight, wasn't it—all the way from Germany without any luggage, only that briefcase? It must have been quite urgent. What was in it? What had he found out?"

"I don't know. He never had a chance to tell me. He started to. He told me where he had been the last couple weeks when everyone thought he had disappeared. He told me he had found something out about Rubicon . . ."

"Rubicon, Senator? What's that?'

"The code name—what we thought was the code name—for what happened in Los Angeles. All I know, all he had a chance to tell me, was that what had happened in Los Angeles was not the end of Rubicon—it was just the beginning."

It was slight, almost unnoticeable, but it was there, real, and in the instant it lasted, painful to see, the way that Leonard Coleman's large, impassive eyes recoiled from what it meant.

"And there are people—in this country—who don't want anyone to find that out?" He bit the inside of his lip and thought hard a moment. "You were in the service. You know the drill. Someone higher up is going to try to take this over. I'm just a cop. The FBI will be on this almost as fast as those reporters out there," he said, gesturing toward the street outside where the television trucks had started to arrive. "Maybe you think that would be . . ."

Hart gave him a rueful glance.

"After what's happened, do you think I trust anyone in the FBI, or any other part of the government? For all I know . . . Stay on this case, I don't care who tries to stop you."

"You don't know me, Senator. We've only just met. Why would you trust me more than . . . ?"

Hart looked straight into his eyes.

"I almost never trust anyone, especially in this town, but I knew right away I could trust you. It's an instinct I have. And besides, what choice do I have?"

He quickly jotted down his cell phone number on the back of his card.

"I don't know where I'm going to be, but you can always reach me at this number. I need to get out of here. There are places I need to go. Am I free to leave? Is there anything more . . . ?"

"No, we're all right for now. Someone will need to do something with those reporters outside. Do you want . . . ?"

Hart thought about what he should do. He was running on adrenaline and he knew it. The death of Dieter Shoenfeld had not really sunk in yet; it was still too much a part of a nightmare that kept playing over and over again in his mind. He turned to Coleman.

"Come with me."

With Leonard Coleman next to him, a half step behind,

Hart stood on the front steps of his Georgetown home and gave a brief explanation of what had happened.

"Earlier this evening, two men broke into my house and murdered my good friend, Dieter Shoenfeld, who was visiting me from Germany. As many of you know, Dieter Shoenfeld was the distinguished editor and publisher of one of Europe's most important journals. The reason for what happened remains unclear. What I can tell you is that this was not an attack by terrorists. I heard their voices and . . ." He paused, wondering if he should say it and knowing that, whatever the risk, he had to. "And I saw their faces. They were Americans, both of them. Given what has happened, I'm sure you'll understand that for the moment at least I can't take any questions. Let me turn this over now to Lieutenant Coleman, who is heading the investigation."

He touched Coleman briefly on the arm and went back inside. Uniformed officers were still moving through the house, gathering evidence. He went directly upstairs, shut the door to the bedroom, and packed a bag. Then he called Helen.

"I'm all right," he told her. "But Dieter . . ." He started to feel it, the first signs of collapse, a wave of fatigue that rolled over him like a thick, dense fog. He tried to shake it off. "Dieter is dead. Look, Helen, I have to go away for a few days. There is something I need to do, but don't worry—I'll be all right. Or I will be, if I know that you're going to be okay."

He listened to her promise, knew that it was a promise she would keep, and, knowing that, managed to find more strength.

"I'll call you as soon as I can."

He took a last look around the room. Then, with the overnight bag in his hand, he quickly went downstairs. He was all the way to the kitchen when he remembered. He went to the living room and reached up on the shelf.

"I better have something to read," he remarked by way of explanation when a young uniformed officer saw what he was doing. He tucked under his arm the book that Dieter Shoenfeld had risked, and lost, his life to bring him, and hurried out the back door.

13

CHANCE WAS EVERYTHING. IF DIETER SHOEN-feld had waited a day, Hart would have gone home by himself and been killed. If Dieter Shoenfeld had waited a day, Dieter would still be alive; if Helen had called just three minutes later, he would have been murdered along with Dieter. Everyone who had learned anything about Rubicon had become a target for murder, and now, strictly by chance, Hart was the only one who knew anything who had not been killed.

He drove through Georgetown and back across the bridge, past the Capitol to the dilapidated building where David Allen had an apartment. He parked around a corner three blocks away, just beyond the reach of the flickering neon light of an old hotel. He grabbed the overnight bag, turned up the collar on his coat, and walked quickly, but not so quickly as to attract attention, to Allen's building.

"I've been trying to call!" exclaimed Allen when he opened the door and found him standing there.

Recently divorced, Allen lived alone in a small one-bedroom apartment. Everything had the look of a temporary arrangement. The bookshelves—the cheap kind you assemble yourself—were filled with congressional reports, legislative proposals, the usual paperwork of a congressional assistant. Allen picked up an armful of newspapers from the only sofa and dropped them on top of another stack near the door.

"Sit down, sit down." He took the overnight bag from Hart's shoulder and gestured toward the sofa. He pulled a chair from in front of the small desk in the corner and dragged it over.

"I kept trying to call, but I couldn't reach you. I was just about to get in the car and drive over."

"I turned the cell phone off. I didn't want to talk to anyone . . . and I didn't want anything traced."

"Traced? The phone?"

Hart glanced around the small, cluttered room. His eyes began to focus.

"Can I bother you for a drink?"

Allen made him a Scotch and water. Hart took a drink and then stared into the middle distance, a study in dejection.

"Dieter . . ." His voice trailed off and the name echoed into the silence.

"You better stay here tonight," said Allen. "The sofa makes into a bed. I've got some clean sheets in the other room. It won't be too bad." He bent his balding head to the side, worried. "You look like you're about to fall apart, Bobby. You need to get some rest."

"Rest? I couldn't sleep tonight if I tried. They came to kill me—two hired assassins. I saw them both. They came to kill me, and they got Dieter instead."

Hart took a second drink, longer, slower, than the first. The cool fire felt good against his throat. He leaned forward, the drink held between his knees, staring into it as he thought about what he had to do.

"I need a favor," he said, raising his eyes. "I need to borrow your car."

"Sure, but you know, it's got a few miles on it, and . . . Why? What happened to yours?"

Hart tossed him his keys.

"It's parked up the street, just past the hotel. I need something to drive to Michigan, and I better not use mine. They have the license."

Allen jumped out of the chair and started to pace, realized there was not room, and sat down again. He looked at Hart, not as the senator he worked for, but as his oldest friend.

"Who tried to kill you tonight? And why?"

"Rubicon."

"You've never told me what it meant, just that it was the code name for the assassination plot."

"Dieter was convinced that what happened in Los Angeles was only the first step, but the first step in what, I don't know. He didn't tell me; he didn't have the chance. The phone rang, and I knew it was Helen and that I had to take the call, and then, when I was upstairs on the phone . . ."

He drank some more, then put down the glass.

"When Caulfield was killed—I know he was murdered— the only logical conclusion seemed to be that someone connected with a terrorist cell had managed to get inside the agency. But what happened tonight was a contract killing. Since when does a terrorist organization in the Middle East hire professional killers to do their work? I don't know who is behind this. I don't even know what they're trying to do. But everyone who has tried to find out anything about Rubicon has been killed."

Hart started to reach for his glass, but then, suddenly, changed his mind and got to his feet.

"First thing tomorrow I want you to fly back to California. It isn't safe here. You were going out anyway in a few days," he said when Allen started to protest. "Do it now instead. Look in on Helen. Make sure she's all right."

Allen knew there was no point trying to stop him. He gave him his keys and told him where the car was parked.

"You're going to see Charlie Ryan. That's why you're going, isn't it? You're not going to try to drive straight through? It's six hundred miles."

Time, distance—none of that seemed to matter anymore. There were no alternatives, no choices he could make. Everything was chance, but chance was fate, and the path now in front of him was the only one he could take.

He drove for hours, deep into Pennsylvania, lost in the constant migration of Americans moving everywhere at once. A little before three in the morning he stopped for gas. There was a small coffee shop at the turnpike station. After he filled the tank he went inside for something to eat. Two truckers were sitting together at the far end of the counter. A middle-aged waitress with a mole just above the corner of her mouth poured him a cup of coffee before he had time to ask. She handed him a plastic menu. He did not bother to open it.

"Bacon, two eggs, and toast."

The eggs were runny and the bacon black and brittle, but Hart did not mind. It was good to be out of the car and able to stretch his legs. He listened to the voices of the two truck drivers with their confident, abbreviated speech and envied a little the lives of normal people.

"You driving all night?" asked the waitress, warming his cup.

"I'm not sure," he confessed.

"How far you going?"

"Michigan," he replied. "Ann Arbor."

She seemed to take it under advisement, like someone

who spent her days—or, rather, her nights—calculating for others time and distance and, depending on the season, the effect of the weather.

"Should be there by noon, if you don't stop anywhere too long. Be light in a few hours. It won't be so difficult then. On the other hand, there's a halfway decent motel not too far up the road. But, as I say, it will be light soon."

The two truckers got up from the counter. Each of them left her a good tip.

"See you in a few days," said one of them with a tired smile as they left.

She cleaned up their dishes and wiped down the counter.

"You hear what happened tonight?" she asked as she came back with the pot of coffee. "Another attack. Not like before—no one blew themselves up—but they tried to kill a senator! Right in his own home! Missed him, got someone else. But right in his home, in Washington, the capital. No one is safe anymore, are they?"

Hart paid the bill and left a couple of dollars next to the plate.

"Thanks," he said as he walked to the door.

"Come back soon," she replied in a dreamy voice. She waved a listless good-bye and leaned against the doorway, watching the endless traffic passing in the night.

The coffee kept Hart going until the darkness broke behind him and the sun began to rise. He made Michigan by eleven and, just as the waitress had calculated, Ann Arbor by noon. It was only when he pulled up in front of Charlie Ryan's large Georgian-style house that he suddenly realized that, just back from the Republican convention and in the middle of his own campaign for reelection, Ryan might be anywhere in Michigan, but certainly not at home.

He glanced in the mirror. His hair was a tangled mess and he needed a shave. He got out of the car, stretched his arms, and walked to the front door. Maybe someone was home and could tell him where he had to go next. The door opened before he got there. Charlie Ryan stepped out to greet him.

"How did you . . . ?"

"David Allen called me, right after you left his place last night. Why the hell did you drive? Why didn't you just call? I would have come, taken the first flight back," Ryan insisted as he shut the door behind them. "We'll talk about this later. Right now, go upstairs, take a long, hot shower, get cleaned up. Go to bed for a while, get some sleep."

"No, I can't—not yet. I will take a shower, however. I must look a wreck."

Half an hour later, showered and shaved and wearing clean clothes, Hart sat at the kitchen table and tried to tell Ryan everything that he knew.

"And you have the book—and the diagram—with you? The things Shoenfeld thought so important."

Hart handed Ryan the leather-bound volume. With a raised eyebrow and a wistful glance, Ryan examined it.

"Plutarch. I haven't read him since college. Though Father Henriot, my ancient history teacher, might have told you that I had not really read him then."

He opened the tattered cover, careful to do it in a way that kept it from falling further apart. A slight grimace broke the even line of his mouth.

"Greek! The only subject I knew less about than ancient history."

"But you know it."

"Know it? I suppose that with the aid of a good dictionary I could probably translate ten or twelve lines in a month or so." He saw the look of disappointment on Hart's dead-tired face. He slapped him on the knee and got up. "But don't worry, I have the solution."

Ryan disappeared into the living room. He came back a

few minutes later carrying a small book in a green jacket. He seemed quite pleased with himself.

"Something I thought I should probably study someday. Still looks new, doesn't it?" He placed the book on the table and opened it at random to show Hart why it would help. "On facing pages: the Greek on the left, the English translation on the right. This should work. Show me the first passage he marked—Gunther Kramer, right?"

Ryan remembered enough Greek to find the corresponding place in the bilingual edition and then the same passage in English. After nearly an hour, he sat back and looked out the window, down to the edge of a creek to a stand of birch trees that had begun to turn yellow. Gray clouds scudded across the eastern sky, bringing with them a sudden chill and, for just a few minutes, the season's first snow flurry. In the cold sunlight the air was crystal, pure, and clean. Winter might come early this year.

"It all seems pretty straightforward," said Hart, while Ryan watched the last of the snowflakes melt on the grass.

"What?" asked Ryan. He turned from the window. Hart was still bent over the Loeb edition, reading again the last marked passage. "Yes, I suppose so. I'm not sure."

Hart looked up. He thought he understood the doubt.

"I meant the passages Kramer marked," Hart said. "The connection they have to Rubicon is another matter."

Ryan tapped his finger, gently and without emphasis, on the table. He tried to think.

"Everyone knows the story—at least everyone forced to read Roman history. But even if you didn't, everyone knows that famous line: 'Vini, vidi, vici'—'I came, I saw, I conquered.' Caesar is talking about what he did in Gaul, but it leads up to what he did later when he crossed the Rubicon. The first passage marked: he crosses the Rubicon. Why was that so important? Because he was told not to, because the army was to be kept away from Rome. But why was a Roman army thought to be a threat to Rome itself? That other passage—remember?"

Hart's gaze drifted back to the text, to the place where Gunther Kramer had carefully and with exact precision drawn brackets. The sense of it seemed plain enough. Hart summarized what it said.

"The early days of the republic, when Rome was smaller, no one commanded an army for more than a few months or a year. But later, as Rome acquired more territory, Rome became an empire and armies had to be sent to places so far away it might take months to get there. The armies became less loyal to Rome than to those, like Caesar, who were their generals. In other words," added Hart, "the threat to the republic began when Rome became an empire."

"Yes, but there is something else," said Ryan. He was not quite certain he could put it into words. "Something about the tone in which it is written. You get the sense that everything that happened was inevitable, that once someone had that much power it was only a matter of time before they were going to do something with it."

"What about all the notes Kramer made in the margin?"

"I don't read German, but a friend of mine teaches it at the university. I'll call him. I wonder what Kramer found so fascinating about it."

"Maybe the same thing we're thinking about: what I had never thought about before."

Ryan gave him a puzzled glance. Hart laughed quietly and with a touch of embarrassment.

"I'm not sure I even knew there was a Roman republic. All I know about Roman history is Shakespeare's play: Caesar murdered, then a civil war. I thought Caesar crossed the Rubicon to deal with his enemies in Rome."

"That's all most people know. What's your point?"

"My point is that I confused the idea of the Roman Empire with the long list of Roman emperors. I didn't realize that the empire came before the emperors, and that the empire made the emperors inevitable."

Ryan nodded in agreement.

"And the lesson from this?"

"That a republic that becomes an empire eventually loses its freedom."

"Perhaps. But notice the next passage Kramer marked. What was not inevitable was the genius of Julius Caesar. He changed everything and made it seem, at least while he lived, that he had not changed anything. He kept all the old forms of the republic: everything was still done according to the ancient formula: 'by the will of the Senate and the people of Rome,' though nothing happened unless Caesar wanted it."

"This is all interesting, Charlie, but where does it get us? They came to kill me last night, whoever they are, and all we have is this book."

Suddenly, he remembered something. He unfolded the thin piece of paper on which Gunther Kramer had written two parallel columns.

"This is in German, too—but Rubicon appears twice: at the top of the column on the left, and at the bottom of the one on the right. Dieter told me that Kramer had worked it all out."

Ryan stood up and stretched his arms.

"I'll call that friend of mine. Why don't you go upstairs and try to get a little sleep." He looked at Hart with a worried expression. "No one knows you're here, except David Allen, which means no one else can find you. Every reporter in Washington is probably trying to get hold of you, get your reaction to what happened last night. If you don't surface sometime soon, they'll start to report that you've gone missing, and you know the kind of speculation that will lead to."

Hart rose from the table.

"Allen will tell everyone that I've gone into seclusion, that the death of Dieter Shoenfeld has been a terrible blow, and that I need a little time to myself. That will buy me a couple of days. I have to get out of the country and no one can know about it. I'll explain later."

Hart went upstairs to the guest room while Ryan made his call. He thought he would lie down for a few minutes and rest. He closed his eyes and tried not to think about anything.

"Bobby," said Ryan quietly, shaking his shoulder. "Wake up. The translation has been done."

Hart did not know what Ryan was talking about. The room where he had fallen asleep was dark. He thought that someone must have closed the curtains. He sat up and looked around.

"How long have I been asleep?"

"Six hours, maybe a little more. Come downstairs. Clare is home. We'll have dinner."

Clare Ryan was a physician, a heart surgeon on staff at the University of Michigan hospital. Thin as a long-distance runner, with large, candid eyes, she had one of the most sharply analytical minds Hart had encountered. She took things in at a glance that most people never noticed. She had understood Helen right away. It was the first thing she asked about.

"How is she? How is she holding up under all of this?"

Clare put her hand through Hart's arm and walked with him from the bottom of the long, spiral staircase to the dining room. The table was set for three people. She gave him a buoyant, yet understated, smile.

"I know you're a mess, but you can take it. My friend Helen, on the other hand, does not enjoy the protection of the various layers of stupidity by which men like you and Charlie here try to pretend that there is no such thing as danger. They really tried to kill you last night? Good God, what's this country coming to?"

She kissed him on the side of the cheek and told him that it might be a good idea if he tried to stay alive.

"Charlie tells me that you have to leave the country," said Clare, shortly after they started dinner. "I have a sister in Toronto, a lawyer who does a lot of immigration work. She might be able to help get a passport, something you can use to fly out of Canada. You can drive across from Detroit to Windsor, and go on to Toronto from there." There was a slight change in her expression. She had just realized something she ought to have known. "Or had you thought of that already?"

The conversation turned to other things, to what was happening in the presidential race, and to what was happening to Charlie Ryan.

"You told me a couple weeks ago that the money out of Washington had dried up," said Hart. "I don't imagine what you did the other night with the vice president is going to help much with that problem. How much trouble are you in?"

Ryan shrugged it off, or tried to.

"There are people here who want to help. What I don't know is how what happened in Los Angeles will affect things, or what effect the presidential race will have. It isn't easy, knowing that Taylor would make a much better president, having to pretend in public that Douglas would not be another disaster."

Clare threw her napkin down on the table.

"God, Charlie, don't you think it's time to stop the fraud? You know that Douglas would be just about the worst thing that could happen. He has not had a thought that has not come out of the White House. Why don't you just come out and say so, tell people what you really think? Someone has just tried to murder just about the only friend you have in Washington and you're still going around mouthing the party line? What for—so you don't lose? What's the point of winning if you can't tell the truth?"

The more she talked, the angrier she seemed to become, the broader the smile on Charlie Ryan's face. He turned to Hart.

"What do you think? Sounds like a hell of a good idea to me."

Clare did not believe him. She believed he meant it, that it would be a good thing to do, but not that he would actually do it, take the chance, risk everything he had worked for. She understood that there were certain rules of the game; she also knew that there were not many men in politics, or women either, who had been willing to break so many of them as the man to whom she was married.

As soon as dinner was over, Clare had to say good-bye. There were patients to see in the hospital and she would not be home until late.

"Here's my sister's address and phone number. I'll call and tell her to expect you, and what you need. I don't want to see you go; but I know you have to, and it's probably better if you cross into Canada at night. I'll call Helen from my office and tell her we took good care of you. She'll want to know that, you know," she said as she gave him one last kiss.

"Thanks, Clare," he said, moved by how willing she was to help and by how much she cared about Helen. "Thanks for everything."

"The translation?" asked Hart after Clare had left. "What do all those notes in the margin mean? And the diagram—does it make sense?"

"The translation is done. Does it help explain? I'm not sure."

They went back into the kitchen and sat in the same

places. The book was there, with the diagram beside it, along with two pages of a hand-printed translation.

"Some of the margin notes were just cross-references to other passages. Some of them just a word or two he wanted to be certain of from the Greek."

Ryan turned the first page of translations so that Hart could see it.

"The long margin note next to the discussion of how the crossing of the Rubicon was the culmination of Roman expansion, the necessary result of empire—it's a note about Iraq."

"Iraq?" asked Hart in astonishment. He read the translation out loud. "'What if war in Iraq was not started because of weapons of mass destruction, or any of the other reasons given. Not talking about oil. Started because it was, they thought . . .'" Hart looked up. "'They thought'? Who are 'they'?"

Ryan told him to keep reading.

"'Started because it was, they thought, the perfect pretext to establish a client state—the way the Romans established client states—a military presence, a model government—a puppet government—a colony, in the heart of the Middle East. The empire becomes more expansive, the people at home kept satisfied with promises of the spread of democracy and oil cheap and plentiful.'"

"The other page, the diagram Kramer drew," explained Ryan. "The first column is a list of what happened in Rome after the Rubicon was crossed. The second column is a list of things that could bring an empire—a republican empire— to that same point. It starts with the Second World War, then the military buildup of the Cold War, then the breakup of the Soviet Union and a world in which there is only one superpower left. Then—read what comes at the very end, the few lines just before the word *Rubicon*."

Hart read quietly to himself, and then out loud:

"'Political assassination—the threat of outside enemies— the case for endless war—expansion—more assassination: everything that brings about the necessity, or, rather, the belief in the necessity, that something drastic, fundamental, something without precedent, has to be done.'"

"Gunther Kramer did not think that Rubicon was the code name for a terrorist plot," said Ryan. "He thought it was a conspiracy to destroy the American republic, but how, and by whom? Something doesn't fit. What happened in Los Angeles was a terrorist attack. We know who the suicide bomber was, where he came from. We even know his name and why he said he did it. Something is missing, Bobby, and I don't know what it is."

"Look at this," said Hart. He handed Ryan the diagram. "At the bottom."

"All it says is 'Rubicon.'"

"No, there's something more. Just below it."

Ryan looked again. It was there, a kind of afterthought that, when he first looked at the translation, had not caught his eye.

"'What al Farabi told me.' What does it mean?"

Hart reached inside his jacket for the notebook he had taken from Dieter Shoenfeld. He turned to the page where he had first seen the name.

"Dieter was supposed to meet Mohammed al Farabi early next week in Rome. I'm going to meet him there instead. He said al Farabi might have the missing piece. That was the phrase he used—'the missing piece.'"

14

HART COULD NOT GET THE WORD OUT OF HIS head. He wrote it on a notepad during the flight from Toronto to Rome; he wrote it in his hotel room after he checked in. What did it mean—Rubicon? It was more than a plot to assassinate a political leader, more than an attempt to sabotage the election. But how much more, and where did it lead? The list that Gunther Kramer had made: assassination, the threat of outside enemies, a case for war, and then more assassinations—all of it to make it appear that something "without precedent" had to be done. What was without precedent, and, whatever it was, how would it lead to Rubicon in a way that ran parallel to what had happened in Rome more than two thousand years ago?

He had two days to wait, two days with nothing to do. He wanted to call home, to tell Helen there was nothing to worry about, that he was all right. It had been nearly a week since the night of the murder, five days since he had last heard her voice, but he had become paranoid, almost certain that someone was intercepting nearly every call. He remembered what Raymond Caulfield had said about Orwell's *1984* and the idea of living under the constant surveillance of some all-knowing power. He had spent three days in Toronto and for almost all of it thought he was being watched and followed. Rome seemed safer, and, more important, closer to what he hoped would be the end of the chase, when he would find out who was behind Rubicon and what, after Los Angeles, was going to happen next.

The hotel where Hart was staying was the same hotel where Dieter Shoenfeld was supposed to meet Mohammed al Farabi early Monday afternoon, the next day. Physically spent and emotionally drained, Hart managed to sleep straight through the night, something he had not been able to do in nearly a week. He had a late breakfast and then decided that he had to get out, that he could not stay all day in his room. He threw on a jacket and a pair of dark glasses, the way any tourist would dress, and walked to the Tiber and took the ancient pedestrian bridge across to the Vatican. The wide avenue that runs from the Castel Sant'Angelo was clogged with Christians waiting to receive the pope's blessing at noon.

There were shops and stands all along the route selling various religious objects and pictures and postcards of the pope. On a sudden whim, Hart bought a postcard which he intended to send to Charlie Ryan.

"The pope asked about you," he thought he would write. "Said he would like to hear your confession but, given what you have to confess, was not certain he could spare that much time."

It gave him a strange sense of the familiar, of being at home. He could almost see the laughter spread across Ryan's freckled Irish face when he read it. He put the postcard inside his pocket, stepped onto a double-decker tour bus, and left behind the crowd at St. Peter's.

The Roman sun felt warm and clean against his skin as

the bus lumbered along next to the Tiber. For an instant, with the heat of it full on his face, he could feel, or thought he could feel, what it must have been like to be part of a returning Roman army when the empire had conquered most of the known world and a Roman soldier always came home in triumph. He wished he had read more, studied more, known more about the reasons why Rome fell. He realized that he knew hardly anything about it at all.

In slow, halting, but quite precise English, the tour guide described each famous place they passed and paid an occasional brief, but necessary, tribute to the utter futility of Roman traffic.

"Three million people; three million cars. It is impossible to go anywhere, and so of course everyone does."

Hart looked down the side of the bus and watched the front fender of an Alfa Romeo come within a fraction of an inch of collision before hitting the brakes and pulling back. The bus plowed forward into a bedlam of screaming, high-pitched engines.

"And here, just to your left—that long line of ancient rubble. This is what remains of the marble bleachers that used to seat two hundred fifty thousand people, here, at the Circus Maximus, to watch the chariot races. It was an eighth of a mile across and a half mile in length."

An older man, with short gray hair and sharp gray eyes, sitting with his wife in the row just ahead of Hart, gestured toward the long, grass-covered field where all that was left of the race course were a few barely discernible ruts.

"When Rome became corrupt," he remarked in a steely British voice; "when there was nothing more to do in politics; when the public had lost all its powers and everything was in the hands of the emperors, then the way to control them, to keep their minds off what they had lost, was to keep them well fed and entertained." He laughed, a thin, brittle laugh wrapped in irony. "Think what they could have done with television!"

The tour bus made a wide, sweeping turn, doubled back down two winding streets, and came out on a wide avenue that led directly to the Colosseum.

"The name 'Colosseum,'" explained the guide on a microphone that emitted a whining metallic sound, "is a misunderstanding. The true name is Flavian Amphitheater. It was the first freestanding structure of its type in the world. It was begun by the Emperor Vespasian in the year 64 after Christ. It was finished by his son, the Emperor Titus, in the year 72 after Christ."

The bus came to a stop. Those who wanted to spend time wandering around the Colosseum got off.

"That was the next stage in Rome's corruption," the Britisher explained to his wife. He seldom looked at her when he spoke, but was certain that she listened. "It was not enough to have the distractions of athletic contests. They needed something to give an outlet for all that pent-up aggression. They gave them slaughter. When the place first opened, there were a hundred straight days of it. They say that Roman citizens came from all over the empire—that is what we forget: that they colonized half the globe and gave citizenship to those who earned it through loyal service—to watch the slaughter of more than five thousand beasts, most of them brought over from Africa just for the spectacle. And it never stopped. Almost two hundred years later, on the one-thousandth anniversary of the founding of Rome, two thousand gladiators fought elephants, tigers, lions, even giraffes and hippopotamuses—just to see the blood flow. And then of course there were the games in which the gladiators killed each other. Do you know, sometimes I really don't think there's much hope for the human race."

"Albert," said his wife, gazing off into the distance,

"that was a long time ago. What the Romans did—no one does that anymore."

"No, that's true. Now we just drop bombs on people and kill them that way. And we don't have to come out to a colosseum to watch it; we can do that right at home in our living rooms, can't we?"

"Well, I really don't see how you can compare things then and now," she persisted. But before her husband could reply, the bus lurched forward and the guide began another short description of the next place on the tour.

What the Britisher had said reminded Hart of what Caulfield had said about Orwell and Huxley: the relentless surveillance of *1984,* and the gentler, but in certain ways more pervasive, control exercised in the scientific utopia described in *Brave New World.* Everyone's need for food and shelter met; everyone satisfied with their place in life by proper conditioning and tension-relieving drugs; sex removed from the constraints of both birth and love; and, shaping everything else, entertainment designed to produce not just an emotional but a physical response, what Huxley in his fable called "the feelies."

He got off the bus at the next stop and for several hours wandered, part of the crowd, through the vast broken monuments and shattered remains of what had once been the capital of an empire that had seemed destined to last as long as there was life on earth. As he walked among the towering cypress and the huge blocks of overturned stone, he worked at the various pieces of what he had heard and what he knew: how Rome had changed from a republic in which every citizen fought in its wars to an empire in which generals led seasoned veterans whose only loyalty was to themselves; from a republic in which—how had that Britisher on the bus put it?—each citizen took part in civic life, to an empire in which citizens were kept obedient by countless mindless games and endless bloody slaughter.

Hart did not stop at the obvious parallels between what happened to Rome when it stopped being a republic and what had happened to his own country after the wars of the twentieth century. No one could argue that democracy in America was what it had been two hundred years ago; the country was too big, too industrialized, too specialized and spread out for that. But that was a far cry from having no democracy at all. No, it was not the same, he told himself; no one was elected to anything in Rome once the time of the Caesars started. There was no freedom of discussion, no real debate, not even in the Senate, once Caesar crossed the Rubicon and power came to depend solely, or mainly, on the possession of force.

Hart turned around and gazed once more at the Colosseum, shining in all its shattered, aging grandeur in the rose-colored sun, and then he started walking back to the hotel.

He was almost there, just the other side of the Piazza Navona, when he saw it on the front page of a newspaper. He would not have noticed, mixed in as it was with the newspapers of half a dozen other European countries, if the editors of the British paper had not run his photograph with the story of how the same U.S. senator who had narrowly missed being murdered in his home was now rumored to be missing and perhaps even dead.

It was the stuff of tabloid journalism. Bobby Hart has not been seen in nearly a week, not since the night that armed gunmen broke into his fashionable Georgetown house and in a burst of gunfire killed Dieter Shoenfeld, one of Europe's best-known publishers. Though representatives in Hart's office claim he went into seclusion the day after the Shoenfeld murder, no one seems to have heard from him since. This has led to speculation—"Speculation!" Hart swore out loud—that something has happened to the senator and that, for reasons of their own, the authorities are not talking about it. Knowledgeable sources insist that there is growing concern that the senator may have been kidnapped by the same people who tried to kill him and is now being held hostage somewhere, perhaps outside the country in some Middle Eastern nation.

"Damn," muttered Hart under his breath as he tucked the paper under his arm and strode in earnest toward the hotel.

The entrance to the Rafael Hotel was on a narrow cobblestone street with barely enough room for three or four cars to park facing straight in. The doorman was leaning against the wall, a cigarette dangling in his fingers, speaking to a dark, well-dressed man in a double-breasted suit. When he saw Hart approach, he ground the cigarette out with the heel of his shoe, and opened the door.

"I wonder, Mr. Hart, if we might have a word?"

The well-dressed stranger had his hand on Hart's arm, turning him back toward the blue Mercedes Hart had just squeezed past. Hart was so surprised at hearing anyone use his name that he was sitting in the back seat of the car before he quite knew what had happened. Then he tried to get out. He reached for the door handle, but the door had been locked. The car began to move, backing away from the hotel, then turning down the narrow cobblestone street. There were two men in the car, a driver, whose face he had not seen, and the one who had forced him inside, now sitting next to him. Hart demanded that he stop the car and let him out. The answer surprised him.

"Why, Mr. Hart? Do you have other plans for dinner?"

"Is that where I'm going—dinner? I didn't even know I had been invited."

The driver navigated several sharp-edged corners until he was out on the thoroughfare that ran next to the Tiber, and then, with St. Peter's Basilica glowing iridescent in the falling Roman sun, turned left and headed toward the Palatine Hill.

"How have you enjoyed Rome so far, Mr. Hart?" He asked this in the casual manner of one who is both interested and thinks he can help. "Probably not a very intelligent question, given the fact you've only just got here, to say nothing of the reason you've come."

He spoke impeccable English, clearer, crisper than an American, but without the traces of a British accent. He had almost certainly gone to school at one of the best universities in the Middle East; probably, thought Hart, in Egypt, where the British influence had produced something more than imitation. His hand lay comfortably on the seat between them. He wore gold cuff links and an expensive but understated watch. Hart thought he knew who he was.

"You must be Mohammed al Farabi."

The question seemed to dazzle the Egyptian by its ignorance.

"Am I . . . ? No. But yes, I can see why you might have jumped to that conclusion. No, I am not; but that is where you are going, or rather, whom you are going to see. Unless, of course, you really would prefer to have the driver stop and let you out." As soon as he said it, he began to shake his head, apologizing for an unforgivable breach of etiquette. "What I meant to say is that we would be glad to take you back to your hotel—if that is your preference. Though, I can assure you, Mohammed al Farabi would be deeply disappointed."

Hart wondered if it was true, if the man really would take him back and then drive away without a second thought. For all this Egyptian stranger's well-bred manners, he had, just a few minutes ago, forced Hart into a car and driven off with him. And now he made it seem like there was nothing the slightest bit unusual in any of it.

"That depends," said Hart with a serious look.

"I'm sorry—what depends?"

"Whether I ask you to take me back to my hotel depends

on what you tell me. First of all, who are you and where are you taking me?"

"My name is not important. It is enough that you know that I am taking you to see the man whose name you just mentioned, Mohammed al Farabi, whom you have come all this way to see. Or are we mistaken on that point?"

Hart ignored the question. There were other things he wanted to know.

"How do you know why I'm here, why I've come to Rome?"

With rare precision, the stranger nodded briefly and exactly. He became quite serious.

"Dieter Shoenfeld had made arrangements—through me—to meet with Mohammed al Farabi, here, in Rome, tomorrow afternoon. There were reasons Mohammed al Farabi was willing to meet with him. He will tell you if he so chooses. But one of the reasons was that Mr. Shoenfeld advised me that he had kept you informed of much of what he had learned. That was why we thought you might come. We knew from all the published reports that Mr. Shoenfeld had been murdered in your home, and that there was some reason to suppose that you had also been a target. Then, when we heard that you had disappeared, that no one knew where you were—it seemed at least a possibility that you would come here; that before he died Mr. Shoenfeld had told you he had a meeting with Mohammed al Farabi and that you decided you should come in his place. We are very glad that you did."

"Very glad . . . ?" Hart started to ask, but the Egyptian gave him a look that told him that the reason would soon be clear.

They were now close to where Hart had been before, the Circus Maximus, or what was left of it.

"Why did you come for me? Why not wait until tomorrow and the original, scheduled meeting?"

"Because it was not safe. We could not know it was you until I saw you. We could not know that someone else had not found out where Dieter Shoenfeld was going—and who he was going there to meet. I can assure you, Mr. Hart, that the same people who had him murdered, and would like to murder you, are more than willing to get rid of anyone else who knows anything about them and what they are trying to do." He looked at Hart in a way that left no doubt how serious he was when he added, "You're really quite lucky to still be alive. If you were a Muslim, a member of the faith, I would have to say that you must be one of the favored few chosen by Allah to do God's work." A thin, enigmatic smile cut across his wide, smooth mouth. "Perhaps, even though you are not a believer, that may still be true."

The driver turned away from the race course of the Circus Maximus and the ancient ghosts of Roman chariots and headed onto the Palatine Hill. Ten minutes later, he stopped in front of the guarded gate of a high-walled villa and rolled down the window. Holding an automatic weapon in his arms, the guard looked inside and then, stepping back, waved them through.

"Dieter told me that Mohammed al Farabi had been in Cairo, but that he now lived here, in Rome."

"Cairo was not safe. It never had been, really, but then, after what happened, after they took him away . . ."

"Took him away?"

The stranger's eyes, so bold and full of confidence, suddenly became modest and self-effacing; his manner, so rigorously correct and self-assured, became almost humble. Hart turned to see what he was looking at, what had produced this remarkable change.

Standing directly in front of the car, with a short cropped black beard and piercing black eyes, was someone who seemed to have leaped straight from the pages of the Arabian Nights. He held his head not just erect, like some well-trained soldier, but with the proud, and indifferent, defiance of a man bred from birth to the habit of command. It was not the command of others that made the habit so impressive; it was the control he exercised over himself. Hart sensed immediately that he was in the presence of a rare intelligence, a man who liked deserts and the cleanliness of barren places, someone who could both laugh and cry at the vanities of the world.

15

"GOOD EVENING, SENATOR HART. I AM MOHAMmed al Farabi," said the man as he stepped out of the shadows. "I was very sorry to hear about poor Mr. Shoenfeld. But I'm glad you're safe and that now, finally, we can talk. Please, come inside. We'll have something for dinner."

They sat on a loggia overlooking much of what was left of ancient Rome. The headlights from the traffic in the distance had the look of a torch-bearing army. The scent of jasmine filled the warm night air.

"Augustus, I am told, was born not far from here and, so the story goes, wanted to live in the same simple house when he became emperor. He was forced, however—perhaps by circumstances, perhaps by his wife—to build a palace instead. The irony, if it is an irony, is that because he did what he had not wanted to do, all the emperors who followed him wanted to do the same thing: build, each one of them, a palace of his own. Most men live by imitation, Senator Hart; the only difference between them what they choose to imitate."

A breeze, gentle as a woman's breath, gave a moment's life to the white silk draperies that hung from the loggia's stone columns, which, taking it in, then let it go and hung limp again. Dinner was served by a small tribe of servants who materialized and vanished in strict accordance with their task. It was as if the air itself were filled with an intelligence that could foresee, and arrange, each thing that was needed.

"My family has always been in Egypt. I am told by those who know such things that there is no record of a time in which the name al Farabi did not exist. There was a man of that name quite famous, nearly a thousand years ago, but whether I am a direct descendant of his or not—I think would be too much to claim." Mohammed al Farabi turned to Hart, sitting immediately on his right, and allowed himself a modest smile. "But I have read his works, or tried to.

"In more recent times my family turned to commerce. My father, and his father before him, were bankers, men of great wealth; and because wealth always attracts followers, men of no small influence. They were prudent men, both of them; men who knew how to keep their own counsel, men who understood—or thought they understood—that there are limits beyond which one must not go in trying to change things. They learned to accommodate those in power. I, on the other hand, was young and of course had nothing like their patience. I was also, to tell the whole truth of it, used to being rich."

The sparkle in his eye showed that he understood that if he had seen things differently than his father and grandfather had, it was only possible because of what they had done for him. Hart was drawn to him in ways he had not expected. He had come to talk to someone he had thought must be one of the dispossessed, an outcast living hand to mouth on the margins of society, and found instead a merchant prince.

"I had money, or rather my family had it. It never occurred to me to think how difficult it had been to acquire or how difficult it might be to keep. I only thought about how to use it; and of course, I used it badly: fast cars, fast women, all the usual things." With a shrug of his shoulders, he mocked any thought that what he had done in his youth required regret much less any need of redemption. "Fast cars, fast women," he repeated, his warm voice filled with irony and nostalgia. "Just between us, I kept a few of the cars."

They talked through dinner, or rather Mohammed al Farabi talked, telling Hart about his youthful indiscretions, but in a way that told more about his education, what he had learned growing up in a place in which being frivolous had at least the advantage of being safe.

"If you had money no one cared what you did. As long, of course, as you paid off all the right people, the people in government who claimed to be your friends. They were always taking out loans from the bank; loans, as both sides understood, that would never be paid back. But what did that matter when there was so much money to go around. I did not notice. That was simply how things were done.

"And then it happened, one of those things that suddenly change everything. A friend of my father's, a man he had known since university, was arrested. This was all the more remarkable because he was the publisher of one of the most conservative newspapers in Egypt, a paper that had always taken a strong line against the fundamentalists and extremists, those who were trying to bring down the government. But he had made the mistake—what turned out to be the very serious mistake—of writing an editorial in which he argued that it was time to begin to lift the restrictions on the right of free assembly and free speech; that the failure to do so would only increase the growing discontent with the government and give support to those who were advocating violent resistance. He was taken into custody. There were no formal charges, no formal sentence. He was just kept there, in prison, and on more than one occasion beaten nearly to death. When they released him, almost a year later, he was just a shell of the man he used to be.

"What happened to my father's friend, a man I had known my whole life, changed everything. I talked to my father about what we could do. He was so angered by what had been done, that he did not hesitate when I told him what I wanted to do, though he knew better than anyone what was likely to happen because of it."

The servants, as if summoned by a wish, cleared the table and brought coffee. With a small silver spoon, al Farabi slowly stirred sugar into his cup. The expression in his eyes became pensive and somber.

"What did you do?" asked Hart, quietly and without hurry. He was interested in what al Farabi was telling him, and understood that it was part of the larger story, a necessary preface, as it were, to what Hart had come to learn. "What was it that you wanted that only your father's anger allowed you to have?"

Al Farabi looked up. A bright smile glittered in his dark eyes.

"I bought the paper."

"You bought the . . . ?"

"Yes, and the first editorial I wrote was all about what the government had done, how they were willing to stifle the voices even of those who supported them the moment there was disagreement on anything."

"What happened?" asked Hart, astonished.

"Nothing, at first. They thought I was a young hothead; a rich playboy with no discipline, who had taken over the paper as a lark, a moment's youthful passion that would never last. I surprised them. Here," he said, smiling gently into the night, "let me pour you more coffee."

For a few minutes he sat in silence, thinking back over what had happened. His eyes narrowed into a look of intense concentration.

"I had known for some time," he said presently, "that Egypt, that the whole Middle East, was stuck between two impossibilities: two types of tyrannies, secular and religious, and both of them doomed to failure. The paper attacked them both, the religious extremists of the sort who run things in Iran and the feudal kings and one-party presidents who rule nearly everywhere else. Some days religious mobs threw rocks through the windows; other days the police came to arrest me. The windows could always be replaced, and, because my family was so prominent, there were certain limits beyond which the government did not think it could go. And then came September 2001, and they suddenly had the chance to be rid of me forever. They took me into custody, told the Americans that I had useful information about terrorism, and then put me, gagged and blindfolded, on a plane. The next day I was in a prison camp in the place you call Guantánamo."

Hart did not want to believe that someone could have made such a serious mistake.

"You were held in Guantánamo as a prisoner of war? There were only supposed to be people who had been taken captive during actual hostilities, captured on the battlefield in places like Afghanistan, members of Al Qaeda who had knowledge of other, planned attacks. I sit on the Senate Intelligence Committee; I have been briefed on—"

He realized what a fool he sounded, what a fool he was. He did not need Mohammed al Farabi to tell him that the full briefings he was supposed to receive had too often been a smokescreen of half-truths and lies.

"Even now, after everything that has happened, I still have a hard time believing that any government of my country could have let something like this take place."

"Yes, it must be difficult for an American, raised to believe that you always fought only on the side of freedom and came only reluctantly to war, to learn that when you think yourselves threatened there isn't anything you won't do to stop it."

He paused after the word *anything*, let it echo with a significance that could scarcely be missed. But Hart had to be sure.

"You're saying you were tortured there, as a prisoner at Guantánamo—tortured by Americans?"

"From the beginning, and at regular intervals. They did not believe me when I told them that I was not a terrorist and knew nothing of any terrorist plot. They may be new to it, these agents of yours—though I think not so new as some would like to pretend—but, new or not, they learn quickly. They have this thing they do—tie you to a board which they then submerge in a tank of water . . ."

"Waterboarding. They claim they got important information, that it helped stop another attack."

"Perhaps; I would not know. It did not seem to work too well with me, but then such things don't, when you have nothing you can tell them. But whether or not it is effective, the virtue of the method is that it does not leave any marks, nothing by which the victim could later prove he had been in any way mistreated; nothing but his word, and who is going to believe anything a terrorist has to say? And we know he must be a terrorist because why otherwise would he be in Guantánamo? Who would ever believe that an innocent Egyptian publisher could be made to lie naked for days in an ice-cold cell, or be held by a steel chain while a guard dog snapped its jaws just inches from his genitals? None of these things ever happened, of course. The American government categorically denies them."

"I'm sorry," Hart mumbled with a bleak, angry look in

his eyes. "I'll do what I can. As soon as I get back, I'll start an investigation, I'll—"

Al Farabi placed a hand on his arm.

"There are more important things you have to do, though they may not be entirely disconnected. I don't mean what they did to me, but the other thing that happened at Guantánamo: what I told Gunther Kramer about, what he apparently told . . ." He smiled at the puzzled expression on Hart's face. "I'm afraid I've gotten a little ahead of myself. Gunther Kramer is the one who saved me."

"Saved you? What do you mean?"

"I mean that if it had not been for him, I would still be a prisoner in Guantánamo."

"But what could Gunther Kramer have done? He used to be an agent in East German intelligence—the Stasi—though for a number of years he had actually been working for the West. My father was his contact. My father was CIA. What did he do to . . . ?"

Al Farabi's eyes lit up. He looked at Hart as if this fact about his father made them more than just acquaintances.

"He told me this, that he was an East German spy who worked for the West. He said he met someone with Western intelligence, a man of great wisdom and insight, but he did not tell me his name. Gunther was like that; he told me much about his life, but he seldom mentioned anyone's name. It was, if I read him right, a habit to which he had trained himself, a way of avoiding an inadvertent slip that might put someone else in danger."

"But he told you that he had been an East German spy who worked for the West. How did he happen to tell you that?"

"I don't know how much you knew of him."

"I knew that he was a gifted musician with a talent for languages. I met him just once, a month ago, in Hamburg.

I was there with him when he was murdered. He came to warn me that there was going to be an assassination."

"His death was a great loss to me. He was as good a friend as I have ever had. We met some years ago, shortly after I became a newspaper publisher and was often in trouble with the law. He had spent most of his life in the Middle East and understood it in a way I'm not sure anyone else ever has. He did not see it in the way of someone born there, who never questions it, nor did he see it from the narrow perspective of someone who only thinks of the interests of the West. He saw it in all its complexity and all its contradictions. He studied it constantly because he knew that what happened in the Middle East would determine much of what would happen in the world."

The Roman night spread over everything. The table, lit with ancient candelabras, became a field of shadows, moving in an endless dreamlike dance. The voice of Mohammed al Farabi, at one moment come from somewhere far away and then, the next, whisper close, was like something heard inside your mind before the words themselves had yet been spoken.

"And he saved you?" Hart heard himself ask. "Got you out of Guantánamo. How was that even possible?"

Al Farabi laughed quietly into the night.

"I think it was not possible; which explains how he did it. I told you that he understood the Middle East in all its contradictions. He complained to a friend of his in Syrian intelligence that another friend of his had been handed over to the Americans by mistake. He was told of course, by this Syrian friend of his, that while this was no doubt quite unfortunate, there was nothing that could be done about it. Gunther insisted that not only could something be done about it, but that he, the Syrian, could do it quite easily and would have not only the pleasure of saving an innocent man, but become quite rich because of it." Al Farabi looked at Hart and sighed. "Gunther Kramer could have written the definitive history of human weakness. His friend, the Syrian, did not so much as bat an eyelash at the thought of saving an innocent man, no matter how little effort it required; at the thought of getting rich, however, he began to sweat ink."

Hart sat back, enjoying every larcenous word of it.

"And how little effort was required?"

"Not very much at all, just a little fabrication, a few made-up documents."

"Showing that you were as innocent as you had always said you were."

"Oh, no; just the opposite! The key to everything was to show that I was an even greater threat than the Americans thought I was." Al Farabi bent forward, his eyes alive at the memory, the sheer temerity, of what Gunther Kramer had done. "This took some time to develop; all the pieces had to be in place. But then, when everything was ready—well, few things are quite so satisfying as a lie perfectly told. The Syrians went to the Americans, informed them that this man they had in custody—this Mohammed al Farabi—had been involved in numerous plots against not only American interests, but governments within the region; that if the Americans had been able to get information out of him, well and good; but if they had not been successful, there were people inside Syrian intelligence who had had some luck with certain methods of their own."

"And that's how you got out of Guantánamo?"

"I think you call it rendition. I was put on a plane late one night and the next thing I knew I was in Damascus. Several weeks later, according to what certain well-paid Syrian authorities told certain gullible Americans, the prisoner Mohammed al Farabi met his death while under interrogation. An unfortunate accident, it was called."

A slight, bittersweet smile drifted across his mouth. He

gazed into the night filled with ancient ruins and ancient memories.

"Only Gunther Kramer could have thought of it; only Gunther Kramer could have pulled it off. And now, because of it, he's dead." He turned to Hart. "If he had not saved me, if I'd been left to die in that place, he never would have learned what I learned inside. It was that knowledge that killed him, Senator: what he learned from me."

"I brought with me—it's in my briefcase at the hotel—a book in which Kramer underlined certain passages and made extensive notes in the margin, and a piece of paper on which he constructed a diagram, two parallel columns that—"

"I know about both those things. The book—Plutarch's *Lives,* the diagram—certain parallels he saw between what happened in ancient Rome and what was happening now in America. That was also because of what I told him."

Hart was not sure what he meant.

"What I told him about what had happened—while I was a prisoner. But how is it that you have these things? You got them, I assume, from Dieter Shoenfeld, but how did he . . . ?"

"Kramer left Dieter a letter about where to find them, along with some other things he wanted him to have."

"Yes, I see, but why did Gunther do that—what was the connection between the two of them?"

Hart remembered the sad, stricken look in Dieter's eyes when he shared with him what he had never revealed to anyone.

"They were brothers, half brothers. They had the same mother."

A strange look entered Mohammed al Farabi's piercing black eyes. Gesturing with his hand, an invitation to join him, he rose from the table and walked to the railing at the edge of the loggia. He stood there, his face rigid and inscrutable. Suddenly, he struck the railing with the flat of his hand and swore.

"If Gunther had told me! If Shoenfeld had told me!" His eyes full of anguish, he looked at Hart. "If I had known they were brothers, I would have agreed to see him right away. I had no idea they were brothers, and so I put him off, made certain he was who he said he was before I agreed to a meeting. If I had seen him when he first asked, he would have known what was going on, he would have understood the danger. He never would have done what he did and tried to see you. He might still be alive."

His mouth twisted into a look of derision and self-reproach. He threw up his hands.

"It is the enigma of existence, doubled by all the secrets we have, and no one had more of them than Gunther. I knew of course that he was a Jew, though the truth is that Gunther did not believe in any religion. He was one of those rare, extremely gifted men who refuse to believe there is anything about which we should not reason. But for all his rationalism, his incredulity with respect to the things that can be felt only by the heart, he was as decent as any man I knew: a Jew who saved an Arab, and for the very good reason that the Arab happened to be his friend."

His hands clasped behind him, he began to walk the length of the loggia. His words were measured and precise.

"Gunther Kramer lived entirely in his mind. He studied constantly, not to learn something new, something he did not know before, but to gain a deeper understanding of the world and the way it worked. He studied Roman history because he thought it might help him understand what would happen to any country once it started on the road to empire. That was why, when I told him what I had learned in Guantánamo, he became so excited, and so alarmed."

Al Farabi stopped moving. He turned to Hart.

"The book—Plutarch's *Lives*—the passages he underlined: all about the turning point, the decisive moment when Rome changed. Am I correct?"

"Yes, everything; the margin notes included."

"And the diagram—the parallel columns you described: what happened in Rome, and then, what was happening, or rather, at the time he wrote it, what was about to happen in the United States. Also correct?"

"Yes, exactly. Political assassination, followed by the case for war, more assassinations, then . . . What did you learn at Guantánamo? What was it that made him become so 'alarmed'?" Hart remembered what Kramer had written at the bottom of the second column. "He made a note, a reference to something he had learned from you."

"Yes, that would be right."

Al Farabi leaned against the iron railing. The lights of Rome glittered in the darkness behind him, but they seemed now a poor thing, a feeble effort, in the immensity of the vaulted starlit heavens. Two thousand years of history were nothing, an instant's reckoning, against the eternity of the world.

"It is a curious thing, the way different men respond to pain. A few will endure whatever is done to them and will think themselves cowards if they hear themselves scream; but most men have their limit, most men can be broken. They broke some of them at Guantánamo, and some of them they turned."

The means were reprehensible, but even Hart had to admit that the end seemed reasonable. What better way to prevent an attack than to have someone working inside a terrorist organization who could tell you what they planned?

"No, that was not what they were going to do. These men they turned, men who would now work for them, had a different mission. They were to recruit and train young

Arab men to attack targets inside the United States. Suicide bombers, Senator Hart, to be used against people in your own country. At first, I admit, I did not understand it; but when I told Gunther Kramer what I had learned, he knew right away what it meant. Or at least he suspected."

"He did not say anything about this when he came to Hamburg to warn me about what was going to happen. He said that everyone seemed to have heard about it, but no one knew who was behind it. But if he knew . . ."

"Would you have believed him?" Al Farabi peered into Hart's eyes, questioning him in a way that made Hart question himself. "Would you have believed a story based on what someone supposedly learned while a prisoner at Guantánamo; someone who had been rescued with the help of Syrian intelligence, someone they then reported as dead? Gunther knew what he was up against. He told you everything he could. He tried to point you in the right direction. He needed you to start the search where he could not do it, inside your own government in the United States."

Hart's mind raced back to what happened in Los Angeles, the calm, undisturbed look in the eyes of the terrorist, so certain he was doing the work of God when he blew himself into a million pieces; a terrorist, it now appeared, recruited, trained, and equipped by the same people who were supposed to be fighting the war on terror. What he still could not understand was why anyone in the government would do it.

"Gunther had an answer." Al Farabi's eyes were grim and unforgiving. "To repeat the terror, and in that way renew the fear. Only when people feel what it is like to be afraid again do they start to think in terms of what is necessary; only when they believe that their own lives are at stake, are they ready to do whatever they have to do to survive. And what is the reason to do that now—to repeat the terror? To have a reason, an excuse, for more war. Iraq is not what the people who wanted it thought it was going to be. But Iraq was never an end in itself; it was always just a part of this 'global war on terror.' Iraq now threatens to undermine that war, make it more difficult to fight. A new justification is needed. Another attack—this time on the political system, an attack that strikes at the heart of your democracy—provides an even better justification than the one they had before. Because now everyone will be convinced that this so-called war on terror—this war to remake the Middle East—will go on, and should go on, for generations."

It explained how the same people who had Gunther Kramer murdered could have had Raymond Caulfield killed; it explained why there had been so many rumors about a terrorist plot and complete confusion over who was responsible. It explained a lot of things, but it did not explain who was behind it, except that, because they had operated at Guantánamo, they were somehow connected to the government.

"It's curious, don't you think, Senator Hart," added al Farabi with a shrewd, probing glance, "that the first assassination also became a means of silencing opposition. Do you think it was just an accident that they killed the candidate who would have changed the current policy in the Middle East?"

Hart thought he gave Alworth too much credit.

"Alworth did not know what he was going to do, about the Middle East or anything else. He only did things he knew would be popular."

"Which it was," al Farabi gently reminded him, "before his murder."

It was late. Mohammed al Farabi called for the driver to take Hart back to his hotel. He walked him down to the waiting car, but seemed reluctant to have him leave.

"I don't have many visitors, men I can talk to, the way

you and I talked tonight. That was something else my friend Gunther Kramer taught me: there are not many sane men left."

They shook hands and Hart turned to go.

"There is one other thing," said al Farabi, walking the few steps to catch up with him. "I'm not sure if it means anything, but it seemed to have some significance for Gunther when I told him. The plan they had, this use of terrorism for their own purposes—they had a name for it: they called it Rubicon."

16

I T TOOK A SECOND FOR DAVID ALLEN TO BE certain it was really the senator. Then it was as if Hart had not been gone at all.

"Nice of you to call. First you steal my car—I got a call from the police in Toronto wanting to know if it had been stolen and, if it had not, why it had been left on a side street a mile from the airport, the engine still running."

"I was in kind of a hurry. Don't worry, I'll take care of it; I'll—"

"Forget the car. Are you all right? This isn't one of those calls like you see in the movies where you're going to tell me that you've been kidnapped and I should pay them whatever they want, is it? Because if it is—well, you've seen the place I live in. You are all right, aren't you?"

"I'm fine. I'm in New York. I just got back. I'll tell you all about it when I see you. But what are you doing there? Why didn't you go to L.A., like I asked you to?"

"You've been away; you haven't seen the papers."

"The stories reporting me missing, saying that I might

have been taken hostage, held somewhere in the Middle East? I heard about that."

"That's been a problem, but there's more—a lot more. All hell has broken loose. Everyone has gone crazy. How soon can you get back? Someone has to stop this."

"What do you mean? What is going on?"

"Read the papers, you'll see what I mean. When can you get here? How soon—tonight, tomorrow morning? We have to hold a press conference. You've got to explain where you've been and why no one could find you."

"I'm not sure; I haven't . . ."

"Look, Bobby, this isn't the time for indecision."

"It's not that. It's what I found out. I'm not sure about the best way to handle it; I'm not sure what to do."

"What you found out—serious?"

"As serious as it gets."

"That makes it easy."

"Easy?"

"Sure. Just tell the truth. Tell everyone what you know."

"You think that's easy?"

"You think you should lie?"

Those were not the only alternatives, of course, and they both knew it; but when Hart got back to the hotel where he was staying and began to pore over the newspapers, he began to see that Allen might be right. In the last twenty-four hours air strikes had been launched against suspected terrorist training camps in Afghanistan and, despite official denials, inside Syria as well. There was talk that both ground and air forces might be sent on "surgical strikes" inside Pakistan and "any other country thought to be harboring terrorists in any way responsible for the attack in Los Angeles." Unnamed sources inside the administration were quoted as saying that there was evidence that Iran had been directly involved in the planning of the attack.

When he turned from the national and international to the political coverage, the stories about the presidential campaign, the news was even more ominous. Arthur Douglas, the Republican candidate, had gone on record in support of "everything the administration is doing," and then added that he would go "a lot farther." Asked if that meant the possible use of everything in the American arsenal, including the use of nuclear weapons, he replied, "I think it would be a mistake to rule out anything at this point."

Whether Douglas had done this out of expediency— the need to separate himself from the president—or out of some principled, if misguided, conviction, the result was that he had now opened a five-point lead over Jeremy Taylor. As one source inside the Democratic candidate's campaign noted ruefully, "No one wants to hear talk of restraint."

Hart's blood ran cold. He could see the eyes of Mohammed al Farabi narrowing down on him with that question, that challenge the Egyptian knew he could not answer: had it just been an accident, a blind stroke of fate, that this terrorist, this pawn in some scheme of Machiavellian dimensions, had stood waiting for Prentice Alworth instead of Arthur Douglas? The question seemed to answer itself. Hart threw the newspaper down on the floor and called David Allen again.

"Can you reach Quentin Burdick at the *Times*?"

"The one who covers national security issues?" asked Allen, just to be sure.

"Call him. Tell him he can't tell anyone why you're calling or even that you have. Tell him I need to talk to him and that it has to be today; that I'm in New York, but only for a few more hours. Tell him to name the place— somewhere this part of Manhattan. Call me back."

"You're going public with this? You sure you don't want to wait for tomorrow? I've already called a noon press conference. I didn't say you would be there, only that there would be an announcement about what had happened. The place will be packed. But if you're going to talk to Burdick at the *Times* first, then—"

"That isn't the reason I need to see him. I'll explain later. I'm taking the train down this evening. Can you meet me?"

Ten minutes later, Allen called back.

"He had to cancel something, but he didn't hesitate. His apartment is on East Sixty-third. He'll meet you there in half an hour."

Quentin Burdick was the kind of man easily mistaken for an effeminate bookworm, someone whose major enthusiasm in life is the poetry of Elizabeth Barrett Browning. Razor thin, with a long, pointed nose, he was invariably dressed in a tweed jacket, button-down striped shirt, and a cheerful bow tie. He was the typecast professor in every movie ever made about life in the shabby gentility of a small New England college. Burdick took a certain pleasure in knowing what he looked like and what other people thought about it. It was like having the advantage of a deception without having done anything to deceive. He opened the door and greeted Bobby Hart like a long-lost friend.

"There were all sorts of stories flying around about you," he said in his dramatic, rather high-pitched voice. "Everything from you were a prisoner of Al Qaeda to you were in a ditch somewhere with a bullet in your head. I'm glad to see that, as usual, nothing that comes out of Washington is true. Now, here, sit down. What can I get you?"

Hart glanced around the living room of the apartment. From the look of it, this had been Burdick's home for some time. The building was prewar and apartments in buildings like that seldom became available. Hart noticed on the mantel above the fireplace a series of photographs, mainly of Burdick with his wife and daughters; but one, barely visible behind the others, held his attention. He walked over and, glancing back at Burdick for permission, picked it up. He looked at it the way someone examines the forgotten record of another man's painful past.

"I was skinny then, too," said Burdick to lighten the mood.

It was a photograph of a young marine lieutenant, standing shirtless with four of his men on a sultry day in a jungle clearing somewhere in Vietnam. Hart wondered how many of the others had come back alive.

"You've been writing a series of articles over the last several months on the treatment of prisoners at Guantánamo and other places. You were one of the first on the story about the use of secret prisons in eastern Europe. And you've written about the way we sometimes send prisoners back to their country of origin so they can be interrogated there."

Hart began to pace nervously around the room. Burdick sat down in an easy chair in the corner. He had known Hart from his first term in Congress; he had gotten to know him much better during his years in the Senate. He had never seen him so intense, or so irritated.

"You know as much as anyone about what's been going on in Guantánamo and places like it."

"You're on the Senate Intelligence Committee," replied Burdick, watching the way Hart's eyes kept darting back and forth. "I would have to assume that you know a great deal more than I."

Hart gave him a jaundiced look.

"I probably knew less about it than anyone—at least until a few days ago. But here's what I need to know: how difficult would it be to find out who was working there—at Guantánamo—interrogating prisoners a year or so ago?"

Burdick folded his hands in his lap. A quiet, thoughtful

smile, the sort that often accompanies an admission of failure or a confession of ignorance, spread across his mouth.

"More than difficult, I would say impossible—for me. What goes on there, who is involved, is more heavily classified than anything I've encountered. But can't you find out? The committee has subpoena power—yes, of course: 'executive privilege.' You could force them to appear, but without a lengthy court battle you can't force them to answer."

Hart was not ready to give up.

"You have sources, people who talk to you, even when they're not supposed to. The stories you wrote about secret prisons and rendition—those weren't based on anything anyone was willing to say in public."

"Yes, but the names of those who conduct interrogations— some of them are CIA, and you know what it means to reveal the name of an agent. No one is going to do it. And even if they did, I'm not sure there is a set of circumstances in which we would print that kind of information."

"Not even if they had been involved in setting up a terrorist organization of their own, the one responsible for what happened last month in Los Angeles?"

Quentin Burdick looked like someone had just told him that his best friend had died. Every part of him wanted to deny it, but he knew it was true. Or at least that Hart believed that it was true.

"How do you know this?" he asked, speaking slowly and with an effort. "What makes you think something like that is even possible?"

"You've been covering foreign affairs, national security issues, for a long time. You were doing it twenty years ago, when Reagan was president, when Gorbachev came to power, when the Soviet Union came apart, when the wall came down, when . . ."

"Yes, I was even there, in Berlin, when it happened, but what does this—?"

"Did you ever hear of someone in East German intelligence by the name of Gunther Kramer?"

"There was a man named Wolf in East German intelligence. He was called the man without a face, because no one in the West knew what he looked like. Kramer on the other hand never tried to conceal his identity. He didn't have to. He spent most of his time in the Middle East where . . . But why do you ask?"

"Because he first warned me that there was going to be an assassination."

"Gunther Kramer? He was supposed to have died back in . . . I see. He knew what would happen to him in the new Germany. So he has been alive all this time."

"Until he was murdered while he was trying to tell me what he had discovered, when he found out what was really going on, when he found out about Rubicon. Kramer was the first. There were others: Raymond Caulfield—"

"That was ruled an accident."

"Caulfield was murdered. He was trying to find out whether the name Rubicon had come up in any of the agency's surveillance."

Burdick stood up. He looked at Hart, a question in his eyes.

"That's the reason I'm here," said Hart. "One of the reasons, anyway. I'm going to tell you everything I know, and you can use it—all of it—but you can't attribute any of it to me—not yet. You can put me in the story, say something like 'it's reported that' I met with Mohammed al Farabi, but you can't name me as a source. Later, if you want, but not now."

They moved into the dining room, and for the next few hours, while Burdick took voluminous notes, Hart told him almost everything that had happened. He did not tell him that Raymond Caulfield had been giving information to him for years, and he did not say anything about how he managed to get out of the country and get to Rome. What Caulfield had done he had done for a reason, but it was a reason that others could easily attack; what Charlie Ryan and his wife had done was no one's business but their own.

"But why did these people come after you?" asked Burdick when Hart's narrative came to an end. "They had to stop Kramer and Caulfield because either one of them might have found out what they had done and what they were planning, but they came after you and Dieter Shoenfeld."

"We both knew something about Rubicon. Dieter had been to his brother's place in Damascus, had found the diagram and the book. He was certain he was being followed. I'd brought it up, raised questions about it in committee. They could not afford to have anyone find out about Rubicon and what it meant."

"You just said that Los Angeles was only the beginning, that there are going to be more assassinations, more attacks. But why?"

"It's that diagram, those parallels, everything laid out with such clarity and precision: political assassination, the case for war, more assassinations. More assassinations! But who, and for what reason? To create more fear? Kramer knew something, but I still haven't been able to figure out what it was."

"Kramer seems to have taken the long view of things, comparing the Roman Empire of two thousand years ago to the American Empire of today. Perhaps he meant that once this started to happen, once you had this kind of conspiracy to assassinate political leaders, there would be no end to it, that it would become the way it was for the Romans, after the Rubicon was crossed. There weren't many emperors, remember, who died of natural causes."

Burdick had another question. But even after all his years as a reporter, he still found it difficult to ask. He put down his pencil and shoved aside his notebook.

"How high up do you think this goes? Do you think people in the White House could be involved?"

Hart laced his fingers together behind his head, brooding over the question. After a long silence, he brought his hands down to his lap and leaned forward.

"My father died nine years ago. He may have been murdered by some of these same people. He was what you might call 'old school' CIA, the first generation, the men who came to it right from the Second World War. I did not tell you this before but Gunther Kramer was working for the West, in the last few years before the wall came down. My father was his contact."

Burdick's eyes lit up. He nodded eagerly.

"Yes, I wondered why Kramer would have singled you out, taken the chance he did by coming back to Germany."

"Kramer is the one who told me that my father had discovered something, an organization, a group, inside the agency that was deliberately using sources that were not reliable, people who had been caught in lies before, sources who would tell them what they wanted to hear. They needed a way to raise doubts, to question any intelligence that seemed to show that Iraq was not a serious threat. My father knew what was going on, and he was just about to prove it when he died.

"I can't prove that he was murdered, I can't prove that these people did it. But all the pieces fit. They understood from the very beginning the importance of getting control of the intelligence. They had to make certain that no one could seriously question the necessity of what they wanted to do. And they got what they wanted, they got the war they thought the country needed. It did not turn out to be the bloodless victory they thought it would, but they still believe—maybe even more than they did before—that if we don't defeat our enemies in the Middle East, we'll have to fight them here at home."

Burdick picked up the pencil. He tapped the eraser hard on the wooden surface. It bounced a little each time he did it. He repeated the question.

"Off the record: how high up do you think this goes? The White House?"

Hart started to shake his head, to dismiss the possibility; but then he changed his mind and told Burdick what he really believed.

"Who are the people who keep insisting that we're in a war of survival, and that civilization itself is at stake? Who said over and over again that we have to use any means necessary, including torture if we have to?"

"You think the vice president . . . ?"

"Who else could have done this, organized something on this scale? Think about what they've done. Someone had to be working for months at Guantánamo, maybe years, to get a few terrorists to turn; someone arranged the murder of Gunther Kramer in Hamburg; someone arranged the murder of Raymond Caulfield in Washington. This isn't the work of some rogue agent, acting on his own; this required careful planning and coordination."

"But what is the point of it? What do they have to gain?"

"If there had not been the attack in Los Angeles, if Prentice Alworth had not been killed, Douglas wouldn't have had a chance. Now he's in the lead. Why would they do it? So the next president will stay with the same policies, the ones the vice president and the people around him, the people who helped fabricate the intelligence that got us into this war, insist will save the country."

Burdick raised an eyebrow.

"Murder a presidential candidate, a vice-presidential

candidate, a dozen other people, and injure dozens more?
No one will believe it, not without hard, incontrovertible
proof." He stared at Hart with a pensive expression. "But I
believe it. That's why they tried to kill you: to make sure
you couldn't prove anything. Be careful. You have to believe they'll try again."

It was nearly five o'clock when they finished talking.
Burdick walked out with him. He had to get back to his
office.

"I have a busy evening ahead of me," he remarked as he
stepped into the street and whistled for a cab. "There are a
lot of phone calls I have to make before I can write the
story that I can guarantee you will be tomorrow's lead."

17

IT WAS A MOB SCENE, MORE REPORTERS THAN David Allen had ever seen at a press conference on Capitol Hill. All the television news shows, the major networks as well as cable, were there with cameras. Reporters tripped over each other, swore at one another, as they jostled for position. They were shouting questions the moment Hart stepped through the door. He ignored them.

"I have a brief statement, and then I'll be glad to take any questions you might have."

The shouting subsided to a dull murmur and then the room went silent. Reading from a prepared text, Hart explained why he had disappeared.

"A week ago yesterday, two men broke into my home in Georgetown and murdered Dieter Shoenfeld. They were also there to murder me. Mr. Shoenfeld had been followed from Germany, and before that, from the Middle East. I had apparently been under surveillance for some time. The reason that someone wanted both of us dead is that each of us had come into possession of certain information about the attack in Los Angeles. Dieter Shoenfeld had discovered, through sources of his own, that what happened in Los Angeles was part of a larger plan and that this plan had a name. It was called Rubicon. The evening he was killed he was about to tell me everything that he had learned.

"I left Washington that same night because there was someone I had to see, someone Dieter Shoenfeld was supposed to meet, someone who had what Shoenfeld called the missing piece of the puzzle." Hart folded up the sheet of paper and put it in his jacket pocket. "That's where I went, and that is what I did, and that is the reason that I did not tell anyone where I was going or when I would be back. Now, I'll be glad to take your questions."

The shouting started all over again.

"But I'll take them one at a time." He pointed to a reporter at the back of the crowd, one of those who regularly covered the Senate.

"The *New York Times* is reporting today that you met with someone by the name of Mohammed al Farabi, and that al Farabi claims that what happened in Los Angeles was not part of a terrorist plot at all: that it was part of a conspiracy here at home. The first question is, did you meet with this al Farabi?"

"Yes, I did, and what the *Times* is reporting—that terrorists held at Guantánamo were used to recruit and train terrorists for attacks inside the United States—is exactly what he told me."

There was a moment's stunned silence, and then the place exploded. Everyone screamed questions at once.

"But, Senator, the real question is whether you believed him. The White House has already issued a categorical denial. They insist—"

"A categorical denial? How would they know what was going on at Guantánamo? They didn't know anything about Abu Ghraib, at least they said they did not," Hart shot back.

"But now, without so much as bothering with an investigation, without taking any steps to find out if someone inside the government, or with connections to the government, could have been involved, they just dismiss it out of hand, issue a categorical denial?"

"Leave the White House out of it for a minute," demanded a cable news reporter. "What made you think that what this Mohammed al Farabi said was credible? What made you think that it was not just some attempt to shift the blame for what happened in Los Angeles from the terrorists who did it? How do you know you weren't being used, Senator?"

Hart surprised the reporter with his candor.

"That's a fair question, and an important one. It's certainly the first question I would have asked if he had come looking for me. But I went looking for him. He did not know I was coming. He had an appointment with Dieter Shoenfeld. So if this was some story, some fiction, he wanted to peddle, he was scarcely making much of an effort to find an audience. But that's not the only reason. What he told me was simply what he had heard. He didn't claim to know who was doing it, he didn't claim to know the reason. At the time he heard it, he didn't think it meant much at all: another rumor that might or might not be true. And that might have been the end of it, even after the attack in Los Angeles, except for the fact that a year earlier, while he was still in Guantánamo, he heard this rumored plan called by the name Rubicon. It did not mean anything to him, but it meant everything to someone who had heard the same name used in connection with a rumored plan to assassinate someone in the United States."

"So you do believe him, that there is a secret organization, here in the United States, that for reasons of its own planned the attack in Los Angeles?" asked a network correspondent with a cynical look in her eyes.

Hart stared right back at her.

"I can understand why there would be a reluctance to believe any of this possible. I was reluctant to believe it. But consider the facts, consider what we know. No group in the Middle East has taken credit for what happened in Los Angeles. As soon as we started looking into Rubicon, trying to figure out what it meant, people began to die. The deputy director of the CIA appeared before the Senate Intelligence Committee and was asked to look into whether that word, *Rubicon,* had been picked up in any of their surveillance. A few days later Raymond Caulfield was murdered . . ."

"His car went off the road," someone objected. "The police said his death was an accident."

"Caulfield was murdered," insisted Hart. "If you want to believe that he wasn't, fine; but then explain who murdered Dieter Shoenfeld and came to kill me. I saw them, I heard them talking. They were Americans, hired killers. Who do you think hired them—Al Qaeda? No, Rubicon was designed and carried out right here at home. Someone in the United States is trying to change the politics of this country, and they don't care who they have to kill to do it."

"I want to go back to Mohammed al Farabi," shouted a determined reporter who had wedged himself into position just behind the first row. "Sources within the CIA claim that there is no record of anyone by that name ever having been a prisoner at Guantánamo or at any other location where prisoners in the war on terror have been held."

A tight, caustic smile cut across Hart's mouth.

"I'm glad to hear the CIA keeps such meticulous records. I'm sure they won't have any objection to allowing a group of reporters—or a few members of the Senate Intelligence Committee—access to all the prisoners who were there at the time Mohammed al Farabi claims he was there.

It would certainly prove one way or the other whether Mr. al Farabi is telling the truth."

Another reporter wanted to know how Hart would respond to the vice president, quoted in the story in the *Times,* who claimed that these allegations were nothing more than—the reporter read from his notes—"a reprehensible and desperate attempt to shift attention away from the failure of the Democratic candidate for president to take a strong stand in favor of the war on terror."

"Prentice Alworth was murdered in Los Angeles. I was there. I saw it. Others have been murdered to keep the rest of us from finding out who was behind it and why it was done. They murdered my friend Dieter Shoenfeld; they tried to murder me. If the vice president thinks I'm wrong, then let him stop hiding behind claims of executive privilege and answer the questions that will help us get to the truth. Or is it possible that the vice president knows more about this than he is willing to admit? I'll even give him an incentive to come forward and tell us all he knows. Prove I'm wrong, Mr. Vice President, and I'll resign from the Senate!"

Hart spent another half hour answering questions, all of them variations on what had been asked already. As soon as he said it, promised to resign if he was wrong, the evening news shows had their opening lead, and Quentin Burdick, writing the next installment of the story he had just started that morning, had his opening sentence.

Finding itself in the middle of a firestorm, the White House softened its approach. They did not deny their categorical denial, they still insisted that nothing like what Hart had said was possible, but they suggested that, as the White House press secretary put it, "everyone should just calm down." Hart was wrong, he went on to say, but it was not his fault. "The senator has been through a lot. We need to understand that. He was there in Los Angeles, friends of his were killed. He himself was one of the heroes on the ground that day. He helped save lives. And then, after going through that, two men break into his house—burglars, killers; we still aren't sure—and shoot to death someone who is a guest in his home. That would have an effect on anyone. Now, why did he then choose to run off to Europe somewhere and talk to this Mohammed al Farabi—if that's his real name—I think you'll have to ask him."

After watching the press secretary on television, Hart turned to David Allen and laughed at the absurdity of it.

"Not guilty by reason of insanity. Don't blame Hart: he's been through too much to know what he's doing."

Allen turned off the television and sat back in his chair. They were sitting in his office, eating a sandwich, while they watched the coverage of what Hart had done that afternoon. Allen thought it had gone as well as they could have expected.

"Better, actually. You got it all out in the open. Now everyone knows about Rubicon. All over Washington, people are trying to figure out what to do next. This story isn't going to go away. It's too big. Whatever stupid things the White House tries to do, you're not some crazy who thinks there is a conspiracy behind every corner. There are going to be investigations, serious ones. The Senate, the House, every committee that thinks they can get away with it is going to want to look into this. The presidential debate is a week from tonight. It's going to be the first question that gets asked. What is Arthur Douglas going to say? That he doesn't think there should be a full investigation? That he doesn't think the CIA and anyone else that has had anything to do with what goes on at Guantánamo should at least tell committees of Congress what they know? He'll get buried if he tries to do something like that, and he knows it."

Hart got up to go to his own office next door. Allen's

telephone rang, the line from the receptionist. He flipped on the intercom.

"Is the senator with you?"

"Right here," said Hart.

"There's someone who has been calling all morning. He called again just a minute ago. He said it was important, and that he was sure you would want to talk to him. Someone from the police: a Detective Coleman, Leonard Coleman."

Hart and Allen exchanged a glance.

"Call him back, if you would. I'll take it in my office."

Two minutes later, Leonard Coleman was on the line.

"I wonder if you could come down to the station." There was a low chuckle as he realized what that could lead to. "No, that's probably not a good idea, is it? Half the press corps in Washington would end up blocking the street. But there is something that I need to talk to you about. Maybe we could meet later tonight." There was a short, awkward pause. "Are you going to be staying back at your house, or are you . . . ?"

"No, not yet. Last night I stayed at a hotel. I'll be there a while longer, I think."

"That's probably a good idea. But if you wouldn't mind, Senator, perhaps you could meet me back at the house, around nine o'clock. There is something I want you to see."

Because he thought it would be painful, and even a little terrifying, for Hart to go back for the first time to where he had nearly been murdered and a friend of his had died, Leonard Coleman got to the house in Georgetown and turned on all the lights. He was sitting on the front step, the door behind him partway open, when Hart came up the walk.

"These places always have ghosts," explained Coleman, as he stood up and shook hands. "Better not to see them in the dark. The back door has been replaced. Everything has been put back pretty much the way it was before. Come out here on an afternoon. Decide then what you want to do."

Hart gave him a look that Coleman had often, too often, seen before. It was a question he had never quite known how to answer.

"Some people, after a thing like this happens, never go back. They put it up for sale and move to a different town, or at least a different neighborhood. Other people, sometimes because they feel that moving would only add another injury to what had happened, sometimes because all the memories of their lives, good and bad, are wrapped up in it, never even think of leaving."

"But you—if it were you?"

"If it were me?" With his hands shoved deep into his pockets, Coleman studied the pavement, wondering if he even knew. "It's like I said," he said finally, "these places always have ghosts. So if it were me, I suppose I'd just put it up for sale and go someplace where every time I turned a corner, every time I heard a noise, what happened would not all come rushing back. But that's just me, Senator; everyone is different."

They walked inside, and suddenly, as clear as if it had been that night, Hart heard Dieter Shoenfeld's voice, telling him he was almost certain that he knew what Rubicon meant.

"I agree with you, Lieutenant. I don't think I'll be coming back here again."

Coleman led him into the dining room and pointed to the crystal chandelier. He reached into his pocket.

"We found this. Tiny, isn't it? But it picks up sound perfectly. We found others, too—listening devices all through the house, and in the telephones as well. I don't know how long they were doing it, but they would have heard everything that was said."

Hart's mind flashed back to the night he and Raymond Caulfield sat in his kitchen, talking about Rubicon and what Caulfield would try to find out. Caulfield never had a chance. They knew what he was going to do before he ever started.

Coleman had left a file folder on the dining room table. He pulled out a chair and motioned for Hart to take the one next to him. There was something else he wanted to show him. Opening the folder, he removed a smaller, manila folder and placed it in front of them. Hart could tell that there were photographs inside.

"These aren't very pleasant, Senator, but I need you to tell me if this is one of the men who broke in and murdered Mr. Shoenfeld."

It was a morgue photo, a man in his late thirties or early forties, lying faceup on a metal table. Part of the left front corner of his forehead had been blown away.

"Shot in the back of the head, execution style. Is he one of the men you saw?"

Hart kept looking at the photograph. He was certain that this was one of the men who had murdered Dieter Shoenfeld and would have murdered him, but there was something else he wanted to see.

"You won't find it, Senator; it isn't there anymore. You can't see it when they're dead."

"Sorry—what?"

"You want to know what makes someone do this, become a killer. You can't see it now; or you can, but it doesn't mean anything. It's only when they're still alive that you notice that their eyes are dead."

"Yes, but how . . . ?"

"Did their eyes go dead? Some of them are born that way;

some of them . . ." He glanced at the photograph and shook his head. "This is Frank DeStefano. Murder for hire was a sign of upward mobility. He started out as a two-bit enforcer, a guy who went around collecting gambling debts, a low-level mobster who took whatever small jobs someone in the New Jersey organization would give him. You were right, when you said you thought one of them had an accent."

Coleman kept the file open, but he turned the picture of the dead man facedown so Hart would not have to look at it.

"DeStefano had a long, relatively uninteresting record— served some jail time, even did a two-year stretch in prison for things like assault, robbery, extortion—serious, but never anything close to murder. If the Mob wanted someone taken care of, there were plenty of other names they would have thought of before they ever thought of his. Then, two years ago, Frank DeStefano disappeared, fell right off the radar. No one knew what had happened to him; no one much cared. Maybe he had been caught stealing from the Mob, maybe he had been killed. No one knew and, as I say, he did not have many friends. And now, two years later, this same Frank DeStefano murders, or helps to murder, someone in a way that involved not only careful planning but very sophisticated surveillance, and then, just days later, he's found in a vacant lot, his hands tied behind his back and part of his head blown away."

Coleman rubbed his chin, and then, both puzzled and amused, he scratched his ear. He looked around the dining room and then through the open doorway to the living room where the murder had happened.

"A guy like DeStefano—all he would have known how to do was pull the trigger, and he probably would have failed at that if he had tried to break in here by himself. But this guy . . ." Coleman pulled a second photograph from the file and tossed it on the table in front of Hart. "This guy could come in here and sit right next to us and we wouldn't even know it."

The photograph was of an army officer in dress uniform. The face was younger, clean shaven, and the haircut much shorter, but Hart was sure it was the other man, the one he had seen with DeStefano.

"Meet Henry Lattimore, former army ranger, former special forces, former—well, we're not sure. Like DeStefano, Lattimore disappeared. Left the army. Strange, though, that he did that, only a year or so before he would have qualified for full retirement. The army has no record of him, no address, nothing. At least nothing they'll tell us."

"But how did you find him? The cigarette, the one you picked up that night?"

Coleman raised his eyebrows, a wry but knowing commentary on the inevitability of chance.

"One cigarette, one mistake. It was the only thing he left behind. He killed DeStefano that same night. It was a couple of days before the body was found, but the time of death seems to match up pretty close. There isn't any physical evidence that says Lattimore did it, but it's the only explanation that seems to make sense. And if that's what happened, if Lattimore did kill him, then it must have been something that was planned from the beginning: use DeStefano for the job—someone no one would miss—and then get rid of him before he did something stupid that would give it all away."

Hart's gaze kept darting back to the living room. The sofa where Dieter had been sitting, when he jumped to his feet after he heard the noise and then saw them and knew what was going to happen; the sofa that had been soaked in blood, Dieter's blood, was gone. It seemed odd that he had not noticed it until now. Coleman had watched his eyes.

"We took it in—it's evidence, but I don't think you'll want it."

"No," said Hart firmly. "When you've finished with it, get rid of it." He moved his chair so that the living room was behind him and his eyes, with their rampant curiosity, could no longer betray him.

"This Lattimore, the one that is still alive . . ."

"We can't be sure of that," cautioned the lieutenant. "From everything we've learned, from everything you've . . ." A soft, shrewd smile flickered at the corners of his mouth. "From what I've been reading in the papers, the people behind this seem to do whatever they have to do to tie up loose ends. Lattimore may be alive, or he might not be. Either way, there is something I'd like to do, but I need your help."

"Anything. Whatever I can do."

"You've identified Lattimore as one of the killers, and DeStefano as the other. I want to give Lattimore's picture to the media, let everyone know this is who we're looking for, for the murder of Dieter Shoenfeld, for the attempted murder of you, and for the subsequent murder of Frank DeStefano."

"Sounds like a good idea to me. But you said you needed my help. What can I do?"

"Two things; one is easy; the other is perhaps more difficult. First, I need you to work with a sketch artist. We have this photograph, but it's old, taken when he was in the army. You can help show how he has changed. Then we can run two pictures, this one," he said, pointing to the army photograph, "and one that shows how he looks today."

"Sure, I'll be glad to. When do you want me to do it?"

"Tonight, if you don't mind."

"Tonight? But how . . . ?"

"The artist is a friend of mine. Said he'd come in late, if that would help. I figured that there wouldn't be so many people around, that we could get you in and out before anybody in the press found out."

Hart gave Coleman a searching glance. He had liked him from the first, trusted him implicitly, and now, more than ever, he knew that his instinct had been right.

"You're always a little ahead of the game, aren't you, Lieutenant?"

"Age and experience, Senator; age and experience—that's all. But there is something I'm not sure about, and that's the second thing—the one I said might be more difficult. This is a murder investigation, and there are certain rules you follow in a murder investigation, but this time there's a little more involved than just trying to catch a killer. If we put Lattimore's picture out there, if everyone knows he's the one we're looking for, we may never find him, not alive anyway. They killed DeStefano; there's no reason to think they won't kill Lattimore if they think he's a liability. Lattimore is no fool. Once he sees his picture in all the papers, he'll know he has to get out; that the people he works for won't be willing to take the chance he might get caught."

"Which means he might decide to trade what he knows for protection."

"Maybe, but I doubt it. A guy like that—trained the way he was—he'll go to ground, someplace he knows he'll be safe, somewhere far away—Southeast Asia, someplace like that. He may be there already, or he may already be dead. There's no way to know, Senator, which is the reason I'm asking."

"I'm not sure what you're asking, Lieutenant."

"Whether we should do it, run the picture, go public. We might have a better chance of finding him if the people who hired him don't think we know who he is."

"But I already told the press that I was there when it happened, that I saw them both."

"Nothing more than a quick glimpse of a face, a face without a name and without any way of finding one. And we wouldn't have, either, if he hadn't stopped to take a few drags on a cigarette so we were able to get his DNA. As I say, this is a murder investigation. Normally, I wouldn't hesitate to run a picture, a description, anything that might help find out who the killer is and where he might have gone. But this time that might end up helping whoever is behind this cover up his traces."

Hart thought about it, but only for a moment.

"No, put it out there, everything you have, everything you know about him. Put the pressure on these people, whoever they are. Let them know that this well-made plan of theirs is coming apart, that it was not even close to the perfect murder they had intended. There's another reason, Lieutenant," he added as he stood up and, this time quite deliberately, stared at the spot where Dieter Shoenfeld had been shot. "Someone out there knows him, or used to know him; someone in some agency, like the CIA, must have worked with him at some point; someone who is not involved in this."

Coleman understood immediately what Hart was really saying.

"Which is what the people behind this will think: that someone who knew him is going to come forward and that it will eventually come back to them. That might make them start to turn on each other, make them start to look out for themselves, and then they'll begin to make mistakes."

"Perhaps," said Hart as they turned out the lights and shut the front door. "At least it might give them second thoughts about trying to kill someone else—or about going ahead with another attack."

Working in a windowless room at police headquarters, Hart spent an hour with the sketch artist. At the end of it, the drawing looked perfect in every detail. Placed next to the army photograph, the changes in the appearance of Henry Lattimore seemed to be exactly of the kind that would have been expected with the passage of time. It would be easy to pick him out of a crowd.

"You're going to release these tomorrow?" asked Hart, just to be sure.

"First thing," replied Coleman. "Along with a release that gives as much of his background as we know."

"And I'll bet that's what you've been doing—isn't it?— while I was in there with the artist."

Coleman's aging eyes took on a youthful sparkle.

"Just finished it, not more than five minutes ago. Want to go over it?"

"No, I'm sure you said it exactly right. Can you send a copy of it, along with copies of the pictures, to someone in New York tonight?"

"Sure. Won't take more than a minute."

"Let me make a call first."

He pulled out his cell phone and moved off to the side of the large open room where a few detectives were still sitting at their desks, writing reports. Quentin Burdick answered on the first ring.

"Working late tonight," said Hart. "Must be some story you're writing. I'll bet it has something in there about some crazy senator who offered to resign if something he said was proved wrong. Well, just in case that isn't enough to write about, I'm sending you a press release and a couple of pictures you might be able to use."

18

BOBBY FOUND HER IN THE GARDEN, CUTTING roses.

"Hello, Helen," he said softly.

She did not turn around until she was sure that it was really his voice and not the one she had been imagining day after day, and then, laughing and crying all at once, she let go of the basket and with roses flying everywhere ran to his arms.

"You didn't call, you didn't . . . I didn't know where you were or what you were doing or how long you would be gone or what kind of danger you were in." She laughed at how the words came tumbling out, how she had suddenly so much to say and could not slow down long enough to say it.

"I'm all right," said Bobby to comfort her. "I'm sorry I had to disappear like that, but there was a reason. I had to—"

"I know, I know. I've watched it all on television; I've read the papers. It's the worst thing ever, isn't it—what those people tried to do. But let's not talk about any of that now. You're home. Nothing else matters."

They picked up the roses and cut a few more from the well-tended bushes. On the distant edge of the Pacific, the sun, almost straight in front of them, was growing larger, the way it did nearly every evening this time of year.

"You really love this place, don't you?"

"More than I ever thought I could love anything but you, Bobby Hart. Remember how we found it?"

"Dumb luck," he said with a casual laugh. "We were just driving around, came around a corner and there it was, a For Sale sign right in front of it."

"Call it luck if you want to. We both know it was fate. You might as well say it was only chance that we ever met. I didn't even want to go to the dance that night; I wouldn't have gone, either, if the other girls had not dragged me with them. But why did I let them do that if I had not known, deep down, that if I didn't go I'd spend my whole life wondering what would have happened if I had. So say what you like, Bobby Hart, we both know there was a reason we went for a drive that day, a reason why we chose that road, a reason why this house just happened to be for sale." She gave him a look of a certainty so great she could laugh away objection. "The For Sale sign had only just been put up. Remember what the real estate agent said: if we had gone driving just an hour earlier we would have missed it?"

It seemed to Bobby that she was right, that it made more sense that way. It made it possible to live a reasonable, decent life if you believed that things happened for a reason, and that your life was not just the plaything of chance.

"And if you had not called me when you did, if I had not gone upstairs to take that call . . ."

"I know," she said quietly; "I know."

And Dieter, he wondered silently, what about Dieter?

Was it fate or destiny, was there a reason for things when they turned out the way you wanted them, and only chance when they did not? There was madness if you looked too closely into the why of things.

For Helen, it was enough that Bobby was alive and that, for a while at least, he was home with her.

They were almost through with dinner when she remembered.

"Clare Ryan called, the night you were at their house in Ann Arbor, the night you left to go to Canada on your way to Europe."

"She said she would. You like her, don't you?"

"She called a couple of times after that, as well. And yes, I like her, I like her more than almost anyone. She isn't like those other women, always trying to size you up, figure out where you are in the great, that is to say Washington, scheme of things."

Bobby laughed gently.

"Maybe that's because, like you, she doesn't live there. She has a life of her own in Ann Arbor."

Helen poured each of them a glass of red wine.

"She said that she and Charlie would like to spend a few days out here after the election. She was funny. She said win or lose, Charlie was going to need a little sun, and someone he could tell the truth to."

Remembering the conversation at dinner in Ann Arbor, Bobby smiled into his glass.

"She thinks Charlie should endorse Jeremy Taylor."

Helen did not see anything wrong with it.

"He's a lot better than Douglas."

"Charlie is a Republican, running in one of the closest Senate races in the country. Endorsing the presidential candidate of the other party hasn't usually been considered a winning strategy."

She looked at him with a puzzled, candid glance.

"Why not? Has anyone ever done it?"

Bobby started to reply, but then he realized that he was not sure what he wanted to say.

"No, or if they have, I don't remember it. But if he did that, a lot of people who are going to vote for Douglas might just decide not to vote for him."

"And a lot of people who don't know who they're going to vote for—who think party politics means thievery and stupidity—might fall all over themselves for the chance to vote for someone that honest."

"You like Charlie a lot, don't you?"

"I'd vote for him, if I had the chance."

Bobby could not resist.

"If he were running against me?"

A thought came to her. She played with it a while, doubting whether she should say it out loud, but then, finally, she refused to lie.

"Yes, I would. Because if Charlie won, you'd be here with me and there would be someone else honest and decent in your place back there."

Bobby looked at her for a long time, envying a little the clarity of her mind, the clean, logical precision with which every problem seemed to have a single, neat answer.

"If Charlie were running against me," he said presently, "I'd probably vote for him myself."

"Why don't you tell him that when you talk to him later this evening," she suggested. "He called earlier."

"He called? Why didn't you tell me?"

"He said you wouldn't be able to reach him—he's in the middle of some campaign thing—and that he'd call back late night, a little after midnight his time. I told him I didn't know if you were getting home today or not. I didn't, you know; though when Charlie called I thought you must be. But then, when you did—come home, I mean—I forgot about everything except how glad I was to see you. There's something else I forgot, something I need to tell you," she went on in the soft, breathless voice that always made him forget everything but her.

"You look wonderful," he said spontaneously.

"I do? But I didn't have a chance to—"

"You look wonderful," he repeated. He stared into her eyes, watching her stare back. "What did you forget, what do you need to tell me?"

"That I love you."

"You forgot that?"

"No, but I needed to tell you that. The other thing I need to tell you is that I've made a decision. After the election, I'm moving back, with you, to Washington. I'll do the best I can, Bobby. I can't stand being away from you, and when that thing happened, when it happened in our house—I felt like I'd betrayed you, left you alone when I should have been there."

"Thank God you weren't."

"No, but with everything going on now, with all these awful things happening, I can't just sit here and dream about the day when it will just be the two of us again. You don't have to worry about me, Bobby. I'm stronger now, stronger than when I was there before, when I had the breakdown."

"I know you are, but let's wait a while before we decide. It's safe here, and I don't know if it's safe anywhere else. We'll see." Reaching across the table, he took her hand. "But thank you for that. I know how difficult it must have been."

She held herself perfectly erect, all her emotions in check. She was stronger now, and more determined to do what she knew was right.

"It wasn't—it isn't—difficult at all, Bobby. I'll go wherever you need to be."

He got up from the table and cleared the dishes.

"I think you're right," he said a few moments later, as he sat down and reached for the wine bottle.

"Right?"

"That it was not 'dumb luck'; that we were fated to have this house. I want to sell the house in Georgetown—after what happened there. We could rent an apartment to use during the session. It might be fun, a small place, to use during the week, and then we'll be here every weekend and during all the holidays. And what I said a few weeks ago: a year, maybe two—long enough to finish what I've started, and then I'm through. After that we'll just be here, all the time, you and I." He gave her a teasing glance. "You might get tired of that, having me around that much. I'm really quite boring, you know. That's why I give all those speeches: people have to listen."

They sat talking for a long time. A few minutes past nine, a little after midnight in Michigan, the telephone rang.

"It must be Charlie. I'll take it in the study."

But it was not Charlie Ryan. It was Quentin Burdick from New York, looking for a quote.

"The vice president has called a press conference for tomorrow morning. They apparently have some information on Mohammed al Farabi and he plans to release it."

Hart stood next to the glass table he used as a desk, drumming his fingers.

"What kind of information?"

"You're not going to believe this." Burdick's voice sounded like a low whistle. "They now admit that al Farabi was being held in Guantánamo, but only for a short time until he was returned to his country of origin to face local proceedings. They supposedly have documents that prove al Farabi was involved in terrorist activities."

"Remember what I told you, how Gunther Kramer got him out? How he used forged documents to make it look like al Farabi was involved so they would send him to

Syria? He did such a good job that now the vice president can use them to prove al Farabi was exactly what he was not. He's good at fabricating things."

"Can I quote you on this: that the documents were forged and that was how they got him out of Guantánamo?"

"Quote me on the whole damn thing: everything I told you about Mohammed al Farabi—why he was sent there in the first place, what he learned about Rubicon, how they got him out—how the only way they could get him out was to tell a lie so that our people—our people!—would be convinced that they had to send him back to the Middle East for more refined methods of torture than what they were using at Guantánamo."

Hart was so angry Burdick asked him if he wanted to think about it before he said anything more for attribution.

"Think about it? No, I don't want to think about it. Mohammed al Farabi was handed over to us for the crime of speaking his mind, publishing in a newspaper what he thought of a government that puts people in prison for having the courage to dissent. He was handed over to us without any supporting evidence of terrorism whatsoever. Ask the vice president why, if al Farabi was such a well-known terrorist, he sat in Guantánamo, not for just this 'short time' they now want to claim, but for more than four years before these documents from Syrian intelligence just happened to arrive?"

Hart stared out the window at the moonlit ocean. He was certain what was going to come next.

"He isn't holding a press conference just to claim that Mohammed al Farabi is a known terrorist, is he? He's going to attack me, discredit me any way he can. He and his people can't afford to have anyone believe that what happened in Los Angeles was part of a domestic plot."

"He's going to say that al Farabi was a known terrorist

and that anyone who would believe what he said—that what happened in Los Angeles was some kind of government plot—is not only out of their minds but is giving aid and comfort to the enemy and that everyone ought to know it."

"First I'm crazy; now I'm a traitor. Ask him this: if what happened in Los Angeles was the kind of terrorist attack he says it is, then who hired Henry Lattimore and Frank DeStefano? Who sent them to my house to kill Dieter Shoenfeld and murder me? Then ask him what he knows about Rubicon—ask him whether all these murders happened at his direction!"

When he finished the call with Burdick, Helen could tell he was upset.

"They only know how to do one thing," he explained.

They were in the room off the kitchen, the sitting room with the long view of the ocean. Helen had put on a nightshirt. She sat on the sofa, her legs pulled up and her arms wrapped around her knees. Bobby opened one of the French doors and took a deep breath.

"They only know how to do one thing," he repeated. "Attack. Everyone is a traitor who does not agree with them. Given all the things that have happened—the number of people who have been killed—the government should be all over this: the FBI working overtime, every investigative agency sifting through every piece of evidence, trying to find out what really happened in Los Angeles and whether that was the end of it or just the beginning. But no one is doing anything."

He looked at Helen as if he suddenly understood something. He stood up and started to walk back and forth. A bitter smile cut hard across his mouth.

"Political assassination: disrupt the election, cause everyone to question whether democracy is even safe; instill such a deep fear in everyone that they won't think to question whatever someone in power tells them has to be

done. That must have been why Gunther Kramer, and
then Dieter, thought there would be more than one attack;
why Los Angeles was just the beginning of . . ."

Helen knew from the look in his eyes that he was holding something back.

"You know who it is, don't you? You know who started
all of this."

"Raymond Caulfield told me, but I wasn't smart enough
to see it. He told me about the people around the vice
president, the ones who talked about an American empire,
who believed that we had the power to remake the Middle
East. He told me something else that at the time I didn't
understand: that for all their reputation as brilliant intellectuals their knowledge of history, serious history, was
almost nonexistent. It all fits," he said with a dismal stare.

"But it's all come apart, hasn't it?" asked Helen. "Everything they tried to do has failed."

"If everything had gone the way they expected, there
wouldn't have been any need of something like Rubicon.
That's what I've only gradually come to understand. The
worse things got, the more certain they became that they
were right, and the more determined to see it through.
They're the ones who have the courage and the foresight to
stay with something for as long as it takes. They think we
would have won in Vietnam if we had stayed longer, if we
hadn't lost our nerve. That's why Rubicon was necessary:
to bring back all the fear that let them start this misadven-
ture in the first place."

"But do you think the vice president . . . ?"

"Someone who divides the world into friends and enemies; someone who does not think twice about suggesting
that anyone who criticizes a policy he supports is giving
aid and comfort to the enemy; someone who talks about a
war of civilizations that will go on for a hundred years. Do
I think that someone like that would tell the people around

him that they had to do everything that was necessary, that the greatest threats to the security of the country were the people who were trying to stop them, that the future of the country and the world depended on it? You bet I do. It has to be the vice president. He's the only one who could have pulled it all together. The only problem is that I can't prove any of it; not yet, anyway."

Bobby glanced at the clock. It was nearly ten, one in the morning in Michigan.

"I wonder why Charlie hasn't called?"

THE NEXT DAY Helen insisted on watching the vice president's press conference on television.

"It won't be pretty," Bobby warned her. He was used to the combat, the sometimes vicious combat that had come to dominate political campaigns. He could take the best, or the worst, of whatever the other side could do. It was something else again when his wife had to hear it. Or at least he thought he would be upset, until he realized that he had seriously underestimated both Helen's resiliency and her sense of humor.

The vice president's prepared remarks were delivered in a flat monotone that, like the voice of an accountant, made what he had to say seem more factual. He may have been accusing a member of the United States Senate of consorting with the enemy, but he made it sound as if there were nothing personal in it.

"It's because he can destroy someone and never think twice about it," explained Bobby.

"That's because for him everything is an abstraction. He doesn't have a sense of the specific," said Helen, her eyes focused on the screen.

"He doesn't . . . ?"

"He was never in the service. He never saw men dying.

He's always been a bureaucrat, whether he was in politics or not. He only knows how to see the world in numbers and categories. The only things he can understand are quantifiable. Everything is mechanical, even the way he talks. It is all analytical. There is no judgment."

At that very moment, the vice president was rattling off the numbers of those who had died fighting the war on terror.

"Thousands of Americans, brave young men and women in uniform, have given their lives in this cause. For someone in a responsible position—a member of the United States Senate—to take the word of a known terrorist and make the claim that the murder of Governor Alworth was part of some domestic conspiracy is either the result of a disturbed mind or an unprecedented disregard for truth and decency.

"Mohammed al Farabi was detained upon credible information supplied by a friendly government. He was sent back to his country of origin where he was later reported dead—mistakenly, as it turns out. He continues his work against the United States, against the spread of democracy, only now he has the assistance of one of the leading members of the Democratic Party. It seems to me, given what this country has gone through, that the leadership of the Democratic Party, as well as that party's presidential candidate, should either denounce the actions of Senator Hart or explain to the American people why they prefer to take the word of a self-proclaimed terrorist over the word of every credible law enforcement authority in the country."

The first question came from Quentin Burdick.

"So you dismiss out of hand even the possibility that the Los Angeles attack was part of a domestic conspiracy?"

"Categorically."

"And this is based on whose investigation?"

"You've seen the videotape the terrorist made. You have

now been given copies of the documents that prove al Farabi was a terrorist, though I should have thought the fact he was held at Guantánamo was proof enough of that."

"According to Senator Hart, those documents were forged, a way of getting Mr. al Farabi, who was a newspaper publisher in Cairo, sent back to the Middle East. You misstated the facts when you said he was sent back to his country of origin. He was sent to Syria where, again according to Senator Hart, his release was obtained through bribery."

Bristling at the suggestion, the vice president denied that he had misstated anything.

"I said he had been sent back to the Middle East where he came from. But with respect to your question, the suggestion is absurd. Why would anyone forge documents to prove they were guilty?"

He turned to a reporter with one of the more reliably conservative cable channels. The question was not what he expected.

"There is still the question, Mr. Vice President, about how to explain the fact that it was Senator Hart who was the target of an assassination plot? Armed men broke into his home, murdered Dieter Shoenfeld, a German publisher many of us knew. The police now have identified the two killers. Frank DeStefano, a New Jersey mobster, has been murdered. Henry Lattimore appears to have had some previous contact with members of the government. There are reports, so far unconfirmed, that Lattimore was someone the CIA once hired for what they are calling 'special assignments.'"

"There is no connection between the two events," said the vice president. "A terrorist—a suicide bomber—was responsible for what happened in Los Angeles. We have the videotape. We know who he was and we know why he did it. The break-in at Senator Hart's home in Georgetown—two men, now identified, shot and killed Mr. Shoenfeld and left Senator Hart unharmed. Why they came to his house, what they were there to do—"

"Rubicon, Mr. Vice President!" shouted Quentin Burdick, determined to bring the questioning back around. "A number of people, including your own deputy director of the CIA who started looking into what was apparently the code name for the attack in Los Angeles, have died. Are you suggesting that all these deaths are simply coincidental?"

"I'm not suggesting anything, except that there is no evidence whatsoever to back up Senator Hart's fantastic and harmful allegations. Not only is there no evidence to support them, the evidence I've given you today proves that Mohammed al Farabi was, and is, a terrorist."

"Do you think then that Senator Hart should resign from the Senate? He said he would if the claims he made were proved wrong."

The vice president never missed an opportunity to say what someone else should do. He looked straight into the camera.

"That's what a man of his word would do."

Minutes after the press conference ended, the telephone started to ring. The first call was from David Allen.

"When I draft the resignation statement, do you want to give yourself a couple of months or shall I make it for immediate effect?" he deadpanned. "Seriously, what do you want me to say? We need to put out something by way of a reply."

Hart held the receiver away from his mouth. He looked at Helen.

"David wants to know what we should say. What do you think?"

"Those documents he talked about, the ones he said prove the man you met was a terrorist—say that with all the vice president's experience with making things up, you would think he would know a forgery when he saw one."

"Helen suggests—"

"I heard. It's better than anything I could have come up with. Bobby, listen, there is one other thing. He must have got wind of what the vice president was going to do. He put out a release the second the press conference ended."

"What are you talking about? Who put out a release?"

"Senator Ryan. It says that anyone who thinks that Senator Robert Hart would ever give aid and comfort to an enemy of the United States does not deserve to hold public office."

"Did he really? Charlie always did know how to start a fight."

He talked for a few more minutes with Allen about the reply that should be made to the vice president's attack. Then he called Ryan. He reached him between campaign stops just outside Detroit.

"Thanks, Charlie, but you didn't need to do that."

"It's the reason I didn't call back last night. The vice president's office sent that statement out to every Republican candidate for the House and Senate. I'm afraid there is going to be a loud chorus of support among all the other know-nothings. I thought I'd get in a first shot the other way. But don't get the wrong idea. This was pure political calculation on my part."

"Calculation?" Hart laughed, waiting for the zany logic by which Ryan could make a generous act seem a monument to his own, purely selfish, motives.

"Several, actually. First, a fairly large percentage of my constituents despise the vice president. A public disagreement with him can't hurt. Second . . ." There was a stifled pause, as if he could scarcely keep from laughing. "Second, in a close race like this, the one thing certain to lose it is to have my wife file divorce papers before the election, which she promised to do if I didn't say something in public about that stupid bastard. And third . . ." This pause was serious, and full of significance. "There wasn't any choice. He's wrong, wrong about all of it. Rubicon is just what you said it is. All these murders are connected. And you're right about the rest of it. It isn't over. I can feel it. I keep thinking about what Gunther Kramer wrote, those notes of his, and that diagram. Rubicon was not just a plan to disrupt the election, to make it easier for one side to win; there's something bigger, much bigger, at stake. Remember what he wrote: assassination, the case for war, then more assassinations. I can feel it, Bobby; someone else is going to be killed."

19

FOR ALL THE CHARGES AND THE COUNTER-charges, for all the poisonous rhetoric, the race for the presidency did not change. Arthur Douglas continued to hold a lead over his Democratic challenger which, though somewhat diminished, was still greater than the margin of error.

"The debate could decide this thing," said Jeffrey Stone with a look of frustration. He turned to Hart, sitting in the passenger seat next to him. "Taylor is a better candidate than Alworth—looks and sounds like a president should. He should be up six or seven points. Douglas is a blowhard, a fool. I don't understand it."

"Of course you do," replied Hart, gazing out the window at the long row of glass buildings on Wilshire Boulevard. "Douglas plays on patriotism and fear. In the fifties there were people like Joe McCarthy who thought there was a communist under every bed; now there are people like Douglas and the vice president who think a terrorist is waiting around every corner."

Hart began to watch the sunlight reflecting off the different-colored glass on the buildings that towered up from the street. There was something almost majestic in the way that, together, the tall angular structures formed a long sweeping line that seemed perfect for the place. It reminded Hart of how the country, at its best, was supposed to work: the parts not always everything you would hope for, but, taken together, a remarkable achievement.

"Until the earthquake," he said out loud.

"The earthquake?" asked Stone, confused.

"Sorry," said Hart, turning to him. "I was just thinking of something."

"You were talking about communists in the fifties, and terrorists now," Stone reminded him.

"My father tried to explain to me what it was like. People had to sign loyalty oaths—as if someone bent on subversion would refuse to sign something like that. Anything the least bit unusual, the slightest deviation from what was considered normal, became a cause for suspicion. Sometimes out of fear, sometimes out of false patriotism, sometimes out of the worst kind of ambition, people reported on each other, became informers. A friend of my father's, a hero in the war, a man who had been with the agency from the beginning, was forced to resign because when he was a student in the thirties he had belonged to a student group that advocated aid for Russia after Germany invaded the Soviet Union."

Hart checked his watch. They were right on schedule. He pulled out the speech he was about to give at the Los Angeles City Club.

"This is all I've been doing, explaining over and over again why I think I'm right and the vice president and the rest of them are wrong. But there is still no proof; everything is circumstantial."

"Most people believe you."

"No, most people believe that the government is hiding something, most people believe there should be a thorough investigation. But on the question whether what happened in Los Angeles was a terrorist attack of the same sort that happened on 9/11 or whether it was part of some domestic conspiracy, there aren't that many willing to believe it could have been done by someone here."

Stone knew the polling numbers. Hart had left out something important.

"It's true only about a third are willing to say they think you're right, but the number on the other side isn't that much greater. All the rest are undecided; which means it wouldn't take much more in the way of proof to convince them that you're right."

They were almost there when Hart's cell phone rang. It was Leonard Coleman. Hart listened and did not say a word.

"Thank you, Lieutenant," he said at the end. He put the cell phone back in his pocket, and immediately began to scribble changes on the speech he was going to give.

The City Club was packed. The entire back of the room was lined with television cameras. Reporters crouched wherever they could find an open spot. Hart sat at the head table, next to the lectern, still working on the speech while everyone else was eating lunch. He glanced at it one last time as he was being introduced, and then slipped it into his jacket pocket.

"At the height of the Great Depression, with millions out of work, Franklin Roosevelt in his first inaugural spoke those much-needed and now famous words, that the 'only thing we have to fear is fear itself.' Thirty years later, at the height of the Cold War, John F. Kennedy, in his inaugural address, reminded the country that in dealing with our adversaries 'We should never negotiate from fear, but we should never fear to negotiate.' Two presidents—two great presidents—both understood that fear only makes a problem worse. Today, however, there are those who believe that fear is the only way they can govern."

Hart reminded his audience what had happened, how the Democratic candidate for president had been assassinated, and how, a short time after that, Dieter Shoenfeld had been murdered in Hart's home just as he was about to tell him what was involved in the Los Angeles attack and who was behind it.

"A few days later I kept an appointment that Dieter Shoenfeld had made. I met with Mohammed al Farabi, who had been held at Guantánamo, and learned from him how terrorists were brought to this country to carry out the plan known as Rubicon.

"I reported all of this in a press conference; I have now been labeled a coward, a fool, and even a traitor. The vice president of the United States has called me all these things; I am still waiting for him to call for an investigation."

Hart paused. His gaze swept from one side of the room to the other.

"Mohammed al Farabi is not a terrorist; he is exactly the kind of man on whom we should be relying, a voice of reason, in the Middle East. Yesterday, he identified the man who murdered Dieter Shoenfeld and would have murdered me. He was interviewed by a member of the D.C. police. He was shown six photographs and asked if he recognized any of them. Without a moment's hesitation, he picked out the photograph of Henry Lattimore. He said it was a face he would never forget, because Lattimore was one of the men who interrogated him while he was held prisoner at Guantánamo."

Hart looked straight ahead, his eyes hard, determined. He spoke in a slow, measured cadence.

"Lattimore didn't get to Guantánamo on his own. He was there because someone in the government sent him.

And that means that what happened here in Los Angeles was not an attack by a terrorist organization, but part of a domestic conspiracy. The only questions still remaining, at least for those who do not suffer from 'a disturbed mind and an unprecedented disregard for truth and decency,' are how many people were involved and how high up into the government this goes!"

Hart left without taking any questions from the press. He had to get back to Washington. Lattimore was the key to Rubicon, the link that connected what had happened to Dieter Shoenfeld, what could have happened to him, and the attack in Los Angeles. Someone had sent Lattimore to Guantánamo and someone had to know who.

The plane landed in Washington a few minutes before eleven o'clock. David Allen was there to meet him. Hart had one question.

"Were you able to do it? Has the chairman called an emergency meeting?"

"Seven o'clock tomorrow night. It gives everyone time to get back. They won't all come back," he added, walking quickly to match Hart's pace. "But most of them will be there."

Hart did not break stride, his footsteps a stark staccato in the dimly lit parking garage.

"And the director? Any trouble?"

"A little. He said it would take a while to pull together the information, that he didn't want to come unprepared. The chairman told him that he was already out of time, that he could either come voluntarily or under subpoena."

Hart slowed down. There was a look of mild surprise on his face.

"That's more than I would have expected. I wasn't sure he had it in him."

"No one likes to be lied to, and after what came out this morning—about Lattimore and Guantánamo—it's hard to believe that Townsend did not know more than he told the committee, hard to believe that, if he was not lying, he didn't do more to find out the truth about Rubicon and about the death of Raymond Caulfield."

They reached the car, Hart's BMW.

"Mine is still in Canada," said Allen.

"Probably a good place for it," replied Hart with a quick, abbreviated grin as he got into the passenger side.

"It got you there."

Hart shook his head at how much had happened.

"That was only a few weeks ago and it already seems like years. Sometimes it's hard to keep everything straight. Everyone should be out campaigning, going to those local events we all like to complain about; smiling, shaking hands, saying all sorts of stupid, meaningless things, and at the same time, feeling more alive than we ever have before or ever will again. But instead, the country is too scared, too worried about what might happen next, too confused about whom to blame for how we got to where we are. It's got to stop." He looked across at Allen. "The lieutenant is expecting me?"

Allen's eyes lit up.

"You know what he said, when I told him you were flying in tonight and wanted to see him? 'Later the better.' That's all. Didn't ask why, didn't complain that it was going to be damn near midnight, didn't even seem to think there was anything unusual about it."

Hart stared into the darkness.

"When he called me this morning, I think he expected I'd be back. He has that instinct for things, a sense of what is going to happen just before it does. Maybe it comes with the territory: spending your life dealing with other people's murders."

"How did he figure out that al Farabi might know something about Lattimore? Why would he even think about the possibility that Lattimore had been at Guantánamo?"

Hart did not respond; he had other questions of his own.

"What's been the reaction? Anything out of the vice president's office?"

"They're sticking to the same line: that al Farabi is a terrorist and no one should take his word for anything; and that even if Lattimore was at Guantánamo at some point, that doesn't prove anything about some conspiracy." Allen turned away from the road long enough to let Hart know that despite that, things had changed. "But they're nervous. They hadn't expected this. No one did. Everyone is waiting for the next shoe to drop, the next revelation. The speculation is endless. It's all anyone can talk about. The circle is closing. It's just that no one is yet certain who it's closing in on."

"It's closing in on the vice president," said Hart. His eyes were cold, determined, full of an anger that was becoming more difficult to repress. "He's behind it, all of it. I know it, and I swear to God I'm going to prove it! There has to be something that connects Lattimore to the vice president."

Allen pulled up in front of the police station. He offered to wait, but Hart told him to go home.

"You're going to need a good night's sleep. There's a lot to do tomorrow."

The station was nearly deserted. Somewhere down an empty hallway a door slammed shut and a shouted voice dwindled into muted insignificance. Leonard Coleman was waiting in his small, private office. He had a larger desk than the ones in the room outside and a comfortable high-backed leather chair. His suit coat, old and threadbare, hung on a rack just inside the door. For reasons that were never explained, Coleman wore both a belt and suspenders.

It gave him a look of cautious efficiency. When Hart walked in he was folding up his handkerchief.

"Allergies," he said with watery eyes and a helpless grin. "Or maybe jet lag, or something I picked up on the plane. Or some lethal disease I got at one of the airports while I waited to get through security." He looked at Hart over the spectacles he wore halfway down his nose. "How did you know this man al Farabi knew Lattimore? That was the only reason I made that trip—flew all the way to Rome, Italy— because you told me you were sure he could pick him out of a photo array."

Hart sat back, started to tell him something that was not quite true—the methodical, logical way he had arrived at that conclusion—and then just shrugged his shoulders.

"I guessed."

"That's what I thought."

"Then why did you go?"

In a near perfect imitation, Coleman shrugged back.

"I guessed you might be right. It made sense, you know. Which is the reason you didn't really guess: you knew something. You knew—you couldn't prove, but you knew—that the murder of Mr. Shoenfeld, the attempt to murder you, were connected to this thing you call Rubicon, and you knew—because al Farabi told you—that part of it at least depended on using terrorists held at Guantánamo. And that means someone from the government— probably someone from the CIA—is involved. Given what you already knew about Lattimore—what he did in the military, how he suddenly disappeared—there would be a reasonable chance that Lattimore was involved in this from the beginning."

"As I say, Lieutenant—a lucky guess."

"Call it that if you want—you were right."

"But does it bring us any closer to catching him, to finding Lattimore while he's still alive?"

"We've got a few leads, nothing definite. A couple people claim they've seen him, but nothing has checked out. We did learn, however, that he once knew this guy."

He reached inside a file folder on his desk and pulled out a grainy black-and-white photograph. Henry Lattimore, dressed as an army ranger, was talking with a civilian, a man of slight build with an intense expression.

"That's H. L. Harrison. He was on the national security staff until a couple of years ago. Where was this taken?"

"We're not sure. Looks like somewhere in the Middle East, or maybe North Africa."

"You're not sure? How did you get it?"

"We're not sure of that, either."

Coleman spread his fingers apart. He began to move them slowly back and forth against each other, barely touching.

"It just showed up, right here on top of my desk one morning, neatly sealed in a plain manila envelope, my name printed—or rather, typed—on the front. No note, no message—nothing. Someone wanted me to know that Lattimore and Harrison knew each other; not only knew each other, but from the look of that picture, worked together at some point. It's what you said when I asked you about giving Lattimore's picture to the press, that someone would remember him."

"Someone in the agency," said Hart. "Maybe someone who knew Raymond Caulfield. But whoever made sure you got it, what about Harrison? Where is he? What have you found out?"

"Mr. Harrison has disappeared, left the country, and did it rather suddenly, the day after Lattimore broke into your house, the day after Lattimore got rid of Frank De-Stefano." Coleman twisted his mouth a little to the side. "The day after Lattimore and DeStefano failed to kill you."

"Have any idea where he may have gone?"

"Could be anywhere. He doesn't have any family. Married once, but divorced a long time ago. The ex-wife wouldn't know anything."

"Where has he been the last couple of years, after he left the government? Wait a minute, I remember: he was at one of the think tanks, then he was with one of the companies, the private outfits, that were supplying security forces in Iraq and certain other places. That would fit. I'll find out what I can."

Hart got up to leave. Coleman, moving in his slow, deliberate way, walked over to the coat rack and pulled an envelope out of his suit coat pocket. He gave it to Hart.

"Mohammed al Farabi." Coleman's dark eyes had a new intensity, a sudden gleam of light. "Now there is a man worth meeting. When I was leaving he gave me this. He said he had remembered something; wasn't sure if it meant anything, but he thought you might be able to make sense out of it."

Hart opened the envelope and removed a sheet of paper on which, in a fine, legible hand, Mohammed al Farabi had written a few short sentences. Hart read it through twice, put it back in the envelope and put the envelope inside his own pocket.

"Just before he left Guantánamo, he heard someone talking, one of the interrogators. He isn't sure, but he thinks it might have been Lattimore. He said, 'When it's over there won't be anyone left.'"

"What do you think it means?" asked Coleman with a worried look.

"I don't know. It could mean a lot of things."

Coleman shoved his hands into his pants pockets and searched Hart's suddenly evasive eyes.

"That isn't what you really think, though, is it? You know what it means, don't you?"

Charlie Ryan's voice was echoing in his mind, the last

thing Ryan said to him the last time they talked. Hart looked at Coleman, waiting, always a little ahead of things with his uncanny sense of what would happen next.

"I think it means that we don't have much time. I think it means that a lot more people are going to die."

20

Ronald Townsend sat alone at the witness table tapping his fingers. Then, as if surprised that he was doing it, he pulled his hand down into his lap. He began to tap his foot.

At exactly seven o'clock, all the members in their places, the chairman of the Senate Intelligence Committee opened the session with a terse statement:

"We now have evidence that suggests at least the possibility that the attack in Los Angeles was part of a domestic conspiracy, though precisely to what end remains unclear. What is clear, however, is that the committee needs to get answers about what the government, and in particular the CIA, knew about this and when they knew it. Director Townsend has agreed to appear this evening voluntarily. He will, however, be put under oath."

Released from his pent-up anxiety, Townsend shot straight up from the chair and raised his right hand.

"Because Senator Hart has done more than anyone to uncover what has been going on," continued the chairman after the oath had been administered, "to say nothing of the fact that he appears to have been one of the targets for assassination, I'm going to ask him to lead off the questioning of the director."

Hart gave one of the clerks a stack of photographs, all copies of the same one, and asked her to distribute them to the members of the committee. Then he turned to the director.

"This morning, I sent over to your office this photograph, along with the names and what was known of the background of the two men seen in it. I see you have the photograph with you."

"Yes, Senator," replied Townsend in a steady voice.

"The two men have been identified as Henry Lattimore and H. L. Harrison. Is that your understanding?"

"Yes, that's correct, Senator."

Hart had worked all day getting ready. He moved relentlessly from one question to the next.

"Henry Lattimore has been identified as one of the two men who broke into my house in Georgetown, murdered Mr. Dieter Shoenfeld and, there is reason to believe, would have murdered me." Hart nodded toward the thick file folder on the table next to the director. "You have been given a copy of the statement I made to the police and the other materials pertaining to the manner in which that identification was made?"

"Yes, Senator, I have. There is no doubt that Lattimore is one of the men who murdered Shoenfeld. Nor is there any doubt that Lattimore is one of the two men in the photograph."

"We'll get to that in a minute, Director Townsend. But first, you also have with you, I believe, a copy of the statement by Detective Leonard Coleman of the D.C. police detailing the circumstances of his interview with Mohammed al Farabi and the way in which Henry Lattimore was identified as having been involved in the interrogation of prisoners at Guantánamo. Do you have that statement?"

Townsend tapped the top of the file.

"Yes, Senator, I do."

Hart looked at the director as if he expected an explanation. The director stared back, a guarded expression on his face. The silence deepened, became profound.

"Senator, I'm not sure what you want me to say," he said finally. "It appears—I mean, there is no doubt that Lattimore was one of the two men who broke into your home and killed Shoenfeld; and it appears that he was at some point at Guantánamo—"

"It appears? I think it more than appears, Mr. Townsend. Look at that photograph again. When I sent this over this morning, I asked if you would try to identify where and when it was taken. Were you able to do that?"

Townsend pulled the file over until it was right in front of him. He opened it and turned to the page he was looking for.

"It was taken approximately three years ago," he reported.

"Just before Lattimore left the military and disappeared," Hart interjected. "And where was it taken?"

Townsend pressed his lips together and appeared to concentrate.

"We think somewhere in Afghanistan, but we can't be a hundred percent certain." His expression became more candid. "But if I had to guess, that is where I would say it was: Afghanistan, three years ago."

"And at that time, three years ago, H. L. Harrison was in what position with the government?"

"He was deputy director of the National Security Advisory Council."

"What exactly is the National Security Advisory Council, Director Townsend? Would you describe it to the committee? It isn't part of the CIA, is it?"

"No," he replied with a quick, sideways movement of his head, eager to distance himself from any connection with it. "The National Security Advisory Council was set up to coordinate the gathering of intelligence among the various agencies. It was supposed to perform the same kind of role played by the office of the National Security Council in the coordination of foreign policy issues."

"The National Security Advisor reports directly to the president. Who does the head of this agency report to?"

"The vice president."

"I see. The vice president. So, H. L. Harrison was working for an agency that reports to the vice president, and three years ago H. L. Harrison was somewhere in Afghanistan where, as that photograph shows, he was deep in conversation with Henry Lattimore, who was then doing something with special forces?"

"Yes, it appears so."

"And then, just a year or so later, this same Henry Lattimore is in Guantánamo, interrogating prisoners. But he was not in special forces then, was he? He had left the military just a year before. He left special forces and went to work for you—for the CIA—isn't that true, Director Townsend?"

The veins on the director's temples began to throb; the muscles around his jaw tightened into knots.

"No, Senator, he did not. At no time was Henry Lattimore ever employed by the agency." He let out a breath, as if relieved of an obligation. "Not directly."

It took a moment for those two words to sink in. When they did, Hart's eyes turned lethal.

"Not directly," he repeated in the same slow cadence the director had used. He bent forward, mocking the director's quiet subterfuge. "Not directly. You mean the CIA did not hire him directly. The CIA hired one of the companies, the private contractors who have gotten rich in this war, and one of those companies hired Lattimore."

"Yes, so it appears."

"So it appears. You hire someone; they hire Lattimore. Then when Lattimore gets caught—when he's identified as the man who committed murder in my house, when he's identified as someone who was at Guantánamo, when it becomes apparent that he's involved in the conspiracy that involved Los Angeles and God knows what else besides—then you and others like you can deny that you knew or should have known anything about him or what he was doing! Only this time it's not going to be so easy to hide from responsibility. What was the name of the private contractor, Director Townsend?"

But before Townsend could answer, Hart threw up his hands in frustration.

"Don't even bother. It doesn't matter. Just tell us this: the company—the company your agency hired—is it the same company that three years ago—which means close to the time that photograph was taken—hired H. L. Harrison?"

Hart asked more questions, narrowing the circle.

"Where is H. L. Harrison now?"

"I'm sorry, Senator, we don't know."

"You don't know, or you haven't looked?"

"We only found out Harrison's potential involvement this morning, Senator—when you sent over that photograph."

"But you do know that he disappeared, that no one has seen him since the night of the break-in and murder at my house?"

Townsend gestured toward the file on the table in front of him.

"That's what the police report says."

"Yes," said Hart dryly, "thank God for the police."

Hart questioned the director for nearly three-quarters of an hour. When he was finished, Charlie Ryan took over. He was even more aggressive.

"The last time you were in front of this committee, I told you that this was serious, that Rubicon involved more than a single assassination, that what happened in Los Angeles might be only the beginning of what Rubicon was about. And yet you have to wait to find out from Senator Hart and the D.C. police that a man who worked for your agency— directly or indirectly, it doesn't matter—a man who worked for your agency interrogated Mohammed al Farabi at Guantánamo and was later involved in the murder of one man and the attempted murder of a United States senator."

"I'm sorry, Senator—is there a question in there some- where?" asked the director with a thin, caustic smile that nearly brought Ryan out of his chair.

"A question? I have a question. Either you're the most incompetent person ever to head a federal agency or some- one has told you not to look into Rubicon at all. Which is it, Mr. Townsend? Is the job too big for you, or are you part of a deliberate cover-up, an attempt to protect certain people, certain high officials, involved in murder and as- sassination?"

Townsend clutched the edge of the table, trying to hold himself back.

"No, Senator, I'm not trying to do any such thing! And I resent—"

The door at the side of the hearing room swung open. A young staff assistant rushed over to the chairman and whispered frantically in his ear. The chairman's face went ashen. He sat straight up and pounded the gavel. The room had already gone silent.

"There has been another attack," he announced, his voice

quivering with emotion. "Another suicide bomber. The reports have just started to come in. We don't know how many people may have been killed. It happened outside a hotel in Atlanta, just a few minutes ago. The only thing they know for certain is that Arthur Douglas is dead!"

No one moved, no one said a word, the immediate reaction a kind of paralysis. Then the committee room was bedlam, everyone talking at once. Townsend scooped up the file from the table and turned to go. Several members of the committee were out of their chairs. The gavel struck again.

"The committee is still in session," the chairman reminded them. "All we know is what I have just told you. I suggest that we stand in recess, but that we reconvene either later tonight or first thing tomorrow morning." He looked at Townsend, standing at the witness table, clutching the file folder in his arms. "At which time, Director Townsend, we will expect a full briefing on everything you have been able to learn."

Reminded by the chairman's slow, deliberate manner of the responsibilities that went with their position, members of the committee left the room in an orderly fashion. They returned, most of them, to their own offices to find out more about what had happened in Atlanta.

Charlie Ryan caught up with Bobby Hart in the hall. He knew what Hart was thinking.

"We don't know anything yet. Another suicide bomber, another assassination—that's all we know. Don't jump to any conclusions."

"We were wrong!" cried Hart. He was angry, angry with himself. "I was so certain, so convinced, that this was a conspiracy to change the outcome of the election! I was so certain the vice president was behind it—but now Douglas?"

Ryan grabbed him by the arm and forced him to stop.

"Listen to me! We don't know anything yet, except that

Douglas is dead. But whatever happened, all the other facts remain the same: all the murders, Lattimore, Harrison—all of it!"

"The facts may not have changed, but they don't mean what they meant before. If Rubicon was what we thought it was—an attempt to keep the presidency in the hands of someone who would not change policy—killing Arthur Douglas is the last thing they would have done."

They started walking again, moving quickly. Ryan shook his head in partial disagreement.

"After Los Angeles, after the first attack—what did we think it was about? An assassination, but not to take out one candidate so the other could win—to create a sense of uncertainty, of fear, so that everyone would think that we were under siege, that we had to strike back, that we really were in an endless war on terror. What better way to do that than to have the next attack, the next assassination, the candidate who kept promising to be the terrorists' worst enemy?"

When they reached Hart's office, he switched on the television set as David Allen quickly brought them up to date.

"Douglas had just finished giving a speech. It happened when he came outside. He was just getting into the limousine. A car, packed with explosives, drove right into it."

Allen nodded toward the images flickering on the television screen. Live pictures from Atlanta showed the charred wreckage of the limousine and numerous other vehicles. The front of the hotel was a tangled mass of twisted steel and chunks of concrete. The ground was ankle deep in glass.

"How many . . . ?" asked Hart, stunned by the devastation.

Allen could only guess.

"They're saying dozens; it could go higher."

"Douglas and everyone who was with him . . . ?" Ryan started to ask, but the question seemed a kind of obscenity, a too graphic reminder of death.

The television coverage moved away from the carnage in Atlanta to a scene in Washington. Allen turned up the volume. Standing in front of the White House, a reporter read the first few lines of a statement put out under the president's name.

"'The enemies of freedom have for a second time assassinated a candidate for the presidency. Arthur Douglas was a courageous public servant and a good and decent man. His death will not go unavenged. The terrorists will be brought to justice.

"'Everyone should now understand—there is no longer any room for disagreement—that America faces an enemy who will do anything to destroy us. The time for discussion and debate is over. No one understood better than Arthur Douglas that America is in a war, a war we have to win. We would dishonor his memory were we to fight it with anything less than everything we have.'"

Hart and Ryan exchanged a glance. They both understood what would happen next. Los Angeles had been traumatic, a blow to the national psyche; but it was still comprehensible as a single, isolated, though tragic, event. No one could think that way about Atlanta; no one could take comfort in the belief that what had happened once could not happen again. Terrorists had murdered first the Democratic, and now the Republican, candidate for president; murdered two men both of whom had been given all the protection the Secret Service could provide. If terrorists could do that, no one was safe.

"I'll tell you one damn thing we better not do," insisted one of the more influential talk radio personalities. "We better not waste any more time listening to people like Bobby Hart. I mean, here's a guy who can't even figure out that a suicide bomber is a real terrorist. This man sits on the Senate Intelligence Committee and what does he do? Does he look to find out who might be threatening the country, who might want to bring us down? No, because he kept insisting that this was all some kind of conspiracy— secret organizations—groups within the government—some bizarre CIA plot—God knows what. And what has happened as a result? How many lives have been lost because the senator was more interested in publicity than in doing his job? We shouldn't have to deal with people like that in this country, and maybe after what's happened now we won't have to."

Even the mainstream media thought that enough was enough. Editorial writers in every part of the country, including New York and California, suggested that whatever may be the truth about the break-in at Senator Hart's house and the murder of Dieter Shoenfeld, the attacks in Los Angeles and Atlanta were clearly the work of Al Qaeda or some other terrorist organization. It was impossible to think they could be anything else.

Quentin Burdick was not so sure.

"I knew H. L. Harrison," he explained. "In my dealings with him he was usually fairly honest. He would tell me when there was something he could not discuss, but he was often willing to explain in great detail the thinking within the administration on some national security issue, though I don't believe he even once allowed me to quote him by name. Always 'someone within the administration,' that kind of thing."

Burdick looked at Hart, sitting across from him in a restaurant on Manhattan's Upper East Side. At three o'clock in the afternoon it was a quiet place to talk. Hart seemed worried. Leaning forward on his elbow, Burdick played with the edge of his bow tie.

"You remember President Truman's line, 'If you want a friend in Washington, get a dog'?"

For the first time in days, Hart cracked a smile.

"There are a couple people left who haven't turned on me."

"Senator Ryan, for one?"

"Charlie Ryan, for one." The smile grew a shade larger. "It isn't his fault, you understand. I think he'd like to turn on someone once, just to know how it felt, but it isn't in him, he doesn't know how. But you were about to tell me something about H. L.—what does that stand for, anyway?"

"Hannibal Lawrence."

"Hannibal." Hart shook his head. "What about him? What about Harrison? No one has found him, have they? I don't imagine now that anyone is really looking. Except the D.C. police."

Burdick reached inside his jacket.

"I dragged this out. It's a speech he gave a couple years ago at a conference sponsored by that think tank he was with. I didn't think much about it at the time. It was the kind of complaint that had become fairly common in those circles. The only difference was the context in which he tried to put it."

Hart looked at the front page, the date and location of a speech that perhaps two hundred people had listened to and most of them had then forgotten. The title of the speech seemed not just generic but dull: "American Democracy, American Empire: A Choice for the 21st Century."

"The complaint," continued Burdick, "was that government had become too cumbersome, too complex, to meet the challenges of the new century; that with interests and responsibilities around the world, the executive could not respond to each new crisis with the kind of energy the framers of the Constitution intended, if it was constantly having to do things the way that Congress insisted. I remember most distinctly—and the reason I pulled it out—" He pointed to the text. "I marked the passage, on the last page. He makes the remark that in the age of terror, any interference with the ability of the executive to decide what has to be done is a threat to national security, and that an empire has to act like one."

Hart did not see the point.

"That argument has been made before. Lopez, the attorney general, testified a couple of months ago in the Judiciary Committee that there is no limitation on the power of the president in a time of war. None. He can do whatever he decides is best for the country. The argument doesn't stand up, but so long as people in power believe they have that authority, the only way you can stop them is either to refuse to appropriate the money they need or take them to court. The argument, if you take it seriously, is nothing short of a claim to a kind of elected dictatorship."

Burdick searched his eyes with an intensity that Hart at first did not understand. Slowly, it dawned on him.

"You don't really think . . . ?"

"Why not?" asked Burdick. "Start with the name: Rubicon. What did it mean—when Caesar crossed it?"

"That a decision had been made, that there was no turning back."

"It also meant that the republic was finished, that whatever forms were kept, the new reality was that Rome was now going to be ruled by one man."

"They could never get away with it," insisted Hart. "We have an election coming up in less than a month. We have . . ."

"An election with only one candidate?"

"The Republican National Committee is meeting this weekend. They'll pick someone else. The election will still take place."

"They pick another candidate, less than a month to go. Are you sure that's going to happen?"

"Of course. Why wouldn't it?"

"That isn't much time. There has already been talk about delay, pushing the election back so that the new candidate—whoever it might be—has a chance to campaign."

"Even if it were pushed back, that still doesn't bring about what you're suggesting."

Burdick seemed relieved that Hart did not think it possible. He signaled to the waiter to bring them another drink.

"But it does make sense, doesn't it?" said Hart, suddenly intrigued. "The parallel would then be exact: what Gunther Kramer wrote, the passages he marked, all about what happened in Rome after the Rubicon was crossed. I wonder how many people then thought it could happen, that what they had known all their lives, what went back generations, four hundred years, could change, and change that quickly?"

Burdick sat hunched over his empty glass, a pensive expression on his narrow face.

"I've been hearing rumors that the White House has been discussing the possibility of martial law, declaring a state of emergency until every terrorist involved in the attacks has been rounded up. I'm also hearing rumors that the Pentagon has been given orders to begin planning an attack on Syria and Iran."

"Because Syria and Iran are responsible for what happened here?"

The waiter brought the second round. Burdick took a

sip and then held it in front of his eyes, watching the way the Scotch and water changed color in the shaded light.

"H. L. Harrison," he mused aloud, "was not, so far as I know, one of those religious types, but there was that same kind of inner certainty in his eyes. He believed in what they were doing, believed quite fervently that it was America's mission to remake the Middle East."

Burdick took another, longer sip. With a kind of nervous excitement, his eyes fastened on a single point directly below him. He seemed to concentrate on it, a way to help him see more clearly what was going through his mind.

"The strange thing," he said presently, "is that I always had the feeling that he didn't know anything. That isn't quite right. He obviously knew a great deal, but all about current things: facts, figures, the various arguments used by each side in whatever debate was going on within the administration. But *democracy, empire, what the founders intended*—just words; phrases he had picked up to make what he had to say seem more important, more historical. That speech—read it when you have the chance—it really doesn't say anything except that we know what we're doing is right and there should not be any limit on our power to do it."

"Even if it involves the murder of a few dozen innocent people," said Hart, shaking his head at the blind and brutal arrogance of it all. He was about to say something else when Burdick's cell phone rang.

"Sorry," said Burdick after he checked the screen. "It's the paper." He raised the phone to his ear. Seconds later the color had gone out of his face.

"What?" asked Hart as Burdick put the phone away. "What's happened now?"

"What we were talking about: Rubicon. You better get back to Washington right away."

"Why? What . . . ?"

"Another attack, another suicide bomber. Jeremy Taylor is dead. In Philadelphia, just outside Independence Hall. There isn't going to be an election. That's what this was all about," said Burdick, anger in his eyes. "Rubicon. You've got to stop it."

21

THE THIRD ATTACK KILLED MORE PEOPLE THAN the first two put together. More than a hundred were wounded. That it happened just outside the birthplace of American independence only added to the feelings of frustration and rage that swept over the country.

Jeremy Taylor had just finished giving a speech, a speech in which he had insisted that no matter how many times terrorists might attack the country, America could never be defeated so long as it did not give up on the principles that had guided it from the beginning and given hope to the world.

His words died with his death. A state of martial law was declared. The National Guard began to patrol the streets, authorized to arrest anyone on suspicion and to shoot on sight anyone breaking the law. All commercial aircraft were temporarily grounded so that the military could take over major security operations at the airports. The White House announced that the president would address a special joint session of Congress the following night.

"Burdick thinks it's what?" asked Charlie Ryan, intensely interested in what Hart had told him.

"He thinks Rubicon is more of a parallel than we thought."

Ryan slipped lower in the leather chair. In a precise, methodical motion, he tapped his fingers together as he stared at the ceiling. He had taken off his jacket and rolled up his sleeves.

"The American Empire." The words rolled slowly off his tongue. "There are some parallels." He gestured toward a stack of books on the credenza behind him. "I've been reading a little, some of the histories I was supposed to read in college. The Romans went to war with their neighbors and kept fighting until they had conquered Italy; we fought the Indians and the British and then the Spanish until we had conquered the continent. The Romans kept expanding—we kept expanding. In both cases, a republic without setting out to do it became an empire, and in the process became powerful and rich." Ryan turned his head until his eyes met Hart's. "Remember, back in school, American history—Jefferson's yeoman farmer: self-sufficient, independent, able to write and speak his mind because he was not dependent on anyone else for what he needed to support himself and his family. And how that all changed with the industrial revolution: how wealth got concentrated in fewer and fewer hands; how everyone became in a certain sense dependent on everyone else. It happened in Rome—great disparities of wealth led to great differences in power; equality disappeared and everything was left in the hands of a favored few. Rome became corrupt, and Caesar triumphed."

"Bread and circuses, and now television," said Hart, remembering what he had heard a British stranger say on a tour bus in Rome. "All right, I agree. The parallels are all there, with one important exception."

Ryan sat up and nodded emphatically.

"Right. Caesar came with an army that was more loyal to him than it was to Rome. That isn't the situation we face. If we're right, Rubicon is a conspiracy designed to produce fear, and to stop, or at least postpone, an election. But why? Why postpone it? What can that achieve?"

"Burdick seems to think—"

"Burdick doesn't know. He knows a lot, but he doesn't know that. If they had murdered Taylor and left Douglas alone, then it would have been obvious that they were trying to decide who would be the next president. But this! No one left alive?"

"That's the phrase al Farabi heard at Guantánamo: when it was over, there wouldn't be anyone left. This was the plan from the very beginning: kill every candidate . . ."

"But for what? To postpone the election until other candidates are chosen—and then what? There is something else, something we can't yet see, something that only works if you have precisely this situation: a presidential election that can't take place, an election that has to be delayed."

Growing impatient, Hart had begun to pace around the room.

"Whatever it is, it's right in front of our eyes and we're too damn blind to see it."

Ryan had an idea.

"If you read those histories, you begin to see that what happened in Rome was almost inevitable: that the decision to cross the Rubicon had been decided a long time before, that when Rome began to send armies far away, when . . . But you see my point. Certain things had to happen, once you had that situation. Why not the same thing here? Harrison—and if it was Harrison, it had to be the vice president—knew how people would react. They knew what would happen when the only question was what we had to do to protect the country against another attack. And look what they've gotten! Martial law, the use of the military for domestic purposes, the virtual suppression of any political opposition. The question is, what else do they want? Something permanent, a fundamental change in the way the country governs itself, but what, what exactly?"

WHEN THE PRESIDENT addressed the joint session of Congress the next evening, armed troops had begun to patrol the streets around the Capitol and tanks were stationed at each of the major intersections. No one was allowed within a quarter of a mile without proper identification. Senators, congressmen, even members of the Supreme Court had had to pass through metal detectors and then were searched.

The mood inside the House chamber was somber, reserved, and, above all, uncertain. Everyone, whatever their party, believed that things could not go on this way, that something had to be done; though no one seemed to have any idea what it should be, or, if they did, were willing to say it.

Speaking with the same stiff rectitude with which he had addressed the Congress before, the president called for tighter security and greater unity, promised retribution, and pledged to continue and intensify the war on terror. He asked for immediate passage of legislation, long stalled in committee, expanding the power of the government to conduct regular surveillance of all telecommunications both foreign and domestic. He asked for a number of things, each of them a power needed to fight terrorism more effectively, and each time he asked, the Congress responded with applause. Finally, at the end, the president spoke about the election and what was going to have to be done about it.

"The tragic deaths of three candidates for the presidency, the cowardly attacks on our citizens, will not be allowed to destroy our democratic institutions. The presidential election will go forward, as soon as it is safe to do so. We will not allow terrorists to dictate the outcome of elections by murder. We will not allow terrorists to prevent a full and fair debate between candidates for the highest office in the land. We will do whatever is necessary to make certain that we have a normal election as soon as it is possible to do so. Democracy in America will be made safe."

The applause rolled over the chamber, spontaneous, prolonged, a great outpouring of support for the president, the leader of the nation, determined, as they all were, to protect the American democracy from anyone who would dare threaten it.

When the speech was over, after the president had left and the House chamber was all but deserted, Charlie Ryan had not moved from his chair. There was a strange defiant certainty in his eyes and a thin, knowing smile on his face. He looked up at Hart.

"'When it's safe.' We're going to delay the election of a new president until it's 'safe.' And who gets to decide when that might be? I think we begin to see where all this is going, what Rubicon was always meant to do." He jumped to his feet. "When it's safe! Who the hell do these people think they are?"

Charlie Ryan was not the only one who had questions about what the president meant. Quentin Burdick emphasized precisely that part of the president's speech in the front-page story he wrote the next morning in the *Times*. Alvin Roth, however, did not need a newspaper to tell him that a serious constitutional issue was at stake. The chairman of the Senate Judiciary Committee thought the administration had better explain itself. Three days after the president addressed the Congress, the attorney general was back on Capitol Hill, listening to another lecture he thought he did not need.

"Attorney General Lopez," said Roth in obvious

frustration, "we have an election—a presidential election—scheduled two weeks from next Tuesday. Thanks to these terrorist attacks, neither party has a candidate. We all understand that the election has to be postponed. What I don't understand is your reluctance to support legislation setting a new date. You agree, do you not, that it's important that we set a new date as soon as possible so that things can go forward in an orderly process—the parties can select their candidates, the candidates can begin to campaign. Electing a president is a very serious business, Attorney General Lopez."

"I'm perfectly aware of that, Mr. Chairman, which is the reason it can't be done."

"Can't be done? I'm not sure I understand what you mean."

"We can't just randomly pick a date. We have to know first that it's safe, that we won't have a repetition of what has just happened. We have to make certain it's safe, Senator Roth. The president made that quite clear in his speech. And I don't think it's irrelevant to note that the great majority of the American people believe we should delay the election until all the terrorists involved in the three attacks are captured and put away."

Roth made an effort to be patient.

"We have never in the history of this country failed to have a presidential election at the time it was scheduled, Attorney General Lopez. We may not have any choice now but to postpone this one, but we ought to set the new date immediately. And it should not be any later than the middle or, at the very latest, the end of December."

Lopez flashed a fervent smile.

"That may be possible, but at this point it's just too early to know."

Roth eyed him coldly.

"It seems to me, Attorney General Lopez, that the Congress has the authority to set a new election date; that the Congress, not the Executive, has the power to decide what is important here: achieving perfect safety before we have an election or running whatever risks are necessary to keep intact our democratic institutions."

Lopez leaned forward, a tight, unfriendly smile on his mouth.

"No one is more committed to keeping our democratic institutions safe than the president, which is the reason we are determined to make certain our elections are safe, Senator. And with respect to your other point, I doubt there is much support in the Congress for legislation that would undermine the president's ability to prevent terrorists from murdering any more candidates for the presidency."

Ryan was not surprised when Hart told him what had happened; nor did he appear to be particularly disappointed.

"Alvin Roth has a fairly limited understanding of most things, including the Constitution," he said sharply. "But his instinct is right. There should be legislation. The president can't be allowed to decide when the next election is going to be held. But Roth hasn't yet grasped that the power to delay, the power to postpone, is the power to prevent. Let the president decide when it is safe to have an election, we might never have another one. Roth doesn't understand that yet, but there are a few things that Lopez doesn't understand, either."

Ryan was almost manic, pacing back and forth, punctuating his speech, inexplicably, with short bursts of laughter and then, suddenly, swearing under his breath. Hart was not sure what to make of it.

"It's all right, Bobby." There was that same look of grim

defiance in his eyes that Hart had seen the night of the president's speech. "I haven't lost my mind." He paused. "Have you ever argued a case in front of the Supreme Court?"

"Argued a case in front of . . . ? I never practiced law. I have a law degree, that's it. Why? What are you . . . ?"

"You're on the Judiciary Committee. That's probably better preparation than a few years in private practice." He said this as if it were a matter of some importance. "The main thing is you're as good on your feet as anyone I've ever seen."

"What are you talking about?"

Ryan came back to the chair in front of Hart's desk. He glanced across at a portrait of the Constitutional Convention that hung above the marble fireplace on the far side of the room.

"I'm talking about that—the Constitution, and what you and I are going to do to save it. We're filing a lawsuit on behalf of the Congress of the United States against the president of the United States."

Ryan reached inside the briefcase next to his feet. He tossed Hart a thick document, the brief he intended to file with the court.

"Read through it. See what you think. If you agree, we'll file it first thing tomorrow morning."

Hart glanced at the cover, and then thumbed through the pages to get some idea how long it was.

"You did this? When did you have time?"

"It wasn't that difficult, once you understand what's really at issue."

Hart could see from his expression that Ryan was not talking about some narrow legal technicality. Ryan was always at his most understated when the stakes were high and the risk enormous.

"What's really at issue?"

Ryan looked straight at him. There was not the slightest doubt in his eyes.

"Whether this country stays a republic or becomes a dictatorship."

"And you're taking this—?"

"We're taking this," Ryan corrected him "you and I. It has to be like that. We'll get some others to sign on, but it's the two of us—one Democrat and one Republican—that are going to argue this thing. This can't be some partisan contest, where it looks like one side is trying to gain some political advantage."

"We're taking this to the Supreme Court? The chief justice was appointed by the president. A clear majority are conservatives."

"That's what I'm counting on," said Ryan as he got up to go. "They're always talking about original intent, what the Constitution meant to the men who framed it. That's the best hope—maybe the only hope—we have."

Hart glanced again at the brief. He turned automatically to the last page, where the plaintiff lays out the relief he is seeking, what he wants the Court to do. He almost came out of his chair.

"You're asking that the Court order that the election go forward as scheduled? That's impossible!"

"No, actually, it isn't," replied Ryan. A crooked grin made a crooked line across his slightly freckled face and gave it a boyish glow. "Read the brief in its entirety. Then you'll understand."

He was almost to the door when he remembered.

"By the way, you better cancel anything you had planned for this weekend. We'll need at least that much time to get ready."

"Get ready? Why, when are we supposed to . . . ?"

"This will be considered an emergency proceeding. The Court will set a hearing for Monday morning."

"Monday morning? This is Thursday."

"And our brief is already written," said Ryan, amused at the look of panic in Hart's eyes. "Think how much work the bastards on the other side have in front of them!"

It was nearly seven-thirty when Ryan left. Hart slipped into David Allen's office and told him what had happened.

"I can't leave, I can't go back to California now."

"There is nothing to do there anyway. No one is campaigning. No one quite knows what to do. They're all just waiting."

Hart tucked the brief under his arm. He looked around Allen's cluttered office, at the files full of legislation, proposed, considered, sent to committee, considered some more, dropped; then picked up again, rewritten, amended, changed into something completely different than what was first intended; and then, finally, passed, become a law—or not passed and become a cause. It was messy, wasteful, hugely inefficient; and still the only thing that worked, the endless battle in which someone won and someone lost and then, armed only with the written and the spoken word, fought some more.

Allen knew what he was thinking. He gestured toward the brief that Hart was taking with him to read through that night.

"You think Ryan can do it?"

"I never practiced law, but I've met a lot of lawyers. Ryan is better than all of them put together. But can he do this? Convince a court like this one that . . . ? I don't know. Maybe. Unless someone on the Court is involved in . . ."

"Rubicon?"

They exchanged a glance. Hart turned to go and then, quickly, turned back.

"Have we heard anything from the lieutenant? Has he called?"

"No, nothing, not a word. Why? Were you expecting to hear something about . . . ?"

Hart shook his head. There was a look of discouragement in his eyes.

"I just keep hoping that something breaks. I don't mind that everyone thinks I was crazy. What I mind is that these people—Harrison, Lattimore, the vice president, and all the rest, whoever they are, however high this thing goes— seem to have gotten away with it."

"They'll make a mistake," said Allen as Hart opened the door. "People like that always do."

Hart was not so sure. Not every murder was solved, not every murderer was caught and locked up in prison. And now, except for Leonard Coleman, no one was even looking. No one was interested in who murdered Dieter Shoenfeld, or who might have killed Raymond Caulfield; no one cared that Henry Lattimore was still on the loose or that H. L. Harrison had disappeared. The country had been attacked, and there might still be other terrorists out there, part of the same network, the same cell, planning another, even more lethal, assault. This was war, not a time for conspiracy theories.

Outside the Russell Senate Office Building, the only vehicles in the street belonged to the army. Every corner was now a checkpoint, no one allowed to pass without proper authorization. Public buildings were no longer open to the public.

The night air was cool and crisp. Hart decided to walk a while. He wanted some exercise and a chance to clear his mind. It was only after he had gone a couple of blocks that he realized that there was no one else around. This time of evening, especially when Congress was in session, the streets were usually full of people who worked on the Hill, some of them going home, finished for the day, others taking a break for dinner before they went back to something they had to have ready the next morning. It was as if the whole town was in hiding, afraid to go anywhere that was not protected by armed security. He turned at the next corner and found himself staring down the wrong end of a rifle.

"Identification!" demanded a young soldier.

"And if I don't have any, what are you going to do, shoot me?" In the shaded light of a street lamp, Hart could see that the question had not registered. "Are you going to shoot me?" he repeated with careless indifference. "If I left my office—just decided to go for a walk—and did not remember to bring my wallet, is that what you're ordered to do—shoot me dead?"

The private was becoming nervous. He held the rifle in a stiff, awkward position.

"Identification!" His voice was thin, hollow, and forced.

The rifle in Hart's face seemed the culmination of every terrible, violent thing that had happened. He did not think about what he was doing; it was all instinct, reaction, an eager belligerence that put aside any thought of his own safety.

"Answer my question, soldier! I don't have the right piece of paper, you're going to shoot me? You don't know who I am, you don't know anything I've done except to walk down the street, and you're going to shoot me?"

The soldier's face was flushed; his hands began to sweat.

"Identification!"

"Is this why you joined up—to shoot other Americans—unarmed citizens—when they don't do what you tell them to?"

The soldier's eyes grew wide. He was scared, and Hart knew it.

"Never mind, soldier. It isn't your fault. If you'll put down that rifle, I'll take my wallet out."

The soldier looked at Hart's identification, and then, just to be sure, looked at Hart.

"Sorry, Senator; I didn't—"

Hart stopped him with a look. He walked away, moving quickly now, anxious to get back to his hotel. When he found a cab, he started to think about how stupid he had been, how easily he could have gotten himself killed; and all to make a point that would have been lost on anyone but himself, a small rebellion against events he had tried, and failed, to control. That was what was making him crazy, the knowledge that he knew what was going on, knew how it had all started, knew who was behind it, and he still could not do anything to stop it. He pulled out his cell phone and called Helen. He tried to sound upbeat and cheerful. He did not tell her what he had done with the soldier.

"I'm about to become a practicing attorney. Charlie and I have started our own firm. Our first case is in the Supreme Court, this Monday morning. By Tuesday," he said, laughing, "we should be out of business."

Helen did not know what he was talking about, but she caught the mood.

"You always used to say that you wanted to start at the top and work your way down. But don't you have to be admitted to practice before the Court? Isn't there some kind of rule about that?"

"Haven't you heard: there aren't any rules anymore." He paused and became serious. "Are you okay—is everything all right?"

"I'm just worried about you, Bobby Hart, I'm just worried about you."

It made him smile a little, the effect it still had on him, the gentle heartbreak of her voice, the soft vulnerability which confessed how much it would hurt if anything were ever to happen to him.

"You're staying at the hotel?" she asked. "You're not going back to the house?"

"I can't go back. It wasn't the same when you weren't there, and now, after what happened . . . No, we'll do what we talked about: rent a place, use it when we have to be here."

"I'm sorry you won't be here this weekend, but it won't be long now. This will all be over soon, won't it, Bobby? You and Charlie, at the Supreme Court . . . You'll win, you know."

"I hope you're right."

"When was I ever wrong—about you, I mean?"

Helen had taken away much of the tension he had felt. When he got to the hotel, he kicked off his shoes, put two pillows behind his head, and started reading Ryan's brief. When he finished it, he went into the other room and sat down at the table. He wanted to read through it again, slowly this time, making notes as he went. It was difficult to believe that Ryan had been able to do this in just the few days he had had to work on it.

Half an hour later, he called room service and ordered dinner. There was not going to be time to go out. He was so engrossed in what he was doing, so caught up in the argument Ryan had developed, that when room service knocked, he kept reading as he walked to the door.

"Just put it over there," he said, pointing vaguely toward the coffee table, his eyes still on the brief.

He had turned and taken two steps when he felt it, the pressure of a gun barrel hard against the back of his head. His eyes darted to a mirror on the wall. The man who held the gun was dressed as a waiter, but he had seen the face before, twice, in two different photographs. Henry Lattimore was still alive.

22

L ATTIMORE SPUN HART AROUND AND PRESSED the gun against his chest.

"Listen carefully. I'm only going to say this once. We're going to leave the hotel and we're going to get into a car that's parked down the street. Then we're going to take a little drive. Do anything stupid and you're dead. It's as simple as that."

He shoved Hart down on a chair.

"Hold your arms straight out in front of you and keep them there."

Cautiously, one eye on Hart, Lattimore looked around the room. He went to the open doorway that led to the bedroom and glanced inside. Hart had left his suit coat draped over the back of a chair. Lattimore took off the waiter's jacket and put it on.

"All right, get up. It isn't far." He opened the door and pushed Hart out in front of him. "The end of the hallway—we'll take the stairs."

Hart was surprised that he did not feel fear, or even

anger. All he felt was an intense curiosity, and not so much about what was going to happen to him, as about Lattimore and what he knew about Rubicon.

"You're in some trouble, Mr. Lattimore," he said as they moved down the carpeted, dimly lit corridor. It astonished him how calm he sounded. "But you have a chance to get out of this. You might even be able to get immunity from prosecution—get away with murder—if you tell everything you know about Rubicon and everyone involved."

Lattimore kept moving straight ahead, the gun placed discreetly in the small of Hart's back. Suddenly, a few steps in front of them, a door opened. A middle-aged couple, tourists from out of town, were leaving their room.

"Good evening," said Hart. He felt the gun press harder against his back.

"Good evening," said the woman. She stared at him a moment. "Aren't you . . . ?"

Lattimore pushed hard with the gun. Hart smiled at the woman over his shoulder. She had seen him, and she had seen Lattimore as well. That was all he had wanted.

"I told you not to be stupid," said Lattimore with a warning glance as they entered the stairwell and started down the steps.

"She was looking right at me. Was I supposed to ignore her?"

Lattimore shoved him; Hart stumbled and nearly fell.

"Move, damn it! I haven't got all day."

They were down the stairs, out through the service entrance, and into the alley behind the hotel. A drunk, resting up for another night's revelry, was curled up behind a stack of garbage cans. A mangy cat jumped from an empty cardboard box and scurried away. Just a few steps up the street, they reached the car. Lattimore opened the passenger door, pushed Hart across to the driver's side, and tossed him the keys.

"You drive."

"Where?"

"Where I tell you."

Hart glanced in the rearview mirror as he started the engine. This area of Washington was heavily patrolled. If he saw a cop, if he could get the cop's attention—give the cop some reason to stop the car . . .

"Drive slow. Don't make any sudden moves."

"Where are we going?"

"It doesn't really matter," said Lattimore with a disquieting sense of finality. "Maybe I should let you decide, Senator. Where would you like to go? Back to your place in Georgetown? Funny thing, that's where I always wanted to live. First time I came to Washington—must have been almost twenty years ago now. Georgetown. It has a nice ring to it. I was just a young lieutenant then, not much chance of living there on what I was going to be making."

With eyes full of contempt, Hart looked across at him.

"Is that why you became a hired assassin? For the money?"

Lattimore glared back.

"Money? You think I did this for money? I did it for my country, I did it to keep people like you from selling us out."

"Selling us . . . ?" Hart gripped the wheel; his knuckles turned white. "You help organize an attack on your own country, arrange the assassinations of three different candidates for the presidency, and you have the guts to talk about people like me selling you out?"

"A few politicians—what's that compared to all the millions of people in this country whose lives are at risk from terrorists that people like you won't let us fight?"

"Is that what Harrison told you? Is that how he got you to start a little private war of your own; recruit a few terrorists and use them to destroy everything this country stands for?"

Lattimore dismissed it with a harsh, corrosive laugh.

"Harrison? You thought that Harrison . . . ? He was just a messenger, and he didn't always do that very well. That guy wouldn't take a leak unless someone gave him permission."

"Rubicon wasn't his idea?"

Hart kept his eyes on the road. Lattimore was still shaking his head at how far wrong Hart had been.

"He did what he was told. We all did." He pointed to a road sign. "Take that exit."

It was the way to the Jefferson Memorial. He remembered the morning when Dieter Shoenfeld tried to warn him that they were being watched; insisting, in that understated way he had, that no one was safe anymore.

"Is that where you're going to do it, where you're going to kill me—at the Jefferson Memorial?"

Lattimore seemed almost amused.

"Do you have a better place you'd like to die?"

Faced with it, the imminent prospect of his own death, he discovered that it was somehow important that he not give Lattimore the satisfaction of a show of weakness. It was important, important to him, that if he were going to die, he do it properly, the way he thought a man should.

"If Harrison was just another soldier—if he was just taking orders—who was in charge of it? How far up does it go? Whose idea was it?"

"You ask too many questions."

Hart forced himself to laugh.

"Who am I going to tell?" He waited for an answer, but Lattimore made no reply. "You killed DeStefano; did you also kill Harrison? Is that part of what you do—get rid of anyone who knows anything after they've served their purpose?"

"I told you, you ask too many questions. But, yeah, there are some people you can't trust."

"Harrison?"

"He got scared. He thought you knew too much, that you were getting too close. He was getting nervous. He couldn't be trusted."

"Who knew about Rubicon? How far up does it go? It's the vice president, isn't it?"

Lattimore looked at him like he was a fool, someone who could not see what was right in front of him; someone too blinded by his own, all too innocent, assumptions, to see what should have been obvious.

"Everyone knew about Rubicon. They all read the document. They all knew what was involved."

"Document? What document? Are you saying this was all set out in writing, that the White House signed off on it?"

"And it's probably still there, in a file somewhere, the contingency plan for what might happen, and what would have to be done about it."

"Contingency plan? What are you talking about?"

"It started right after 9/11. You were around. You remember. There was an election scheduled in New York—some people thought it should be delayed. Others, including Giuliani, thought there should not be an election at all so the mayor could stay in office. That's when it began: a contingency plan for what to do if there was a terrorist attack just before a presidential election, how the government would function if an election could not be held."

Hart vaguely remembered some talk at the time about what might happen if a situation like that should arise.

"But that isn't—"

"But it is, Senator; it's exactly what has happened. When you have a contingency plan, all you have to do is create the contingency."

"Whose decision was that?" demanded Hart. "Everyone may have known about a contingency plan—what might have to be done after another attack, if an election had to be delayed—but everyone didn't know about Rubicon. Who was it, Lattimore? Who is behind Rubicon? Tell me! It's the vice president, isn't it?"

They were in a park, the other side of the basin from the Jefferson Memorial. The statue of the third president, the one that Dieter Shoenfeld had so much admired, was lit up inside the columns, a beacon in the darkness.

"Park over there, just past those trees," he ordered. "What difference does it make whether it was the vice president or whether it went higher than that? It's too late. You can't stop it."

"Harrison worked for the vice president, so it must . . ."

A cruel smile creased the broad and arrogant mouth of Henry Lattimore.

"I told you. Everyone knew."

"You mean it wasn't just the vice president, it was . . . ?"

"Get out," ordered Lattimore. With the gun pointed straight at Hart, he eased himself out the passenger side door.

There was a chance Hart could make a run for it. It was dark and the trees were just a few yards away. It was a chance, the only one he had. Lattimore was an expert marksman, a trained sniper, but it was still a chance.

"Keep your hands where I can see them," said Lattimore as he moved around the front of the car.

Hart darted a glance over his shoulder, measuring the distance, trying to calculate the odds. It was too late, and he knew it. All he could think about now was Helen, whether she would be strong enough, whether the news of his death would be more than she could handle. He tried to concentrate on the single thought of her, wishing with his dying breath to send her all the strength he had.

"Stop! Stay there."

Lattimore held his arm straight out and pointed the gun. Hart stood still, unresisting. It was over. He was about to die and he was not afraid and he was proud of that. Everything came down to this, the last moment you lived, the way that in the end you faced your own death. He raised his chin and waited.

A giant whirring motion almost knocked him off his feet. There was noise everywhere, a strident blast on a loudspeaker, and then a blinding flash of light. Lattimore staggered back, waving the gun wildly over his head. Hart dove to the ground.

"Put down the gun!"

Lattimore dropped to his knees, firing at the helicopter swirling above him. He looked for Hart, swung the gun around, ready to fire. And then, suddenly, he jolted forward and fell facedown, dead before he hit the ground.

The helicopter hovered overhead while a dozen police officers converged on the scene. An unmarked police car drove up behind them. Leonard Coleman got out and walked over. Hart was clasping his hands tight together, trying to stop the trembling that had only just started.

"Hasn't been a very good night, has it, Senator?"

Hart opened his mouth, but nothing came out. Coleman put his arm around his shoulder.

"Come on. I'll get you a cup of coffee. We can talk about this later."

Hart's voice came back to him.

"How did you . . . ?"

"It isn't just the bad guys who know how to do surveillance. I figured that whoever wanted you dead wasn't going to stop just because they didn't get you the first time. I've had someone following you every time you were back in Washington."

"A few seconds later and . . ." He took a breath.

"Harrison is dead. Lattimore told me that he killed him, the same reason he killed DeStefano: to keep him from talking, from making a mistake."

Coleman looked across to where Lattimore lay face-down in the grass.

"Did he tell you who he was working for—who else was involved? Lattimore didn't do this on his own."

It was the same question the reporters wanted answered. Within minutes, they had started to arrive. Standing at the edge of the road, a few yards from where Lattimore had forced Hart to park the car, Coleman tried to fend them off with a brief description of what had just transpired.

"Henry Lattimore, wanted in the murder of Dieter Shoenfeld, and in the subsequent murder of his accomplice, Frank DeStefano, has been killed in an exchange of gunfire with the police. Lattimore abducted Senator Hart from his hotel, forced him at gunpoint to drive out here, just across from the Jefferson Memorial, where he planned to kill him. As I'm sure you can all understand, the senator has had a difficult—"

"No, I'm fine," insisted Hart, turning to the gathering of reporters. "I'd be glad to take any questions you might have."

But first there was something he wanted to say.

"This should be all the proof anyone needs that there has been an organized attempt to prevent the presidential election from taking place. Three candidates for the presidency have been killed in attacks planned and organized by a domestic conspiracy that included among its other participants Henry Lattimore and H. L. Harrison. Lattimore admitted to me that he killed Harrison. He did so because certain people were afraid that Harrison might get caught and tell everything he knew. Lattimore also told me that Harrison, far from being one of the principals in this conspiracy, was just someone who took orders."

Hart's pulse was still racing. All around him were the flashing lights of cameras taking his picture, while the mournful siren of the coroner's ambulance, come to take Lattimore's body away, screamed in his ears. And yet he felt a strange, inner calm. He knew exactly what he was doing. He listened to what he was saying as if the words were being spoken by someone else. He watched with a spectator's curiosity how quickly the reporters seized on what he said, and how easily they were led to the one question he wanted to answer.

"You just said that Harrison was someone who took orders. Who gave the orders, Senator? Did Lattimore tell you who else is involved in this?"

Hart did not hesitate.

"Lattimore told me everything. He was going to kill me, he didn't care what I knew." He paused. "He told me the names of everyone involved."

"Who are they?" a reporter shouted. "Who was involved in this?" another one demanded. "Aren't you going to tell us?" yet another one cried out.

"Each of these people will become the subject of an investigation. It would threaten the integrity of that investigation to release their names before I've even had a chance to turn them over to the proper authorities."

"Were people in the White House involved in this?"

"I can't say anything more than I've said already. But I don't think you'll have to wait too long to find out who these people are. Once they understand that it's over, that Lattimore talked, I imagine at least some of them will try to save themselves by coming forward with what they know."

"Was anyone from the vice president's office involved?"

"As I said—"

"Was the vice president himself involved?" Hart did not say anything. "Then the vice president was . . . ? What about . . . ? Does it go even higher?"

Coleman stepped in front, waving his hand to signal that the senator had to go. He did not say anything to Hart until they were in the car, driving away.

"Lattimore told you he got rid of Harrison—right?"

"Right."

"And he told you that Harrison only did what he was told?"

"That's what he said."

"But he didn't tell you the rest of it, did he? He may have told you that this thing went as high as the vice president or maybe even the White House, but he didn't give you any names, did he?"

Hart was not surprised that he knew.

"How did you know I was lying?"

"I'm not sure you can call it lying when it may be the only way to get to the truth," said Coleman, pondering what Hart had done. "Everyone involved in this thing is going to wake up in the morning and—if they haven't seen it on television—read in the paper that before he died Henry Lattimore told you who they were."

"You still haven't told me how you knew."

"Instinct, I guess. That, and the fact that I knew you were smart enough to figure out how you could take advantage of Lattimore's death."

Hart made two phone calls when he got back to the hotel. The first was to Helen to tell her that he was all right and that, despite what she might see on television or read in the papers, he had never been in any real danger.

"Why do you lie to me like that?" she asked after a long pause. "It isn't because you really think I'll believe it, that I'll think you weren't in danger. It's so that I'll know you're all right now, that you aren't falling apart because this madman would have killed you if the police had not stopped him at the last minute."

Sitting on the edge of the bed, his elbows resting on his

knees, he stared down at the floor. Leonard Coleman knew by some instinct when he was lying; Helen knew it by experience. He decided to tell her the truth.

"I wasn't scared while it was happening; I was scared to death when it was over, when I knew I was safe. There's something else, something I want you to know. When I thought I was going to die, the only thing I worried about was whether you'd be all right, and whether you would know that the last thought I ever had was you."

The second call was to Charlie Ryan. It was in a different key altogether.

"You know, Hart, you always did have a talent for publicity. No one gets the kind of coverage you do."

Hart sprang to his feet and went hopping into the other room. A smile shot across his mouth. He fought it hard, trying not to laugh.

"I almost get my head blown off and all you can think about is how this could change the whole nature of campaigning in America?"

"Listen," replied Ryan confidentially, "if it works, you know someone will try it." There was a brief pause, a sudden change of mood. "You're back at the hotel? Pack your things and check out. I'll pick you up in half an hour. You stay here this weekend. We need to work anyway."

"No," protested Hart. "The hotel is fine. There isn't any reason . . ."

"Do you think Lattimore is the only hired gun these people have? I'll be there in thirty minutes."

Ryan had an apartment two blocks from Dupont Circle. It was quiet, out of the way. Most of those who lived in the building were diplomatic personnel on assignment with their country's embassy.

"I get invited to all the best receptions," remarked Ryan with a broad grin as he led Hart inside.

He tossed Hart's bag on the bed in the guest room, got

each of them a beer from the kitchen, and they went to work. They quit at two o'clock and were at it again at nine the next morning.

"They'll hit us with questions before we get two sentences out of our mouths. Turn every question into a variation of the only question that counts: what are the limits on the president's authority. Lopez will argue that in a case like this the president can do whatever the president thinks best."

It was midafternoon. Bread crumbs on an empty dish, left over from a sandwich, and two empty coffee cups had not been moved since lunch. With his fingers laced together behind his neck and his legs stretched out in front of him, Ryan leaned against the straight-backed chair. Hart slumped over the table, his cheek in his hand.

"It's like being back in law school, isn't it?" asked Ryan, amused at the look of discouragement on Hart's face. "The day before finals, when you suddenly discover that after a whole year you know less than when you started." He bolted forward. The front two legs of the chair crashed hard on the floor as he leaped up and stretched his arms. "But you always knew you were going to pass, didn't you? And this time you know you're going to win." He started toward the kitchen, thought of something, and looked back at Hart. "Unless they shoot us first!"

On a different level, Hart took it seriously.

"That's one thing that won't happen." He nodded toward the newspaper that had been tossed on the far corner of the dining room table. "Everyone involved in Rubicon is too worried about what's going to happen to them, to think about getting rid of us."

Ryan shook his head in admiration.

"You really made all that up, just minutes after he was about to kill you? And you're worried about a little hearing, a couple questions from a few judges?"

"I didn't make it up. He as good as told me that it doesn't stop with the vice president, but he wasn't specific. He didn't name names, he didn't give me details. He wasn't going to give me that kind of satisfaction. He wanted me to die wondering."

Hart got up and walked past Ryan on the way to the kitchen. He needed more coffee. He stopped just long enough to give him a look that said they both knew what was at stake.

They worked late into the night again, well past midnight, going over every line of the brief, trying to imagine every question that might get asked and every answer they wanted to give. On Sunday, at Ryan's insistence, they worked only until the end of the afternoon.

"It comes down to this," said Hart. "The law, or what there is of it, doesn't matter. The issue is whether the Constitution provides a remedy for a situation that the framers of the Constitution did not foresee."

"Exactly; and the answer . . . ?"

Hart knew their case backward and forward now; he could have answered the question in his sleep.

"The same answer Lincoln gave."

Ryan nodded thoughtfully, full of quiet confidence. He stood up, placed his hands on the sides of his hips, and threw his shoulders back.

"Tell me, when you first ran for Congress, did you ever think it would come to this—that it would be up to you to save the Union?"

Hart was thinking of something more immediate.

"If we lose tomorrow, if the Court doesn't do what we're asking it to do, if there is no election, then they will have gotten away with it. Lattimore and Harrison are dead, and despite what I told the press, despite the fact we both know damn well that the vice president and his people were in this up to their eyeballs, and maybe the president as well, we'll never be able to prove it. Worse than that, if we lose tomorrow they'll be on their way to stealing the country once and for all."

23

THE CHIEF JUSTICE LEANED FORWARD. WALTER Devlin had been on the Court for sixteen years. With high, sharp cheekbones and ice-blue eyes, he had the ascetic look of the scholar, a man of letters who had spent his life surrounded by crumbling manuscripts and dusty books. When he spoke, his voice had a kind of creaking sound, like a door, closed for centuries, shoved open. He was old and seemed older than he was. Oliver Wendell Holmes had been on the Court when he was ninety, but seemed remarkably young compared to the venerable Walter Otis Devlin who was only seventy-six. Like Holmes, however, Devlin lived for the law, and expected everyone who brought a case in the Supreme Court of the United States to feel exactly the same way. A lawyer who did not know what he was talking about was, for the chief justice, no lawyer at all.

"This is a case brought on behalf of the Congress of the United States," he announced in a flat tone, "against the president of the United States, asking that the Court set aside as against the Constitution of the United States an executive order postponing the scheduled presidential election and asking for certain other remedial relief as well. Because of the urgency of the matter, we depart in certain respects from our usual practice this morning. The Court, having read plaintiff's brief and being fully advised in the premises . . ."

Devlin droned on, threading his way through the tangle of jurisdictional issues, until he got to where he thought the argument should be joined.

"So, Mr. Lopez, let us begin with the question whether the president has authority to delay an election. Under what federal statute, or under what provision of the United States Constitution, do you find a grant of this power?"

The attorney general rose from the table and went to the podium directly in front of the long, curving bench at which the nine black-robed justices sat waiting.

"The president has declared a state of emergency and imposed martial law," he began in a slightly hesitant voice. He paused, collecting himself. "It is inherent in the executive power, conferred on the president by Article II of the Constitution, to do all things necessary to protect the people of the United States. No other branch of government can—"

"That wasn't what I asked," Devlin interrupted. "I asked you to cite the precise statute, or the specific provision of the Constitution, that allows the president to decide that an election will not be held. It is a simple question, Mr. Lopez. Perhaps you might be so good as to try to answer it."

"I believe I did, Chief Justice Devlin. Article II of the Constitution confers the executive power on—"

"On the president—yes, believe it or not, Mr. Lopez, I was vaguely aware of Article II even before you were kind enough to bring it to my attention."

The chief justice, who had been bending forward,

slowly drew back. Crossing his arms in front of his narrow chest, he scowled at the attorney general.

"Humor the Court, Mr. Lopez. Where precisely in Article II do you find this authority?"

"As commander in chief, the president has the exclusive authority in wartime to decide what needs to be done to protect the United States. That includes, by necessary implication, the power to protect the institutions of government and, in this instance, the integrity of the elections by which those who head those institutions are selected. Even were we not in a state of war, the executive power of the government can only be exercised by the president. In a situation like this, where the candidates for the presidency have been murdered and there isn't time to replace them, and where, even if there were time, it would not be safe to do so, someone has to decide what to do and that can only be the president."

"But, Mr. Lopez," said Justice Brandes, "you must be aware that there is an amendment to the Constitution that specifically states that in the event a candidate or candidates cannot serve, the Congress is to select a date for the next election."

An associate justice for fourteen years, Kathryn Brandes was a small, tightly controlled woman with a waspish smile and dark, penetrating eyes. She spoke in a slow, measured tone, but in a manner so decisive that she actually seemed to grow larger and become the dominant physical presence in the room. Through years of listening to oral argument, she had acquired a disconcerting habit of waiting for an answer with a look of unwavering skepticism.

"The amendment was intended for what I might call the usual case," replied Lopez, meeting her glance with a look of practiced innocence. "When a candidate, after winning the election, but before assuming the office, dies or becomes disabled. It does not address the situation in which, unfortunately, we now find ourselves. The country is under attack. Three candidates have been murdered in terrorist attacks, and there is no reason to believe that other candidates chosen to run won't be murdered, too. We have to make certain that this won't happen, we have to—"

"None of that has anything to do with the issue, Mr. Lopez," insisted Justice Caruso in the cheerful booming voice with which he regularly destroyed the arguments, and the confidence, of lawyers who had taken the wrong approach to constitutional interpretation. "Nothing whatsoever. The issue has nothing to do with whether the country is under attack. The issue is whether the president has the authority to delay an election, and, if he does, whether he also has the authority to decide when that election should then be held. The issue, Mr. Lopez, is whether this is part of the executive or the legislative power, and, as Justice Brandes observed, there is an amendment that would seem to suggest that it is up to the Congress, not the president, to determine the date."

Lopez seemed stunned. Caruso was an outspoken conservative, a strict constructionist, a brilliant if at times belligerent advocate for the position that the Constitution could only be read in terms of the intentions of the men who wrote it; that the meaning of the words, far from changing with the times, never changed at all. If Caruso had doubts about this assertion of presidential power, Lopez was in trouble.

"Granted, the Constitution cannot, and should not, be read in light of the particular circumstances of a national emergency, the Constitution was clearly intended to provide a remedy for any such emergency. The president is required to preserve and protect the Constitution of the United States. Obviously, that includes the duty to protect the integrity of the method by which the president himself is chosen."

"I'm not sure I quite agree with Justice Caruso's suggestion that the events creating the present emergency are irrelevant to the issue before us," said Justice William Paulson.

Cautious in his judgments, Paulson was considered a liberal by conservatives, while liberals were never quite certain where he stood. But no one, liberal or conservative, had ever doubted the almost mathematical clarity of his mind.

"There is a point that seems to me of particular importance that I should like to have you address. As you know, there is in equity that well-known principle aptly called 'clean hands.' If you ask the court for a remedy you must yourself be innocent of blame. Now, what I would like to know is this: when you say that the president has the authority to postpone the election for his successor until a day that he shall determine, and you say this is necessary because the candidates for the presidency have been killed in terrorist attacks, would you still insist that the president has the power under the Constitution if the president himself—or if not the president, someone in his administration—had been responsible for those deaths? I mean exactly what I say, Mr. Lopez. In your view, does the Constitution allow—no, authorize—a president to decide at his sole discretion when the election will be held, should he in fact have been the cause of the very emergency that brought about the necessity that you speak about?"

The courtroom, crowded to capacity, was, more than silent, subdued, by the terrible possibility that had now for the first time been uttered openly. Lopez stood tense with the effort of keeping himself under control. With a few well-chosen words, Justice Paulson had put him on the defensive, made it seem that the attorney general was arguing the case, not for a president, but for an assassin.

"If a president were ever to be guilty of such a monstrous

crime, the Constitution provides a clear remedy: impeachment. The constitutional powers of the executive, however, cannot be limited by the possibility that such powers might be abused by a criminal act. That would be to argue that no powers could be conferred."

There were other questions for the attorney general from other justices, and then, finally, the chief justice looked up and with a bare nod of his ancient head invited the other side to plead its case.

Hart got to his feet; Ryan did not leave his chair. Hart looked at him with surprise and then, when he saw that Ryan had no intention of joining him, with a sudden sense of panic. Ryan's eyes were full of confidence.

"They only allow one attorney at a time," he explained. "I tossed a coin. You lost."

"Mr. Hart, if you're ready," said the chief justice in his throttled, threadbare voice.

"Yes, Your Honor," said Hart, standing at the lectern.

The chief justice seemed amused.

"You're not a practicing lawyer, are you? Never appeared before this Court—or any court—is that correct?"

"Yes, that's true; but—"

Devlin held up his hand as if to make an important announcement.

"Because this is your first time, Mr. Hart, you are subject to the two-minute rule." He was leaning forward, a shrewd, playful grin on his thin, desiccated mouth. "It's the way we show fairness here, the way we make sure that the experience of one side does not gain an advantage over the inexperience of the other. We give you two minutes to make as many mistakes as you like. It is only after that—a full two minutes—that we then treat you like we do everyone else and begin to crucify you for any, even the slightest, error you might make. That seem fair to you, Mr. Hart?"

"Perfectly fair, Mr. Chief Justice."

This was not some peculiar quirk of the chief justice; it had been done quite on purpose, a way to cut the tension that had held the courtroom in its grip; a way to give a pause, a respite, to the forced discipline of oral argument. Hart had understood immediately from the sparkle in Devlin's wintry eyes what it was about. And he had understood as well the second meaning in what the chief justice had done: made him feel that he was as welcome as anyone else who had ever made an appearance.

Devlin sat straight up.

"Good. Now, what would you like to tell us? We've all read the brief submitted, but what would you like to say?"

"That we agree with the attorney general. The Constitution does indeed provide a remedy for the situation in which we find ourselves. This is a case, perhaps more than any other, where the original intent of the founders is the only thing that will save us."

Caruso stopped him before he could say another word.

"We're aware of the remedy you're asking for, Senator. The question, however, is whether, as part of the inherent power of the executive, the president, in time of war, can postpone an election."

"Our position is that he cannot. It has never been done before. It was not done in 1944, during the Second World War. It was not done in 1864, during the Civil War."

"But in those instances, none of the candidates had been assassinated. There was no reason not to have an election." Caruso gestured emphatically with his hand. "Assume a situation in which the day before an election, both candidates for the office suddenly die—murdered, killed in some natural disaster; it doesn't matter: both are dead. What then? Are you saying that even in that situation the president could not postpone the election?"

"That's exactly what we are saying. Because even in that situation, the president would have to first consult with the leaders of both houses of the Congress before he could postpone it. And it would then be the Congress—not the president—that would decide the date for the election. The point, Justice Caruso—the single, overriding issue—is that we cannot allow, the Constitution does not allow, the president or anyone else to exercise an unlimited power to decide not just when, but whether, to hold an election for the presidency."

"Do I understand you correctly?" interjected the chief justice. "You're saying that the power to determine the date of the election is the power to avoid having any election at all?"

"Yes; exactly. Because the argument isn't just that the president has the authority to postpone the election to another date. The argument is that the president, acting as commander in chief, has the authority to decide when it is safe to have that election. Which means that so long as the president insists that it isn't safe to have an election, we won't have one; which means that—"

The chief justice held up his hand. He turned his eye sharply to the attorney general, sitting alone at the other table.

"Mr. Lopez."

Startled, Lopez rose from his chair.

"Mr. Lopez, I want you to respond to this. Yes, I know this isn't the normal way we do things," he said in answer to the puzzled, and slightly irritated, expression on the face of the attorney general. "But then this isn't exactly the normal case, is it? Now, if you would: explain precisely what happens if the president is allowed to do what you say he should. How long can the president postpone the election?"

"Until he determines that it is safe to hold it."

"And by safe, you mean safe from the threat of another terrorist attack?" asked Justice Brandes, lifting her chin a skeptical half inch.

"Yes, of course; until it's possible to guarantee that the election can be held without the threat of violence."

"But that might never happen," said Justice Paulson. "This war on terror might last generations, according to what, if I'm not mistaken, you yourself have said in testimony before Congress."

Lopez fidgeted with his hands. A nervous smile flickered half an instant on his face.

"I think these are two different issues. The war on terror may very well last generations, but the situation we're dealing with here is much more isolated, the work of a single cell, from everything we have been able to gather—"

"Organized and controlled by people inside the government!" cried Hart before the chief justice silenced him with a quick glance of disapproval.

But Lopez would not let it pass unnoticed.

"Whoever is responsible—no matter who it is—is going to be prosecuted to the full extent of the law!"

"Enough!" said the chief justice. "Now, Mr. Lopez, that still does not answer the question. If the president refuses to set a new date, would we then not be in a position of having no election and therefore no one to head the executive branch of government?"

This was the moment Charlie Ryan had always known had to come. It was, as he had told Hart, the secret that, once understood, explained what Rubicon had always been about.

"That of course would not happen," said Lopez with complete assurance. "The president would continue in office."

"Until when?" asked Justice Caruso. His gaze seemed to become more piercing, more intense, as he moved forward, centering his shoulders over his hands, kept folded on the bench below him. "Just how long, under your theory, does the president remain in office?"

Lopez seemed confused, not by the question, the answer to which he thought obvious, but by the fact that anyone, especially a conservative justice, would even think to ask it.

"Until the next election, Justice Caruso. Until his successor is chosen. The Constitution does not allow a vacancy in the office."

Caruso drew back. He turned to Hart.

"Would you agree with that?" he asked in a thoughtful voice. "That the president would remain in office until his successor was chosen?"

"The Constitution is quite explicit on this point," said Hart without a moment's hesitation. "Section 1 of Article II sets the term of the president at four years. Section 1 of the Twentieth Amendment states: 'The terms of the President and the Vice President shall end at noon on the twentieth day of January.'" His eyes moved from one justice to another until he had, for a brief instant, looked at all nine of them. "Three candidates for the presidency have been killed, along with dozens of their fellow citizens, not because a group of terrorists wanted to show that even in America democracy could be dangerous, but to make us cross a Rubicon of our own, leave behind the Constitution and everything it means, and surrender ourselves to the false promise of a kind of elected dictatorship in which the president himself decides how long he holds office.

"They argue that it isn't safe to have an election; they argue that the president can be trusted to decide when we should choose his successor; they argue—as the attorney general just did—that even the Constitution cannot limit the power of the president to do what he likes. The Constitution says that the president leaves office at noon on the twentieth day of January; the attorney general says the president stays in office because someone has to conduct the business of government. Three men were murdered to stop us from having an election; and now it is argued that we have to get rid of the Constitution so that we can continue to have a government.

"The only legitimate way to interpret the Constitution is the way Lincoln said it had to be done: it has to be read in light of the principles set forth in the Declaration of Independence, the enduring principles of freedom and the rights of man. The requirement of election, the limit on the term of office, these are things meant to protect our freedom by preventing the very thing the attorney general tells us we should now allow: a government that decides for itself what it can do and how long it can do it.

"When Caesar crossed the Rubicon, the Roman republic died and the age of the emperors began. We now stand before a Rubicon of our own. Cross it, and the American republic will be dead as well."

24

QUENTIN BURDICK WAS NOT SURE IF HART WAS telling him the truth. It was not that he thought he was lying, but rather that he was not giving himself nearly enough credit.

"And all of it was Senator Ryan's idea?" he asked with a gracious skepticism. "You argued the case. He didn't."

They were having breakfast across from the White House at the Hay-Adams Hotel, the other side of Lafayette Park. Hart laughed as he buttered his toast.

"I didn't know that was going to happen until I stood up and Ryan didn't."

"Are you serious? Did you think—?"

"That we were going to argue it together? That's exactly what I thought in my ignorance. I thought he would do most of it, and that I might just add something once in a while. I'm not sure I could have done it, if he had told me in advance that I was going to have to do it alone. Which, I suppose, is the reason he didn't tell me until it was too late for me to do anything about it. I'd never argued a case in my life."

Burdick's thin eyebrows shot up.

"And you ran away with it, made Lopez look like a fool."

Hart was not that optimistic.

"The Court hasn't ruled yet."

"You argued it yesterday. I'm told the lights were on at the Court until nearly one in the morning. It's almost certain there will be a decision before the end of the day."

Hart took a bite of toast and wiped his mouth with a napkin. He wanted to make certain that whatever happened, whatever the Court decided, Burdick, and through Burdick the country, knew what Ryan had done.

"I answered a few questions. That was my contribution, and I was only able to do that because of what Charlie taught me. Do you think I could have come up with . . . ? I could have worked until kingdom come and never seen it, never understood how remarkably simple it all is once you go back into it, remember how the process was supposed to work in the beginning. We all think of the electoral college as an anachronism. Charlie Ryan knew better than that."

Burdick had scarcely touched what was on his plate. He was too caught up in the still unfolding story to think about food.

"However much credit you want to give Senator Ryan, all anyone is talking about is the argument you made before the Court."

Hart finished off his eggs and shoved the empty plate aside. Leaning forward on his elbows, he fixed Burdick with a look that left no doubt that he was in earnest.

"Start to finish, this was Charlie Ryan's case. He drafted the brief. He handled all the preparation. I agreed with everything he wrote—every line of it. The only reason I was involved was that he thought it important—and I agreed—

that on a matter of this magnitude, with the stakes this high, the case be brought by representatives of both political parties, joined together to fight what the president and the vice president were trying to do. This was Ryan's case; it was never mine."

A whimsical smile flitted over Burdick's narrow mouth.

"He denies it."

Hart rolled his eyes and with a helpless grin shook his head.

"He's a liar." He started to look away. Suddenly, he turned back. "And you can quote me on that."

"He said you were the one who remembered—during oral argument—the language of the Twentieth Amendment, the fact that the term of the president ends at noon on the twentieth day of January."

Hart waved his hand, dismissing what he had done as unimportant.

"Ryan was the one who understood that under the Constitution the electoral college chooses the president. It's become a rubber stamp, a mere formality, and so we hardly think about it. We count up the votes in each of the states and we're done with it. But Ryan understood that if we didn't have candidates able to run, if we couldn't have an election in which people could vote for the candidate of their choice, we could still choose electors in each of the states to meet together in the electoral college. Only this time, instead of deciding who won a majority of the electoral votes, they'll have to decide—as the Constitution intended they should—who among us is the best qualified person to become president of the United States."

"It's been a while since the electoral college had to do that," noted Burdick dryly.

"Yes, but the last time they did it we got George Washington. But whatever happens, whoever they select—if the Court gives us what we asked—it will be a good deal better than letting the president stay in power after his term is over."

Hart looked around the dining room, full of lobbyists and power brokers, part of the Washington establishment that, in the most fundamental sense, cared nothing for politics because it traded only in favors. Sometimes, watching them in their smug indifference to anything but their own small ambitions, he remembered a line—"What's a Constitution among friends"—that had seemed to capture more than the mood, the method, of so much of what was done here. He turned again to Burdick.

"What do you think is going to happen? You were there yesterday. What do you think the Court is going to do?"

Burdick placed his index fingers together and rubbed them against his chin.

"With that Court—I don't know. But I can tell you this: the White House is worried. No one has admitted to anything—yet—but after you were almost killed by Lattimore, after what Lattimore told you about Rubicon and who was involved in it . . . Everyone I've talked to thinks that, depending on what the Court does, it may be only a matter of days before someone is arrested and the investigations start."

"And if the Court decides the president can delay the election and decide when we'll have another one," Hart reminded him, "there won't be any arrests, and there won't be any investigations. They'll hide everything behind executive privilege."

When Hart was finished at the Hay-Adams, he went directly to his office. There were dozens of phone calls, but he did not want to talk to anyone. He sat alone, wondering how long it would take the Court to decide and what he would do if they lost. There was no point to it, he decided after an hour of agonizing. It was like waiting for the election results after the polls had closed. It was out of his hands; there was nothing more either he or anyone else could do. He might as well go home.

And that, suddenly, was the only place he wanted to be.

"Get me on a plane," he shouted into the phone to David Allen. "The next one there is."

Allen had him on the next plane to Los Angeles. Helen met him at the airport after the short connecting flight to Santa Barbara. He did not say very much as she drove along the narrow winding road through the tan-colored hills. His mind was still on what had happened, and on what might happen next. When they reached the house, he turned on the television just long enough to find out that the Court had not yet announced a decision.

He did not know what to do with himself. He insisted that they go out to eat, then, two minutes later, changed his mind and suggested they stay in. He sat down on the sofa, then got up and started to walk aimlessly around. He sat down again, shook his head at his own impatience, jumped to his feet and swore out loud.

"Sorry," he said, embarrassed. "I don't have any idea what I'm doing."

Helen looked at him and smiled.

"Charlie called me last night."

"And what did Charlie have to say?"

"He called to tell me that he had been a lawyer all his life, but that what you did at the Supreme Court was the finest thing he had ever seen. He said he had never been as proud of anyone as he was of you. Now, why don't you just sit down—I'll get you something to drink—and you can tell me all about what happened yesterday. And then I'll tell you why you're going to win."

She had always been able to make him forget everything but her. He talked, and she listened, and all he heard of what he said was what he saw said back to him in her lovely, gentle eyes. At the end of it, after he had told her everything that had happened, he had forgotten all the anxiety, all the misgivings and the doubt, about what he had done and how it might turn out.

They ate a quiet dinner and went to bed early. When the telephone rang at seven in the morning, he had already been up for an hour. It was Charlie Ryan.

"The Court has a decision. It will be announced in two hours, at noon, nine A.M. out there. We won, Bobby. I got a call a few minutes ago from someone I know over there. They gave us everything we asked for. They ruled that the president doesn't have authority to delay or schedule an election, and that the electoral college has the responsibility to choose the president, whether or not candidates are available to run in an election. The phrase they used was 'The Constitution of the United States does not just apply when people find it convenient, or even safe, to follow it.' There's something else," said Ryan in a confidential tone. "The decision is going to be announced as the unanimous opinion of the Court. It was not. The vote was five to four. Devlin, the chief justice, insisted that once they had a majority, whatever that majority was for, there would be only one opinion and that everyone had to sign it. He told them a divided Court would divide the country. But that's how close it was, how close these people came to getting away with it, taking over the government. If it had not been for you, for what you did in Court, we would have lost."

"I didn't do anything, Charlie, and you know it. You won this thing. You won it all by yourself."

Two hours later, Hart sat next to Helen on the sofa and watched on television the formal announcement that the Supreme Court had ruled against the president, and that the presidential election would now proceed in the manner prescribed by the Constitution. An hour later, Charlie Ryan called again.

When he hung up, Hart walked over to the glass doors

that opened onto the patio. For a long time he stared out at the ocean shimmering blue and silver in the distance, wondering at the vanity of men, driven by dreams of glory that almost always ended badly.

"What is it, Bobby? What happened?"

"The vice president's chief of staff. They found him in a parked car near the Potomac. It looks like a suicide, but Ryan thinks it's murder. We weren't the only ones who were told in advance about the Court's decision. They're covering their tracks now, or trying to; making sure that no one who knew anything about Rubicon will ever tell what they know."

"But doesn't that mean that it's over, that Rubicon is finished?"

He remembered what Ryan had told him about how close the decision was on the Court.

"They almost got away with it. Another attack, a real one; enough fear, a few people who have power and want to keep it . . ."

"Don't give up, Bobby. Don't leave the Senate. I don't want you to. This used to be a great country. It can be a great country again."

Bobby Hart put his arm around her, grateful that she still loved him, grateful for the strength he had not known she had.